Edward A. Robinson, George A. Wall

The Gun-Bearer

A Novel

Edward A. Robinson, George A. Wall

The Gun-Bearer
A Novel

ISBN/EAN: 9783337041878

Printed in Europe, USA, Canada, Australia, Japan

Cover: Foto ©Andreas Hilbeck / pixelio.de

More available books at **www.hansebooks.com**

THE GUN-BEARER.

A Novel.

BY

EDWARD A. ROBINSON

AND

GEORGE A. WALL,

Authors of "The Disk," etc.

WITH ILLUSTRATIONS BY JAMES FAGAN.

NEW YORK:

ROBERT BONNER'S SONS,

1894.

I SEE the cloud of battle and the flame.
  I hear the cannon roar, the crackling note
Of rifles and the clash of angry steel.
My pulses quicken and my brain is wild
With frenzied shouts and yells of men in strife.
There father, son and brother fearless stand
For all men hold most dear.
There, right and left, brave men are stricken down
Beneath the banner that they love so well!
And all the while, pulsating with the shriek
And hiss of shot and shell, with cries and groans
Of wounded, dying men, the sulph'rous air
Speaks to each sense, as if in thunder tones:
The price of peace is blood.

THE GUN-BEARER.

PART I.—PROLOGUE.

CHAPTER I.

"WAR! *Ledger!* Midnight edition! Fort Sumter fired on!" was the cry which, at two o'clock on the morning of the 13th of April, 1861, aroused the slumbering village in which I lived. It was a cry which stimulated and thrilled every fiber of my being, as I ran, splashing through mud, darkness and rain, toward the Waytown Arms, our village inn.

I had recognized the hoarse, familiar voice shouting this stirring news as belonging to old Joe, the paper-carrier, and though I was but a boy, I knew the storm that had been threatening the safety of the Union had burst upon us.

Joe was standing on the seat of a light wagon in the open roadway before the tavern. His vehicle was drawn by two small mules, whose sweating bodies threw up clouds of steam, which the lantern in the hands of the innkeeper scarcely penetrated, and in which old Joe's form towered black and gigantic.

A surging crowd of hurriedly dressed men had already gathered around the wagon, and I could see the gleam of papers as they were passed from hand to hand.

Drawing near, I saw there was another person in the wagon who was distributing the papers—old Joe, maintaining his lofty position above the heads of the encircling crowd, and, whip in hand, as if impatient to be off, had but the one care on his mind, to rouse the heaviest sleeper in the village with this dreaded news.

A moment before silence had reigned in the unsuspecting security of our village, and I, too thoughtful for sleep, by reason of the excited talk which we boys, imitating our elders, had been indulging in at our surreptitious meeting that evening, was standing by the window of my room up under the roof, looking out into the darkness and listening abstractedly to the drip, drip of the rain from the eaves. Not a light was to be seen anywhere; utter gloom and, save the noise of the rain, silence everywhere.

After a while I fancied that the echo of another sound mingled with the patter of the water. It was like the blast of a horn. I opened the window, that I might hear better, and, listening with suspended breath, heard the sound again, this time more plainly.

Toot! Toot!

It was a horn, surely, but still far away.

Later I could hear the muffled rumble of wheels and the thump of hoofs in the covered bridge at the north end of the village and, when that ceased, the rattle of wheels over stony ground and the sound of a hoarse voice shouting something.

Others were waking in the village; lights gleamed

from many windows, and the heads of many people appeared, some with night-caps and some without. Meanwhile the noise of hoof-beats and the sound of wagon-wheels grew louder, the shouting more distinct, and, when the team turned the corner, came full and strong the cry of "War."

I made a short cut to the ground by way of my window, the porch underneath, and a drop from the edge of that to the soft lawn below, and in a very short space of time was, as you see me at the beginning of this story, splashing through the darkness and mud on my way to the inn, where I had rightly concluded Joe would rein up.

By the time I arrived, however, the demand for papers had been satisfied, and old Joe, anxious that no one should get ahead of him in the village beyond cried :

"Ready, boys! G'lang !"

Then letting the whip fall on the steaming mules, and with a final cry "War !" he went rattling and splashing away into the darkness.

As Joe drove off, the crowd which he had called together began to diminish, some going one way and some another, all anxious to know the particulars.

Many of the villagers went into the tavern, whither I followed, but on presenting myself at the door of the bar-room, where they seemed to have assembled, admittance was refused me.

"The room is already too full," they said.

On trying the office, I found gathered there several of the boys whom I had left only a little while before. They were all in one group at the end of the room, watching with a mixture of diffidence and curiosity a strange man who was reading one of Joe's papers by the light of the desk-lamp.

Curiosity at last getting the best of every other feeling, little Tommy Atkins ventured to break the silence and ask the stranger the meaning of all the excitement.

"It means war, I suppose, boys," he said, in a kindly voice, looking toward us; then, probably surmising that we were anxious to know all about it, he added: "but would you like to hear what the paper says?"

"Yes!" we cried, in chorus.

"Very well; you sit down, and I'll read."

We scattered to seats, and the stranger, springing to a place on the desk, by which he had been standing, drew the lamp toward him, and holding the paper sidewise, so that the light would fall strong on the print, read:

"'SPECIAL DISPATCH TO THE LEDGER.

"'*Charleston, S. C., April* 12, 1861.—The rebels opened fire upon Fort Sumter at 4:30 this morning. The first shot was fired from Fort Moultrie. The iron-clad floating battery and the heavy batteries on Mt. Pleasant and Cummings Point immediately followed suit. The encircling guns poured such a storm of shot and shell upon the loyal fort that only the cannon in the casemates could be used,'" etc., etc.

But everybody has read these first dispatches, and been as excited over them as we were. Our youthful spirits under the weird spell of the early morning hour could not be held entirely in check, even by the magnetic charm of the stranger's voice and manner or the strange news that he was reading, and broke through all restraint at times. We were enthusiastic partisans of the northern cause, and understood, in a youthful way, the nature of the crisis. Yet I am sure none of us really grasped the whole significance of this news. The novelty wore away somewhat, I confess for myself, as the stranger went on reading, and my attention wandered occasionally to outside matters.

I heard a wagon rattle up to the door, saw the postmaster come into the office, take his hat and coat from a peg, and go out again. He was evidently thinking deeply about something, for he took no notice of the stranger, who kept on reading, nor of us boys sitting around in silence. In a little while I heard the wagon rumble away.

Again, the stranger had not long been reading before Joe Bentley, the blacksmith's son, who was sitting astride a chair, with his elbows resting on the back, began fumbling about in his pockets. Bringing forth, at last, a short clay pipe, from which he carefully shook the ashes, he crowded down what tobacco there was in it, fished out a live coal from among the ashes in the big fireplace, and proceeded to light it in an abstracted sort of way. Then placing the pipe in one corner of his mouth, where neither it nor the smoke could interfere with his vision, he fixed his eyes unwaveringly on the stranger.

Joe was the biggest and oldest one among us, and we always looked up to him a little on that account; but now he seemed more than ever sedate and trustworthy.

War and the horrors prophesied by the paper might seem unreal and overdrawn to the rest of us, but Joe must realize them, I thought, as I watched him sitting there so stately and thoughtful with the stump of a pipe between his teeth.

Tommy Atkins also seemed to realize something of the terrible news. He, too, seemed absorbed by it, and sat on the end of the newspaper-table, swinging his feet and twisting and untwisting his cap, from which he had long ago wrung out every drop of moisture, utterly unconscious of everything about him except the words of the stranger.

During this time it was evident, from noises which

came to us from the bar-room, that the older people
there assembled were not without their excitement.
First we would hear an indistinct roar, as if all were
talking at once.   Then came a more decided shout,
with stamping of feet and thumping of chair-legs.
After this a short silence, and then the indistinct tones
of a single voice murmuring on, sometimes undisturbed,
sometimes interrupted by applause, and in one or two
cases completely overcome by noises of an opposite
character, not quick and soon over, like applause, but
slowly growing from a mere murmur persistently
louder and louder until the one voice was swallowed
up and lost.

This effort to drown the speaker's voice occurred but
twice.   At the end of the second time I heard a scuf-
fling of feet, a crash as of breaking furniture, followed
by a loud, angry voice, shouting: "You lie! Take
that!"   A pistol-shot added to the confusion, and as I
heard some one cry out: "Murder!" the stranger
jumped to the floor and darted through the doorway
leading to the bar-room.

Curiosity overcoming my judgment, I followed just
far enough to see the cause of this disturbance, and
there, close by the door, struggling in the grasp of two
of the worst roughs that ever disgraced the quiet of a
mill-village, was old white-haired Deacon Miller, his
face streaked with blood, his coat torn to shreds, his
hat off and a crowd of dazed and seemingly helpless
men watching this unnatural combat, yet making no
effort to offer the help that was needed.

Pressing through the crowd, the stranger jumped
like a tiger at the bully nearest him, and, with a well-
directed blow, knocked him senseless. Before the other
villain could appreciate the situation, he, too, received
a well-merited punishment, and the deacon, faint with

exhaustion, would have fallen to the floor had not the stranger caught him in his arms.

A murmur of approval went up from the crowd, and Billy Green, of the variety store, shouted:

"Kick the rascals into the road! Hang 'em to the sign-post!"

"Silence!" thundered the stranger, in a commanding tone. "Can't you act like men? Landlord, get out your carriage and help me take the deacon to his house. And you, sir," addressing Billy Green, "get me a basin of water and a sponge."

It was soon discovered that the Deacon had received only a slight flesh wound, and that, aside from the damage sustained by his clothing and the exhaustion resulting from rough handling, there was no serious damage done.

After the carriage with the deacon, the stranger and the landlord had rolled away, the two miscreants, who by this time had gained their feet, muttered threats of dire vengeance upon the deacon.

"You'd better let him alone," said Joe Bentley, who was standing behind me. "If he can't take care of himself, he's got a friend who can take of him."

The roughs looked at Joe angrily an instant, then turned and left the tavern.

"They're a bad lot," said Dick Wentworth, the station-agent, as the door closed after them—"a bad lot and they ought to be watched. They're mean enough to do anything."

"Who are they, anyhow?" asked Billy Green, rather out of contempt than for information.

"Jail-birds—a couple of jail-birds of the worst sort, just two weeks out of jails, where they've been boarding for the past three years for setting fire to the deacon's mill."

"They 'll get another three years if they don't make themselves scarce 'round these parts," said Billy.

"Like enough—like enough," answered Wentworth, meditatively; "but they'll be up to some deviltry before they go. You see if they don't."

An hour was spent discussing the war-news, during which the situation was viewed from every stand-point.

The village orator, Bert Smith, who, by the way, happened to be town-crier, had a good deal to say about the Stars and Stripes, the scream of the eagle for liberty, and rounded out his speech with the solemnity of a prophet.

"I see," he said, "this beautiful land of ours deluged with blood; our sons slaughtered on our own hearth-stones; ruin, wretchedness, tears, despair and death, everywhere."

Just as he had finished the landlord returned, and, rushing into the room, shouted excitedly:

"The rascals! What's become of them? Where are those brutes that struck the deacon?"

"Gone!" answered Billy Green. "They left just after you drove away."

"Boys," replied the landlord, "there's going to be trouble to-night, sure; and those villains are going to make it."

"What's the matter now?" asked Billy.

"Matter enough. The stranger and I took the deacon home, and were coming back through the woods. When we'd got as far as Paddock's, I saw two men sneak in behind the big stone at the bound'ry line and crawl off into the darkness. The stranger also saw them, and said: 'Landlord, you'd better turn and drive me back to Miller's house. Those imps mean mischief, and the old man may need help. I'll stop with him to-night?' So I drove back, left him, and he's there now."

"What's that?" said Billy, from the west window. "The moon?"

"Moon!" replied the landlord, going hastily to the window. "Moon don't rise in the west. My God, boys! They're at it; they've fired either the mill or the deacon's house. Come on; help me out with the big wagon; and you, Billy, run for the sexton, get the key to the church, and ring the bell, quickly! Away with with you!" noticing a little hesitation.

Willing hands helped the landlord get out the big wagon, to which were harnessed a fresh pair of horses, and into which sprang half a dozen men, eager to render whatever assistance might be needed to save the mill, upon which so many of the townspeople depended for their daily bread.

Just as the horses were put to a gallop toward the fire, the old church-bell rang out an alarm, which aroused every able-bodied man in the village.

While I stood in the doorway, watching the teams disappear in the rain and haze which were reddened by the light of the distant fire, and was debating with myself whether or not I should run after the other boys, I distinctly heard the thump of a crutch on the floor behind me. There could be no mistake about this, and I at once became conscious that my father was near me, as he was the only man in the village who used a crutch.

I was proud that I could show my father that his own interest in affairs of state, as well as of local importance, were finding a ready second in the person of his son; but I was also aware of a little inward trembling for all that.

My father was one of those men who could never be

depended upon beforehand to look at anything in any
particular way. Of a very nervous temperament, and
made irascible by chronic ailing and loss of property,
his views, I often thought, were colored by his feelings;
and as I was an only child, and babied, as the boys say,
it occurred to me that he might think this a fitting opportunity to reduce me to my proper place, as a person
of no importance, and, more's the pity, I was right, for
hardly had he caught sight of me when he cried:

"You here? This is no place for a boy on such a
night as this. Go home!"

Why didn't I run before I was discovered! To say I
was vexed would be putting it too mildly. It seemed to
me that I was old enough to be allowed some rights,
and had about determined to resist parental authority
when my father took me by the shoulder, and pushing
me, said:

"March!"

I went, and felt then as I have felt since, my body
move forward, though my spirit rebelled and bade me
stay.

CHAPTER II.

When I again came out of the house, although the morning sun was high in the heavens, I noticed that the village was unusually quiet. Everybody seemed to be asleep; but, without pausing to wonder at the unwonted stillness that reigned all around, I went to the barn and began work on the horses, finishing with my mare; for I liked to spend all extra time on her.

In the next house to ours lived Mrs. Atkins, Tommy's mother. Mr. Atkins had died in debt, father said. Consequently, Tommy's mother was compelled to depend upon her own exertions for a living, and called upon Tommy to add to the family treasury all he could earn by driving the grocer's wagon, and doing any other light jobs that came in his way.

Out on all occasions and in all kinds of weather, Tommy improved a happy faculty for picking up little bits of news, to which his ingenuity and imagination added many interesting details, and therefore, though the youngest boy among us, he was generally the best informed as to whatever was of current interest.

But he was a little too conscious of this superiority, we sometimes thought. We did not like to have to listen to him always.

Tommy's bedroom window was just opposite the doorway of our barn, and the noise I made over the horses, and the low whistle I kept up to drive the dust from my mouth must have aroused him, as he appeared suddenly at the stable-door.

"Hello, Tommy," I cried, on seeing him.

"Hello yerself. I say, Dan, 'twas too bad yer had to go home. Yer missed all the fun."

"Did you see it all?"

"Did I see it? Wa'n't I out all night?" Tom, indeed, did look as though he had been out, as he said: "Gosh! wa'n't it lively, though?"

"Well, what was it burnt?" I asked.

But Tommy was not going to tell the whole secret or any part of it in a hurry, so he passed over my question as though he had not heard it.

"D'yer s'pose I'd gone home, 'nd left a big red sky like that? Not much! It beat all the Fourth-of-July fireworks you ever saw, all holler."

I was breathless with impatience to hear about it, but saw Tommy had made up his mind to tantalize me, and at the same time show me how much more independent he was than I. It would not do to allow that; besides, I knew that if let alone he would give me the whole story in time. I said nothing, therefore, but applied myself more closely to my work. I was rubbing down the mare's hind legs at the time. This gave me a chance, as I bent over, to watch Tommy under my arm, and by saying "Whoa!" now and then I seemed to acquire independence and carelessness, as it were.

Tommy at first seemed disturbed, because I did not show more enthusiasm, and I became almost afraid that he was going to disappoint me, and go away without giving me the news; but the desire to air some of his knowledge conquered all other inclinations, and, taking up a position on the mealchest, he began:

"Yer know the stranger who read to us. Yer remeriber him, don't yer?"

Of course I remembered him. Was not his face, with its black hair and glittering black eyes, the clearest thing in my mind of all last night's excitement? But I simply said :

"Yes."

"Well, he's a brick." Tommy shut his teeth, winked his eyes, and shook his head convincingly. "You know, of course, 'bout his killing the rough?"

I was startled from my forced calm, and straightening up stared over the mare's back at Tommy sitting on the chest. Tommy saw his advantage and sneered.

"Don't even know that, hey?" I went back to work in a hurry. "Yer a pretty feller to be 'round when there's anything goin' on."

"Whoa! Stand still, can't you?" said I to the mare.

"Well," said Tommy, with a gleam of satisfaction in his eyes, "when we left the tavern the landlord whipped up his horses, and away we went in fine shape, I tell yer."

"But you weren't in the wagon, were you?" I asked, remembering distinctly that when the wagon started Tommy and the other boys were afoot.

"No; but they hadn't reached the corner before I was with them."

"I suppose they needed you," said I, determined to get a fling at Tommy.

"Of course," answered Tommy indifferently, as if that were a matter about which there ought to be but one opinion, and that further remarks on that subject were unnecessary. "But don't bother me, Dan, if you want to hear what happened."

"Go on, then!" I muttered.

"Well, 's I was sayin', we went off in fine shape. We

picked up some of the mill overseers on the way, and by the time we got clear of the town we had a dozen men in the wagon. My, but it was dark and drizzly when we got into the woods! Just after we got through them, and came out at the top of the hill, we could see the blaze over the tops of the trees that stood between us and the mill. One of the overseers said: 'It's the mill, boys, sure enough!'"

"'The rascals!' said the landlord, sharp and angry like. 'Keep a sharp eye along the roadside, boys, for two of the meanest skunks that ever went unhung. Don't let 'em get away. It'll be some satisfaction in running those fellows in.'"

"'Better hang 'em,' said Billy, 'and run 'em in afterward.'

"A little turn in the road as you reach the mansur house brought us into a full view of the fire, which proved to be"—here Tommy began to mount his high horse again—"but what are you looking at me in that way for, with your mouth wide open, and your eyes fairly sticking out of your head?"

"Stand still there," I cried to the mare. I had to say something to cover my excitement.

Tommy waited an instant, just to bother me, and then said:

"Well, it was the—"

"Whoa! Be quiet!" I shouted to the mare, as Tommy again paused, with a smile at my eagerness to catch every word.

"The barn. The mill was all right, but the deacon's house was in danger. The barn is close to the house, yer know, and well filled with hay. It made a mighty hot fire. We could hear it roar as the big waves of flame, all edged with a fringe of sparks and smoke, rose high into the air."

I had now stopped work and was standing, curry-comb and brush in hand, staring at Tommy. Tommy, warming to the subject, for the moment forgot his superiority, and, not noticing my attitude, continued rapidly :

"When we turned into the mill road we heard a couple of explosions. Some of the men said 't was powder in the barn ; others said 't was more like the crack of a rifle. When we reached the house we saw the stranger, the deacon and a couple of his men throwin' water on blankets hung on the side of the house nearest the barn. Edith and the servant girl were there, helpin' carry water from the well to the house.

"Our comin' was a lucky job for them, for they were all tuckered out. In a few minutes the old hand-engine arrived, the suction-pipe was lowered into the well, the breaks were manned, and when the leadin' hosemen got a stream on the fire they began to get the best of it.

"By George," said Tommy, as the whole scene seemed to come into his mind, "what a sight that was and how we all shouted when the flames died down and we knew the house was saved !

"After the fire was all out the deacon opened a barrel of cider and everybody drank his fill."

"Did they get the horses out ?"

"Yes, got 'em all out. Ah, I thought there was some-thin' else. The explosions we heard"—here Tommy looked at me, as if meditating another triumph.

But I was ready for him, and had resumed work on the mare.

"The explosions were caused by the stranger's firin' at the two roughs who attacked the deacon at the tavern."

"Did he hit them ?"

"You bet he did," replied Tommy. "He killed one of 'em stone dead, and he hurt the other so he couldn't get away, and we brought him back with us."

"What were they trying to do?"

"Set fire to the house, of course. They'd piled a lot of straw against the rear of the house, and with a card of lighted matches were goin' to set fire to it when the stranger, who'd been watchin' 'em and was all ready, up and fired. The ball passed right through the neck of one feller and broke his spine, so he died at once. The other one was hit in the leg and fell, so they captured him. He's an ugly feller, that rough; but they'll fix him now."

Just here Mrs. Atkins called: "Tommy!" Tommy heard her and said:

"But perhaps you haven't been interested in what I've been tellin'. Look at yourself."

I did not look at myself, and I did not want Tommy to go away without telling me the rest, for I was interested to know if there was anything more, so I said:

"Anything else happen?"

"Can't stop any longer. There's mother callin' and I'm late to work as 't is."

Tommy sprang down from the chest and started home on the run; but as he was passing out of the door an idea seized him and, catching hold of the door-post with one hand, he swung the upper part of his body into the barn.

"Say! Come round to the store this afternoon, and if I'm there I'll tell you the rest."

He winked one eye at me and grinned. I let the currycomb fly at him, but he dodged it easily, disappeared, and in a moment I heard his feet strike the ground on his side of the fence.

CHAPTER III.

"Daniel, come to breakfast!"

It was my mother calling from the kitchen door.

As I entered the house, mother, who was taking breakfast from the stove, turned to say:

"Don't make any noise, Daniel. Father didn't sleep much last night, and he's abed now."

"Is he sick?" I asked, knowing the contrary, but hoping she would tell me what I had failed to learn from Tommy.

"No; but news was brought last night that Fort Sumter had been fired upon. Deacon Miller's barn was also burned. There were great doings in the village last night."

"I know that," I said, taking a seat at the table; "but what about the stranger and the man he killed?"

Mother was just stooping over the stove with a towel in her hand to open the oven door for the potatoes, but hearing my question, she straightened up and looked at me with astonishment.

"Why, Daniel, this all happened in the night."

She did not know that I had been out at all—a bit of evidence that father must have been thinking of something else when he came in or he would have told her.

"Who told you about it?"

"Tommy Atkins," I replied. "He came over this morning when I was cleaning the horses, and told me all about it; besides, I was in the village part of the time, myself."

"You were? I did not hear you come in," she said, and bent over the stove again. Breakfast was soon upon the table, and by the time we began to eat, a door opened and father appeared.

I expected to be scolded, and watched him from the corners of my eyes. He looked tired and cross, and the moment he noticed me he was evidently reminded of where he had found me last night. "Look here, young man," he said, harshly, "it is time for you to be in bed at two o'clock in the morning."

"But, father"—I objected.

"No 'but' about it, sir. I don't, and what's more, I won't have any more of these goings-on."

"He did not think you wouldn't like it," interposed mother.

"Didn't think—he'd no business to think. Why, I found him at the tavern wet through, just as the tavern keeper with his big wagon and half a dozen men were starting for the fire. A minute more and he'd been off with them, as big as you please. Look here, young man"—father always began with this phrase when he wanted to reprove me—"you've got to grow before you'll be of much account."

"Dan'l wanted to see what was going on, I suppose. You must remember, father, we were all children once."

"That is all very true, but no excuse," and while he was saying this, he leaned his crutch against the wall and slowly lowered himself into his chair at the table. Hardly had he turned around and faced us, before the crutch fell with a crash to the floor,

He jumped in his chair as though a pistol had been fired, and turning, looked at the fallen crutch as if it had been a dog ready to bite him. This seemed so funny that I would have laughed, vexed as I was, if a scared, troubled look on mother's face had not stopped me; the look made me realize that father's nerves were all unstrung with disease and trouble and sleeplessness, and that he was not himself.

But the unfavorable view he had taken of my presence in the tavern the night before and the way he had talked to me about it had driven all desire for news out of my mind, and turning my attention to the breakfast, I discovered I was quite hungry.

Not so with my father; nothing seemed to please him. The beef was too tough, the coffee too hot, or the potatoes too soggy. "Why can't we have as good beef here as in the city?" was a standing question with him.

He was never satisfied with the meat to be had, and every time he returned from his periodical trip to the city he had a great deal to say about it. Mother always bore all this complaining patiently. It must have hurt her feelings, yet she did not seem to mind it much, or else I did not see it. Her face in these years had always a careworn expression, and her eyes the same watchful look that was in them when I was recovering from the scarlet fever.

Father finally pushed away his plate, remarking, as he did so: "Oh, I don't want anything. I'm not hungry." Yet he had eaten half of what he had helped himself to.

"I hope Deacon Miller feels well this morning," he said, after a pause.

"Why, he was not hurt much last night, was he?" asked mother, a little anxiously.

I began to be interested again, but knew enough to keep quiet and let them talk, undisturbed.

"Hurt, no; but he's lost a pretty figure by the fire; and to a man who loves money as he does, it's enough to make him sick. It's lucky for him the stranger happened around as he did; he'd have lost his house, and the mill, too, for aught I know. Well, he's got money enough—he can stand it."

"Yes, father; but think of the people depending upon that mill for their bread and butter."

"Of course, I'd be sorry for the mill people," said father; "but I haven't any sympathy for the deacon. He has none for me. He'll foreclose on this property the first chance he gets, and there's no need of his being so grasping. His clerk told us yesterday that he'd more orders on hand than he could fill for a month."

Father waited for mother to speak, but she only looked worried, and said:

"I am sorry for Mrs. Miller."

"Sorry for Mrs. Miller? Yes; I suppose you are. That's just like a woman. Do you suppose she'd be sorry for you if the deacon foreclosed to-day?"

"Yes, I do," said mother, bravely.

"Oh, you do? Well, I don't. There's no difference in them. They're all in the same boat—deacon, wife, Edith and all—grasping, grasping, getting all they can out of everybody."

"You ought not to be so hard on the deacon," said mother. "He loaned you money when you needed it, and it's not his fault that you have been sick and that things have gone wrong with you. Don't fret, father: things will come out all right when you get well. What started the row at the tavern?"

"Why, the deacon was talking about the war—what

secession meant, how the price of everything would go up, and how long it would be before manufacturers could pay any more for help than they were paying now. That was about all he had to say when one of the roughs jumped up and, running to the deacon, shaking his fist in his face, said :

"'I know you, Deacon Miller! Yer a slick, palaverin', lazy aristercrat, too lazy to do anything yerself, an' too mean an' stingy to want an honest laborin' man paid full wages for an honest day's work. Yer always robbin' somebody an' tellin' 'em yer a frien', an' I tell yer yer lie !'

" Just then he pulled a pistol from his pocket and pointed it at the deacon. Wentworth, who was standing close by at the time, knocked the pistol up just as the fellow fired. Another rough—companion to the fellow who fired the pistol—jumped for Wentworth, and in a minute there was some pretty tall fighting. It didn't last long, for no sooner had some one shouted: 'Murder!' than the stranger rushed in like a mad bull and put an end to it all. The tavern-keeper told me after he came back from the fire this morning that the stranger killed one of these two men just as they were firing the deacon's house, and that he shot the other, wounding him so he was captured, and he 's now in the calaboose. But that don't matter much. Those fellows deserved putting out of the way, both of them. The thing we now have to face is war—a war that has come to stay until the cause has been washed out by blood. Civil war," said my father, dropping his voice to a meditative tone. "Civil war ; grim-visaged, fratricidal, terrible. But," turning suddenly to me, " aren't you going to do any work this morning?"

" The chores are done, the horses cleaned and the stable put to rights," said mother, interfering.

"It 's a wonder," said father, disappointedly.

"You are not going to the mill to-day, are you, father?" asked mother. "I wouldn't."

"I don't believe I will. But that grain must go up the river to-day. That must be done. Here, Daniel, you take the double team and carry it yourself. Be sure that Granger gives you a receipt for the right weight. There's more than I usually carry in. Tell him there 'll be less next week."

"All right," I said, and left the room ; but he could not let me go without a parting shot, and shouted after me :

"Look here, young man, I don't want any mistake about this. It must go to-day."

I hurried off. I could see before me a pleasant drive, and a chance to hear what the people thought of the war.

*   *   *   *   *   *   *

It had come. That crisis which the wise had foretold, and which the thoughtful, earnest few looked forward to as a means to the end they desired; that reality which the great body of conservative, well-fed, unsuspecting populace had pooh-poohed at, and refused to believed in, had come at last. War, with all its horrors, was at the door.

The little fleecy cloud that had crept up above the nation's horizon, unperceived by any one but the most weather-wise, had suddenly taken on enormous proportions, and become terribly visible to all. Broad, black and ominous, it covered the whole heavens, pregnant with rain and hail, hiding, in its shadow, destructive winds.

I, as a boy, lying at ease upon a wagon-load of grain, as my two horses plodded slowly along the river bank that pleasant spring morning, felt something of the excitement in my blood, looked at the approaching tempest with steady, curious eyes, and waited somewhat impatiently, not knowing the frightful power behind it, for the first tangible signs that it was a reality; a fearful fact and no empty though exciting dream.

PART II

CHAPTER I.

Three years have passed since first the country responded to the call to arms; three years since first was raised the cry of "On to Richmond;" since the setting in of that tide of war, which has ebbed and flowed along the coast and rivers of the South and among her mountains, on the plains and valleys of the Mississippi, of Tennessee and of Virginia; which has broken over Maryland into Pennsylvania and rolled along northward until it threatened to submerge Washington and Baltimore; three years of fatiguing toilsome march; of camp, of bivouac and of battle. Hundred of thousands of brave men have bared their breasts as a bulwark for the cause they loved. Tens of thousands have been swept resistlessly onward to die upon the field of battle, to languish in some gloomy, far-off hospital or pestilential prison pen. Again and again have the voice and bloody arms of war been raised for men, more men.

The lines are more contracted, but the battle cloud that has hung so long in the southern horizon has not yet lifted; the smoke and gleam from a country ravaged and burning has not yet faded away; there is no near prospect of peace from the shock of battle.

The North is determined, strong; the South is defiant, desperate.

Three years next month old Joe roused Waytown with the cry of "War." Since then how changed the village grew. So changed and strange I did not care to stay there.

Seventy-five thousand men were called for, and my comrades, all who could, enlisted. Almost everybody said : " Pshaw ! the war will soon be over ;" but when we received the report of the attack upon the Sixth Massachusetts regiment in Baltimore, and soon afterward news of the fight at Bull Run, our people began to realize that war was really at the door, and that, perhaps, it would be long and bloody.

In a few days a pine box, large enough to hold a man, came in on the train.

The whole village knew it almost instantly.

"Who is it?" somebody whispers.

"Mike Clancy, one of the volunteers from Miller's factory."

Then a half dozen Irishmen called for the pine box and carried it away to the north end of the town.

The next day a funeral, with many over-crowded wagons and raw-boned, knock-kneed horses crawled slowly down Main street out of the village to the Catholic graveyard on the hill.

No one thought of the shabby, strung-out pomp. It was a soldier's funeral, the first offering of our village on the country's altar.

A cheap cotton, star-spangled banner gleamed through the glass sides of the hearse.

Children, barefooted and bareheaded, stood by the gateways or climbed the road-side fence to watch with wide-open, calm but wondering eyes the sad procession. The busy housewife forgot for a moment her morning cares and from her windows watched it crawling by. She saw it climb the hill, pass through the graveyard gate, and turned away with apron to her eyes. Farmers suspended work, and with rake or hoe in hand watched it in silence out of sight.

Months passed, and the people grew silent, anxious and impatient. Newspapers were eagerly scanned and passed from hand to hand.

The Ball's Bluff battle was reported.

Many faces in Waytown turned pale, for "our boys" were there. And in the next few days, "He is dead," "He is wounded," "He, too, is dead," were the sad whispers which passed from mouth to mouth. Billy Green and Baker, the sadler, were shot there, and Joe Bentley, the big-hearted, big-bodied blacksmith's son, was wounded.

These dead were not sent home, and all that the fathers and mothers could say to inquiring friends was that their comrades have written us how Billy stood to the first shock like a man ; how, almost immediately after it, he was seen to drop, never to rise again ; how, near the end of the fight, Baker was seen standing with the rest, waiting for the charge, with blood running from his cheek and from his shoulder, two places where bullets had hit him ; and how, after the charge, when the rebels had fled and the smoke had lifted a little, he was found, dead. This was all they knew, all we could learn of the men of our village sent out to the war. Two, at least, Baker and little Billy, would never return.

Thus the war became a more personal matter while such news was going the rounds—a struggle not to be fought out by strangers and to end soon in hurrahs and holidays, but a reckless, hand-to-hand conflict, which threatened to draw every one, man, woman and child, in some way into the vortex of strife.

From the faces of the men around me I saw hope fading, to give place to a settled, anxious but determined look, while the cheeks of anxious women, of widows and of fatherless children, were pale and tear-stained.

After months more of waiting Joe Bentley came limping home, pale and weak, having been for a long time in the hospital, recovering from an amputation.

Old man Bentley had mounted his big horse long ago and ridden off to the South, and now, at long intervals, his daughter—for he had no wife—would get letters from him, saying that he was making a dash into the enemy's country or quietly shoeing horses.

With Joe and his father both away, the blacksmith's shop had been left to itself. Across the dingy windows spiders had spun their dusty webs undisturbed; the big loose-jointed double doors, which Mr. Bentley had swung groaning to, on the day he rode away, were now as he had left them, closed and barred, and through the many cracks and crevices in them you could see, in the dim twilight which reigned there, no matter how bright the sunlight might be outside, the forge, grim, dirty and cold; the big bellows, collapsed and gray with dust; the noisy hammer, now lying silent, across the anvil where the blacksmith had left it.

Nor was the appearance of the adjoining house, where the daughter and her aunt lived awaiting the return of father and brother, scarcely less gloomy, with its green blinds carefully closed, and the sparkling whiteness of its walls staring out cold and lifeless from the shadow of the waving trees above.

When Joe appeared in Waytown he seemed to have grown suddenly much older, and his face, though tired and worn, looked nobler and wiser. The village folk would never have grown tired of asking him questions

if he had cared to answer, but he had no stories to tell
them.

I remember that Parson Slim once asked him what
he thought of the war.

"Parson," said Joe, harshly, with no reverence in his
voice, and pointing to his stump of a leg, "it is a hard
fact," and he turned and limped away.

Joe soon got strong again, and the forge was no
longer deserted. The big double doors were thrown
wide open, letting in the daylight; the bellows groaned
and wheezed; a bed of live coals sparkled and glowed
in the center of the forge so lately cold and grim;
sparks flew out from the red-hot iron, and once more
the sharp ring of the anvil, under the heavy blows of
Joe's hammer, sounded along the quiet street.

Tommy Atkins and I were the only boys of our
crowd left. Perhaps Joe felt more friendly to us because we had been so much together before the beginning of the war. At any rate, however silent he was
with others regarding the scenes he had taken part in,
he seemed quite willing to tell us about them when
there were no others about.

Often in the long dark winter twilight, when his
work was done we three met by the side of the forge,
and he told us of war and its horrors. As the twilight
deepened and the night closed in, war seemed to over-
shadow us also; and while Joe went on, I could hear
the drums and the trumpets. I saw woods sparkling
with the flash of rifles, and with clouds of smoke drifting off through the trees. I saw the grassy plain
strewn with the dead and wounded and the earth red
with blood.

Did I fear war? Was I afraid to go? I think not;
but I did see more clearly, and began to realize the hard
fact that the highway to a soldier's glory leads through

the valley of the shadow of death. Thus the first flush of enthusiasm left me, and I began to look on war as a business, for I was still resolved to go, if, when I grew old enough to enlist, the fight was still on, resolved that no one should point a finger at me, when the struggle was over, and ask, "And where were you all this time—you who had the opportunity? Why didn't you go?"

But my father would not hear of my going. War was banished from all conversation at home, and I was forced to wait in silence, with the echoes of battle shouts and of rattling drums ringing in my ears.

But the excitement of those times, so powerful over every one, combined with Deacon Miller's foreclosing the mortgage he held on our property, affected my father's health very sadly. He became quite ill and took to his bed. We could see that he was failing day by day; doctors and nursing were of no avail, and we, mother and I, were forced to watch his decline, helpless, until, at the end of March, about a year after the firing on Fort Sumter, he passed away.

A sad time that was for us the spring of 1862. Many and heavy were the cares that were thrust upon my young shoulders, under the ever increasing burden of which I must struggle on for the rest of my days, but in those stirring times no one could remain long a boy.

By the end of September, 1863, our affairs in Way-town having been settled, and with barely enough to meet the expense, we were ready to leave for Kentucky, where mother intended to live with her sister. The war was still going on, and I was old enough to enlist. How eagerly I longed for the departure!

CHAPTER II.

We arrived at my uncle's place in Kentucky after a tedious trip in the cars. Delay, delay at every turn, especially when we came near our destination, explainable only from the tumultuous nature of the times and the moving across our way of troops and provision trains.

We were getting into the domain of war, and as its spirit took possession of me the sorrows of my private life faded away.

Mr. Nichols—my uncle's—family consisted of himself and wife, both much older than my mother, and an adopted daughter, Mary. There were two sons, Charlie and Fred, each of whom had shouldered his musket and departed at the beginning of the war, and neither had, as yet, returned. From the last of Fred's letters, which came at rare intervals, they judged that he was, about the time mother and I arrived at his home, somewhere in Eastern Kentucky or Tennessee. Of Charlie, the elder, they had heard almost nothing since the first year of the war. He disappeared in a battle, and all search for him having been given up for a long time, they came to think him as dead. Judge of their surprise, however, when a half-demented tramp, wandering aimlessly through the village, brought word that Charlie was a prisoner. As may be imagined, much of the time after my arrival was spent in trying to devise some means of determining Charlie's whereabouts, so that they might get word to him in case he was suffering, and do all they could to relieve him. This did not prove to be an easy matter, and they finally concluded to wait until Fred came home, as his three years of service had about expired. We were, therefore, looking impatiently forward to his return, as he would be likely to know, better than any one, how to go to work to find his brother. In the meantime, I was making preparations in secret for entering the service, and cogitating the best way to do so.

But while waiting for the time to come when I should be ready to depart, I could not help feeling that this going away would not be the easy matter I had once thought it.

How could I say good-by to the good, kind mother with the tears in her eyes that I knew would come, and how could I bring myself to turn my back on this pleasant, hospitable home? How would I feel when, taking Mary by the hand and looking into her eyes, I should try to say good-by, knowing that it might be good-by forever? The more I thought of it the more difficult did it appear, until I became at last disgusted with myself. I was thinking too much of Mary's handsome face and her sweet voice.

In the early morning, when the sun was bright and everything was glaring and unromantic, I suffered from the consciousness of having been a fool the day before, and determined to be one no longer. I decided that I would attend to business for that day at least.

After breakfast I strolled down the street and watched the long trains bearing soldiers and supplies to the front. At noon I returned for luncheon, and after it strolled up to Fred's room with my pipe, for I was a smoker now. Mary would, of course, appear there; but how could I help it, I asked myself. I was not obliged to shun her; besides, her presence was very agreeable to me. She generally brought some of Fred's letters, and the two or three that Charlie had sent home, and we read them there together, she explaining what the letters left unsaid, and telling me about the country, for she had been through and was familiar with that section; and so, however strong my determination had been in the morning, by dinner time, which came on the edge of evening, I was as much under her control as ever, and when we went for a walk afterward my hopes and plans were almost forgotten, and I re-membered only at long intervals that over there beyond the moonlit hills were fire and smoke and blood and duty.

I went to bed to dream of her, and awoke next morn-ing to the same round of savage resolution, battle and defeat.

At length Fred arrived, travel-stained, sun-tanned and hungry. But what stories he had to tell—stories to make us laugh, stories to make us weep and stories that made the blood tingle in my veins! I could see how proud the father was of his son, and the mother too, despite her tears; and Mary—what would I not have given to bring for myself such a look of interest into her dear face.

One morning, soon after Fred's arrival, I found him in the barn, enjoying a quiet smoke.

"Well, Fred, what are you going to do?" I asked, striking a match on a post to light my pipe.

"I'm going back; I don't feel at home here, and so much going on down yonder."

"Why, I thought your time was up? Are you going to re-enlist?"

"I have already re-enlisted," he replied. "You see, most of our fellows were awfully tired of tramping. We had been at it three years pretty steady, so when they asked us to veteranize, we said we would, if they would agree to give us horses, make us cavalry, or mounted infantry."

"Are they going to?" I asked.

"I don't know about that. They promised to, so we veteranized; that is, re-enlisted."

"Then it is all settled. You are going back?"

"Yes," said Fred. "This is only a furlough of thirty days. They don't know it in there," motioning toward the house, "and how I am going to tell them without having a scene I hardly know. 'T was a terrible scene indeed when Charlie and I went off. I don't want to go through it again."

"Well, what am I going to do? I'm going into this thing."

Fred looked at me, his mouth opening in surprise.

"Why—what—you are too young!"

"That's all right. I'm not too young. I'm big enough, and it's no use to say no. My mind is made up."

"Now, don't be in a hurry, Dan," said Fred, looking serious. "This a bad business."

"That's all very true; but what am I to do? You know as well as I that there are younger fellows in the army."

Fred nodded assent.

"Then that is no reason why they wouldn't take me. I want to go—have been wanting to go ever since the war began, but I could never get the chance. Now mother's with her friends, I'm going to skip, if I have to do it when they are not looking."

"Better not do that. They'll let you go if you stick to it. After all, if you've made up your mind, it would be best to let you go. They'll see it in that light, only there'll be the usual amount of crying."

"I suppose there will ; but it can't be helped."

"But think a moment, Dan ; there are many sides to this thing. A bullet through your lungs or liver or heart or your head torn open with a shell, isn't the worst of it. Camp life isn't all that it's cracked up to be. And then the endless tramps !"

I shuddered, but did not waver.

"But you say you are to have horses. Why couldn't I go with you ? Wouldn't they take me ?"

"Why, yes, and it's a good regiment to join, but it's not so sure that we are to have horses. They said so, and there'll be a row if we don't ; but we may not get them, after all. But if we do, there's the camp and the mud and wet and disease and wounds and prisons. There's much to be thought of."

"And I've thought of it. Why did your regiment go in, if they once got out of it ? For the thirteen dollars a month ?"

Fred scratched his head and answered :

"It's hard telling what most of us joined again for. I suppose most of us couldn't stay away if we tried. The thirteen dollars had mighty little to do with it. A fellow don't stand up to be shot at for thirteen dollars a month, if that's the end of it."

"But somebody must have found a reason. What did they say ?" I asked, pressing the point.

"Most of 'em said they were not going to quit now ; they would see it through. One man, when asked if he was going to put his name down, said : 'Yes, if I was out, I couldn't stay out while this thing is going on.' One fellow, who lost his two brothers on picket at Stone River, said : 'I owe the Johnnies something, and I'm going to stay to pay it.' One man came out of

the hospital and put his name down. I heard another
man say he re-enlisted because the others did ; but
perhaps the greatest sacrifice of all was that made
by Eli Norcross. His mother is old and feeble in
health; his wife and children poor, and looking with
hope and longing for his return to their midst.
The boys all watched him as he came forward; with
the perspiration starting from his face. His hand
trembled a little as he leaned over the roll, but he
signed."

"These fellows know all there is in it; they don't
hesitate. I want my share. Now don't try to persuade
me not to go," I said, noting Fred was about to speak ;
"my mind is made up to that ; but help me to go away
easily."

"All right, I will, Dan. After all, you wouldn't be
much of a chap if you did not want to go. I was not
as old as you when I went. Now, what do you know
about handling a gun ?"

"O, I know a little. There were few boys East who
could not go through the manual of arms with a broom,
and I learned it with the rest."

"That's good, you've got the motions, eh? Well,
now, I will get a musket somewhere and help you a
little, for even if we have horses, it won't hurt you to
know how to handle a gun; and if we're made cavalry,
we've all to learn to drill."

We kept silence about our plans and went to work.
A musket was obtained and kept hidden in the barn,
except in the morning when no one was around. Then
it made its appearance, and I went through the drill at
the bidding of Fred. He seemed to take delight in
teaching me ; whether his mind was on such things, and
this gave him an opportunity to relieve his pent-up
feelings, or whether he tortured himself for my benefit,

I do not know. At any rate, in a very short time I
grew accustomed to handling the gun.

Meanwhile, all knowledge of our doings was kept a
profound secret. We were going to put off telling the
folks until two or three days before the time should
come for us to leave, as we did not wish the time for
grief and tears spread out any more than was necesary.

I had been going through this exercise daily more
than a week, when one morning, while we were hard at
it, and more than ever oblivious to everything else,
something was wanted of Fred at the house and he
was called for. As no answer came to repeated calls, it
occurred to Mary that she had seen him strolling toward the barn a short time before, and starting out to
find him, caught us at work.

I was not quite as quick as usual ; at any rate Fred
found fault at the slow time I made loading the gun.

He was saying : " That's too slow," taking the gun.
" It goes to count like this—one, two, three, four,"
speaking quickly. " So now, then," handing it back to
me, " try it again."

As he stepped back to give me room I saw Mary
standing in the doorway behind him. The light was at
her back, so that I could not see her face.

" Fred," she said, in a soft, sad voice, " mother wants
you."

I felt that she knew all. And when, after Fred left
us, she came up to me, I could see that her face was
pale, that her lips quivered and that tears were trembling on her eyelids.

" You are going to the war," she said, laying her soft
little hand on my arm.

The blood rushed to my face, my heart seemed to
come up into my throat, and for the first time I felt
sorry for the step I was taking, realized what I was

breaking away from. But it was only for an instant, although it took all my strength away and forced me to sit down. Mary took a seat beside me.

"And Fred is going, too," she sobbed, turning her face away.

I took one of her hands and drew her a little toward me without her noticing it. My voice was scarcely steadier than hers when I began, although it grew stronger.

"Yes, Mary, we are both going. Fred, although he did not tell you, re-enlisted before he left his regiment. He could not stay, and when he goes to join his regiment I'm going with him."

"And you would not tell us, Dan !" she said, reproachfully.

"It would have done no good. If we had, the fact would have spoiled Fred's furlough. We were going to keep quiet until two or three days before the time came for us to leave."

Mary could not stop her tears. I was beside myself, not knowing how to comfort her. I felt as if I had done her an injury, drew her closer to me and tried my best to change the current of her thoughts. We began again to talk, and, once started, I could not stop until I had told her everything. Many things I said that I had never expected to say to her.

The sun was shining brightly that pleasant day. The dry and withered grass seemed just beginning to turn green, I thought. The air, the sky, the distant woods and hills seemed just ready to burst into the beauties of spring. My own life seemed rather strange, as my eyes wandered from the quiet village outside to Mary's head with its sunny, waving hair, resting upon my shoulder. Yet I never wavered in my purpose to take my musket in hand and depart when the time should come.

In the sweet, sad days that followed Mary gave no sign to the others of what Fred and I had in view; only her eyes were sometimes red in the morning, as if she had been crying, and once in a while I found her sitting silent, her hands, from which the work had fallen, folded in her lap, and her eyes dim and blank.

But we were more together now than before. I did not try to avoid her any longer. There was a promise between us, that if I escaped the clutches of war I was to call for her. She would wait for me.

So these little scenes of comedy and tragedy were enacted in and around that Kentucky home, and yet unnoticed; hours of drill in the use of the gun in the morning; long walks or drives with Mary in the afternoon when the weather was pleasant.

But the time came when they had to be told—the fathers and mothers, I mean. Fred and I came off victorious from the struggle; but let me pass over it in silence.

Two days later came the hour of parting. It was a dark and dismal time, especially for me. Fred had been anxious for the time to come. True, he was leaving home, but he was going back to the camp of old companions, to scenes he had grown to love. I was going into a new country, to new scenes, regions of death and horror, leaving behind me home, pleasures, love—all for what?

At that time I could find no answer to this question. But I would not turn back, and Fred and I departed, going south.

CHAPTER III.

About two o'clock in the afternoon of the following day we reached Lebanon, a large town at the terminus of the railway. The houses were old, dirty and dust-covered; the streets were thick with a fine yellow dust which the feet of hundreds of mule teams and the wheels of army wagons were grinding still finer and throwing into the air until it was loaded with a yellow haze that filled the lungs and settled like a mantle upon everything.

At the quartermaster's department we learned that a train was about to leave for our point of rendezvous on the Cumberland River. We started out to find the train, but it was almost sundown, and we were just about to give up the search when a voice from a passing wagon hailed us:

"Hi, Fred, hello there! Whoa! Where you going? Here, this way!"

Looking through the clouds of dust in the direction of the voice we saw a man standing on a wagon tongue, leaning over the back of a mule, and gesticulating frantically.

"Come here!" said the voice through the dust.

"Who is it, Fred," I asked.

"It looks like Jack Maddox," answered Fred; "but

[45]

he's so thickly covered with this infernal dust that his own mother would not know him. Let's see," said he, walking toward him.

I followed and soon saw Fred grasp the fellow by the hand, and heard him say:

"Jack, I would not have known you for dirt."

"Well, there's a heap of dirt here for sure, but it's better than mud. Goin' back to the company?"

"Yes. But what are you doing here, driving a team? Haven't left the company, have you?"

"Yes. You see, Fred, the horses haven't come, and it didn't look to me as if they ever would. I'm sick of tramping, so when this chance opened in the quarter-master's department I got the detail."

"Like it?" Fred asked.

"Like it! Well, I don't like it so well as I should like to be with the boys if they were made mounted infantry. One horse is easier to take care of than half a dozen ugly mules. But things don't look first-rate for the horses, and I'm not goin' to take any chances; 'sides, I get better feed where I am, sleep in the wagon, and don't have to tramp and carry everything on my back."

"There is no doubt about our horses, is there?"

"They haven't come yet," and Jack shrugged his shoulders.

"What do they say about it?" Fred asked.

"I heard one of the officers say t'other day that General Potter had promised in writing that horses would be furnished and the regiment should be mounted."

"There is no danger but what they'll get 'em, Jack; they would not get us in under promise of giving horses and then back out."

"Well, I hope they will; but I am trusting Jack Maddox, just now. But," he said, lowering his voice, and looking toward me, "who's that with you?"

"That's my cousin. Here, Dan," said Fred, turning to me, "this is Jack Maddox. You remember I told you about him. He's the fellow who did the good turn for me at Mill Springs. My cousin, Jack; he's going to enlist in our company."

"It's a good company," said Jack, nodding his head, taking me by the hand and looking me over seriously. "There are no better men in a skirmish, and no better men in a fight than those men; they hang together, somehow, better than most men, and you can't skeer 'em a little bit."

"Same officers?" Fred asked.

"Pretty much. Of course you know of the new captain. Hartee's his name. Nobody knows anything about him, except he's seen service. He's a good talker, and if it hadn't been for him and the way he talked about the horses at Strawberry Plains, I don't believe so many of the men would have 'listed again. But come, if you're goin' to camp right away you might as well get on and ride; it's a heap easier, and it's a right smart tramp to the river."

We climbed to a seat beside the dusty, good-natured driver, and while Fred and he discussed the probabilities of the company being mounted, and all the little odds and ends of camp gossip he had picked up relating to the question, I lay back against a barrel and listened, with my eyes closed.

Mile after mile of that dusty road we passed, nor did we stop until long after sundown, when he came to a halt by the side of a creek. Here we washed, built a fire, made coffee, and fried pieces of beef, which, with soft bread, completed our supper. Here also we slept, wrapped in blankets—thanks to Maddox—by the fire. Early the next morning, about daylight, after a hasty bath and breakfast, we were on the road again.

Up and down hill we went, with nothing but the creaking of the wagon frame, groaning under its heavy load; the rattle and clatter of camp kettles, frying-pans and buckets that were hung from beneath, the shout of the driver, the crack of his long whip, or an occasional remark from him or from Fred, to break the monotony of the ride. On we went through Liberty, Mount Gilead and Somerset, until, on the afternoon of the second day, we came in sight of the river where Jack Maddox, pointing to the side of a distant hill, said :

"There's camp."

"What have they got, tents or log-houses?" Fred asked.

"Tents. We can see them a little further up on the road," Jack answered, and we relapsed into silence.

Perhaps half a mile further, and we were at the top of the hill, from which we could look across the little valley to the camp.

I saw that it was situated on the north side of the Cumberland River, on the hillside plateau above the road, and that it overlooked the river, valley and away to the hills and mountains beyond.

I could make out lines and rows and squares of small tents, a group of larger tents, a flagstaff from which floated the Stars and Stripes; while here and there the smoke from a burning camp-fire drifted lazily along on the still air.

"So that's camp, is it?" said I, partly to myself, and yet loud enough for Fred to hear, who answered :

"Yes, good place, isn't it!" he said, with a tone of approval in his voice.

"It's out of the dust; that's one good thing about it," said I, "and has a good prospect over the surround-ing country."

Then Fred and Jack compared its location with some

other place they had camped in, while I, partly listening to them and partly wondering what my first duties would be, said nothing more. When we reached the foot of the hill leading up to the camp we left the wagon, to ascend on foot.

At the top we paused to look over the scene, and I saw men moving about, building fires, carrying wood and water, cleaning guns, putting up tents, &c., &c.

"You never saw a camp before, did you, Dan?" Fred asked as we stood there. "When the regiment is full each company has fifty tents, divided into five rows, and, with the exception of a company street, sometimes twenty-five feet wide, a space of about six feet between them. The officers have their tents near their companies. Over there," said he, pointing to a row of larger tents at the further end of the line, "is the regimental headquarters. Just back of that, in that large tent, is the sutler, where we can buy condensed milk at fifty cents a can; molasses cakes, not more than a mouthful, at thirty cents a dozen; canned meats, oysters, fish, preserves and jellies of all kinds; even butter and fresh milk and extravagantly high-priced eggs, and not warranted good at that, are also sold there."

"What is that vacant space over there?" I asked, pointing to the open end of the plateau.

"I suppose that will be used mostly for exercising us in horse-movements. But come, let's go to the captain's tent and report. There you can sign the roll, and we can get orders for tents, blankets and so forth."

We approached the camp, where Fred was pleasantly greeted by members of the different companies through which we passed.

"Where's company D," he asked of a man who had been tightening up one corner of his tent, and was driving the pins into a new place.

"Lower end of the line," the man replied.

We soon came to the company, and after an introduction and a hearty shake of hands all around, we went to the captain's tent, where I discovered what was necessary to complete my formal joining of the company.

I signed the roll, and as I made the last strokes to my name I happened to look over the heads of the officers sitting by the camp-table, to the back end of the tent, and there saw somebody just lifting up the flap, to come in. As he straightened up inside the tent, I recognized, much to my astonishment, the stranger of the Waytown Arms. But he gave no sign that recognition was mutual. No doubt the face of the boy who had listened to him reading the news of the war had long since passed from his mind. I, however, knew him at once, although he had grown older and bigger. He evidently did not notice me or the stare with which I honored him, for he turned to speak with some of the officers, and I, pulling myself together, followed Fred out of the tent.

"Who is that man?" I asked Fred, as we came outside.

"That's Captain Hartees, our captain," he replied carelessly.

The conversation stopped here, and we followed the sergeant, who took us to the quartermaster, where I received a suit of army blue, overcoat and all—haversack, knapsack, canteen, rubber blanket, woolen blanket and half of a shelter-tent. Fred took the other half—a tin dipper that would hold at least a quart and a tin plate.

At Fred's suggestion I had bought at Louisville a knife, fork and spoon that folded together completely. In addition to the other things I also received a gun, a

bayonet, a belt, bayonet-scabbard, and cartridge-
box.

With this load we followed the sergeant back to the
company, where our position in line was pointed out,
and I took my first lesson in tent-pitching.

First we obtained, from the woods near by, two
forked sticks for the two standards, and a straight stick
to serve as a ridge-pole. The forked sticks were then
driven into the ground, and the ridge-pole laid into the
crotches of these uprights. The two tent halves were
then buttoned together, thrown over the cross-poles,
and the ends brought to the earth, where they were
pinned tightly, forming a regular pitch roof.

All around our tent, which was about six feet long,
five feet wide, and just high enough in the center for
one to sit down inside and not have his head touch the
ridge-pole, we dug a deep ditch to receive and lead
off the water in rainy weather. On the inside, close to
where the cloth was pinned to the ground, we banked
up the earth to further insure protection against water.

From Jack Maddox we obtained all the hay we
wanted. This we spread on the ground, under the
tent, and covered with a rubber blanket. Our canvas
home was hardly completed when some one said:

"There goes the grub-call, boys. Better go up and
get your coffee."

"What, already?" said Fred. Then, turning to me:
"Get your dipper and plate, Dan, and let's go."

With our new tin plates and dippers, Fred and I
hastened to interview the cook.

As we approached the fire, already surrounded by
men drawing their rations, I saw a stalwart negro, on
his knees, holding over a bed of red coals a frying-pan,
the sizzling contents of which he was turning with a
fork. The man was jet-black, apparently oblivious of

his surroundings, and was singing, in a low musical tone :

> "Nebber min' de wedder, so de win' don't blow;
> Nebber min' de wedder, so de win' don't blow;
> Nebber min' de wedder, so de win' don't blow;
> Don't yer bodder 'bout yer trouble till it comes."

"Same old song, Lige," said Fred.

The man grinned, rolled up his eyes, and nodded in assent; then, starting quickly as he glanced at me, said :

"Golly! Dat you, Maws' Dan? I's glad ter see yer. 'Deed, I is."

"How's this, Dan?" said Fred. "Do you know black Lige?"

"No. I never saw him before."

"What! Don' yer know me, Maws' Dan? I's Lige—brack Lige, whose ole mamma used to tote yer in her arms when yer wus a pickerninny. Don' yer 'member her?"

"Mistake, Lige. I am Daniel Wright; came from the North, where I was born."

"Bawn in de Norf? Wasn't raised 'round yuh? Das jes like yer—foolin' ol' Lige."

"No, Lige; I'm not fooling."

"Well, I thought yer was my ol' maw's boy; yer does look pow'ful like him for sho." Then turning his attention to the frying-pan, he added: "But I s'pose yer wouldn't be 'round yuh, do; yer wouldn't be 'round yuh?" Saying which, and as if dismissing the subject, he sang :

> "Nebber min' de wedder, so de win' don't blow;
> Don' yer bodder 'bout yer trouble till it comes."

"I say, Lige," said Fred, after a while, "sing the other one. I want Dan to hear it."

"Long 's Maws' Dan done born in he Norf," said Lige, after a moment of hesitation and with a quizzical

"GOLLY! DAT YOU, MARS' DAN?" *See Page* 52.

look at me, "I's bound ter sing it. But dat's more'n a song, Maws' Fred; mor'n a song."

Taking from the fire the pan he had been tending he stood erect and fixed his eyes steadily on mine. His gaze was sharply questioning, almost fierce at first, but soon turned into a vacant, far-off stare, broken at length by a sudden flash of expression, when, throwing back his head and fixing his eyes on the sky, he broke forth into a strain so abrupt, impassioned and of an energy so wild that it seemed inspired by a soul too large for mortal form. It was not Black Lige's voice we heard, but the voice of his people, the cry of an oppressed race, struggling, striking and dying for liberty. It rang out in trumpet tones, drawing and thrilling the entranced listeners, who came softly stealing up from all directions.

As the chant moved to a close the voice swelled with the waxing theme, and Lige stood like one turned to stone; then, as tears started from his eyes, the tones became more tender and subdued, dying away at length in a hoarse whisper. Even after the song was ended Lige's glance did not wander from the heavens. His lips moved and there was a look in his eye as if he saw in the air above a something that was vanishing, yet he could not look away from it till it was quite gone from view. When he did turn to the circle of silent and awe-struck soldiers gathered round him he looked dazed; and sinking to the ground, he covered his face with his hands. After a moment, when most of the soldiers had gone away, Lige got up and resumed the work that our coming and the song had interrupted.

"Who is that man, Fred?" I asked, after we received our rations of coffee, hard bread and fried beef, and had moved away from the fire.

"The captain's cook; got him somewhere in Tennessee,

a year ago. Do you know, Dan, I've heard Lige sing that last song of his three or four times, and each time I hear it there seems to be something new about it. He's a whole-souled fellow, is Lige, wonderfully clever; got lots of good sense, and does about as he pleases. He is quite a favorite with the boys. They never mock him or impose on him in any way. He's manly and commands respect, in spite of some of his oddities. Then, too, he will find things to eat when no one else can. The captain fares well with Black Lige to care for him. Funny he called you by name."

"Merely a coincidence," I responded.

"I suppose so." Then, as if noticing for the first time the contents of his plate, he continued: "This is pretty good, Dan; we don't get fried meat very often."

"What do you get?"

"Coffee and hard-tack."

"A simple meal for a hungry man."

"Yes, rather; but to-morrow I'll get a junk of salt pork; that's the stuff; that'll give us a meal fit for a king. There's nothing like salt pork for a regular 'stand by.' With that, either fried, broiled, toasted, boiled, baked or raw and a little hard, or even a little soft tack to eat with it, a man always feels well, can stand any amount of marching, and is never hungry. You can do anything in the line of cooking if you only have a little salt pork. If you have beans to cook, it's the pork cooked with them that makes the beans fit to eat. If you want a little fat to fry your meat in, if you want to fry pancakes, or do anything else under heaven for which fat must be used, pork is the article you want. It is the only butter a soldier gets in the field. Depend upon it, Dan, there's nothing like pork."

By this time we arrived at our fire, where we found three of Fred's friends (Alf Kimball, Dick Taylor and

Jake Bence), Fred's crowd, as he called them, already seated on the logs about it, each busily discussing his ration of beef and coffee.

Fred introduced me in an off-hand manner, and, as I took my seat, I became so much one of them as if we had known each other for years; for formality, especially at meal time, has no place about a soldier's camp fire. A man's heart naturally expands as his stomach fills; the fresh air flavored with odors of burning pine, steaming coffee and frying and broiling meat lends its charm; an atmosphere of bohemianism, a spirt of romance, and a sense of companionship in a dangerous calling—all combine to find the "good fellow" lurking (sometimes pretty well concealed in some of us) and drag him into view.

Kimball was a good-natured, fine-looking fellow, easy-mannered and possessed of a happy faculty of giving conversation on unpleasant subjects a turn to keep it bright and pleasant. He was always ready to take things as they came, whether it was a plump goose, a fat hog or an order to march.

Taylor was quiet, good natured, always ready to do a favor for any one, and was popular with all.

Bence was a big-boned mountaineer and inveterate growler. To give Fred's own language: "He's a good feeder, brave to recklessness, good on a forage, but he can outgrowl any other man in the regiment."

He had the reputation, also, of being able to get at all there was going on among the officers; and if there was anything to be done, Bence was sure to know it before any one else—excepting, perhaps, Black Lige.

I shall never forget this, my first meal in camp, as I sat with these men on the logs by our fire, drank my coffee and ate my crackers and beef.

The sun had set. In the fading light the distant hills

came out in bolder outline, and seemed to draw near,
while the intervals up and down the valley and along
the river deepened in color until they gradually disappeared. In silence I listened to my comrades chatting
good-naturedly over the incidents of their short furlough—of their homes, of the camp and its surroundings and of their probable future.

Everything was so new—my uniform, belt, tin dipper, plate, the faces of the men about me, the surroundings—even the coffee, the hard bread and the fried beef
were a revelation to me.

And this was camp-life. I did not think it at all
disagreeable. In fact, it was a pleasant hour to me,
tired as I was with the excitement of new scenes, new
work. It was a pleasant sight, the fire in front of me,
around which our fellows were lounging ; the other
fires further off, with their groups of men against a
background of tents ; the clear night, with the evening
star as large as a lantern ; the night wind whispering
in the woods.

Of all, the hardest thing to realize was that I was a
soldier—not my own master, but a man bound to obey
orders—to mount and ride into the teeth of death if
need be. I turned this strange phase of a soldier's
character over and over in my mind, the voices of my
companions gradually fading from my ear, and in such
cogitations I went back to the first results of war I had
known—to the funeral of Mike Clancy at Waytown, to
the columns upon columns of reports I had read about
the battles and desperate charges of cavalry ; about
infantry facing, undaunted, storms of shot and shell
that were slaughtering them by the thousands.

But what had I to do with this ? Then I was a boy ;
now I was a soldier. Come what might, I would follow
my company.

Then Mary, in all the loveliness of her youth, glided into my mind. Should I ever see her again? But I put that thought quickly away. What was she doing then? I wondered. And as I thought I seemed to see her, as I had found her once in a while, when we were together, sitting by herself, dreaming, and her vague, tear-dimmed eyes fixed on the southern hills. And I fancied myself at her side, although I knew those same southern hills spread wide between us.

CHAPTER IV.

"Come, Dan, turn out; there goes the roll-call!" said Fred, the next morning, punching me in the side with his elbow. I awoke while the last notes of the bugle sounding the reveille were echoing up and down the river through the valley below. The sun was already up and shining into our tent through the open end.

"Come, Dan, come! A soldier is up at reveille," he cried again, giving another poke to assist me in collecting my drowsy senses. Throwing off the blanket I crept out of the tent and looked about me. All over the camp men were crawling from tents, rubbing their eyes, and assembling in little groups in the company streets.

"Good-looking men, Fred," I said, for want of anything better, and accompanying the remark with a yawn, still feeling decidedly sleepy and, withal, a little chilly at being forced to leave a nice warm bed for the cold morning air from the river.

Fred, on the other hand, was all life and activity.

"No better men in the country," he responded briskly as he dragged our accoutrements out of the tent. "These men are mostly from the mountains of Kentucky, thorough Unionists and brave to a man. But come, fall in ; there's the sergeant, and he's going to call the roll."

I was soon in line with the rest of our company, responded to my name when it was called, and then returned to the tent to roll up my blanket and clean my musket, which, with Fred's, had lain between us all night. While at work over it, I paused often to survey the scene before me. The sun was shining brightly over the tops of the hills, upon the woods and meadows, and making luminous the thin wreaths of mist hanging above the river. In the camp our little dog-tents looked clean and white in the fresh morning light, and, like the grass, sparkled with beads of dew. The moment was one of life and activity, our camp presenting a most animated scene.

Never during a whole day does a camp look so populous as in the early morning hours, when every man is up and busy about his tent, bringing things into order for the day. From one end of the encampment to the other men were scattered in all sorts of positions, some cleaning muskets, as I was, and others building fires, still others bringing wood and water. In some places men had assembled in little groups and gossiped as they worked ; but, as a rule, we were separated, each man working by himself.

Working over a gun is good exercise ; at least, it soon brought my blood into better circulation, filled my lungs full of the fresh air, and in consequence dispelled much of the discomfort of mind and body.

"Clean mine while you 're about it," said Fred at that moment, coming up from the direction of the cook's fire, and indicating his gun, leaning against the ridge-pole just outside the tent. "How's this for a piece of pork?" he cried exultingly, holding up a piece of salt pork that would weigh at least four pounds.

"What are you going to do with that?" I asked.

"Show you when breakfast is ready if they don't give us beef."

"Which I sincerely hope they will, for I don't want to commence on pork before I have to."

"I hope you may always get as good, my boy," said Fred, his face assuming a serious look. "I have seen the time, more than once, when I would have given almost anything for a piece of pork like this. I'll take care of it now. It'll keep and come in handy before long." And he stowed it away in his haversack.

"How much longer do we have to wait before breakfast is ready?" I asked, having an inward feeling that that subject was not receiving all the attention it should

"Oh, somewhere between half-past six and seven o'clock. It'll soon be ready now. Some of the boys went down to the river for water right after roll-call, and as soon as the water boils and the coffee is made breakfast is ready."

"You don't need to do anything but wipe the guns, do you, Fred?" I said, after having wiped away every sign of moisture from the barrel.

"Not while they are new," he replied. "After they have seen weather and the fire-bronze is worn off it takes a little elbow-grease to keep them clean. As long as you can keep the bronze on, wiping is good enough. Most of the boys prefer to keep their old guns to having new ones. They know them, you see, and what they can do with them, but they have to work a little harder to keep them in shape."

I gave my gun an extra rub, rested it against the ridgepole and began on Fred's. "What follows breakfast?" I asked him, after a pause.

" Guard-mounting, I suppose."

" What is that?" I asked, having, however, a fair idea of what he meant.

" Relieving the guard that have been on duty all night."

" That is what I supposed. But is there any particular parade about it?"

" Usually there is," he replied. " But how is that, sergeant?" he cried to the orderly sergeant, who was passing at that moment. " Are we to have guard-mounting this morning?"

" No, not until all the officers and men are in. Until then the guard will be detailed from the different companies, without parade. It was our turn last night."

" Then we won't come in for it again for a week," said Fred. " Well, I don't know if that is anything to crow over ; we'll get our share in time, and not have to forage for it, either."

After a while the men most interested in the preparations for breakfast began to gather around the cook's fire, where they stood dreamily gazing at the smoke from the burning wood as it curled up into the air, or watched the steam rise from the kettles as the water in them began to boil. To those who preferred it a ration of uncooked beef was served instead of fried meat. It saved the cook just so much labor if the men took it raw, and many of us preferred to cook it in our own way.

Fred and I, for instance, availed ourselves of the privilege, and took our meat with a pot of hot coffee, some hard bread, and a can of condensed milk, purchased of the sutler, to another fire.

There, with my coffee resting on some hot coals that I had raked from the fire, I placed my piece of beef upon the end of a pointed stick and held it near the flames to broil.

It was an interesting sight to see at least a dozen men squatting round the fire with a dozen pots of coffee resting on little piles of hot coals similar to my own; a dozen outstretched hands and sticks holding as many pieces of beef that shriveled, sputtered, smoked and blazed in the flames, and the men, without an idea of the ludicrous side of the picture they were making, gazing seriously and earnestly at the sizzling beef.

The lower part of the beef cooked, the ends were reversed and returned to the fire until the rest was done. Then, with a little salt for seasoning, the meal was ready, and, with an appetite sharpened by the clear morning air, I fell to. Never did beef, coffee and hard bread taste so good. The beef was cooked to a turn; the coffee was fine; and the hard tack was fresh and crisp.

Breakfast over, the awkward squad was drilled by a corporal, who acted as instructor. At first, we made more or less awkward work of it; but, by persevering, our showing, in time, was good.

After this came dinner, which, while we were at this place, usually consisted of some sort of stew, made of fresh beef, potatoes and onions; stewed beans and pork, or salt beef and vegetables, with an occasional treat of boiled rice to give a variety.

Day after day we went through this sort of thing, becoming more familiar with the use of a gun, and getting an infusion of military experience, discipline and skill in maneuvering, that in every way fitted us to drill with the company whenever they began.

As stragglers kept coming in all this time, our ranks were soon full, and all the officers present—the colonel coming almost the last of all. Everybody was on the watch for him, and his arrival was known almost instantly throughout the whole camp, although we were busy with our supper at the time.

"Now look out for battalion drills and see if our horses don't soon show up," remarked Fred.

"Yes, if we are to have them!" growled Jake Bence, at my elbow, never taking his eyes from the beef he was holding to the fire. "They've as good as lied to us, and I tell you, Fred, I'm getting mighty sick of it," and there was a sour expression on his face which corresponded strictly with the sentiment and tone of his grumbling.

CHAPTER V.

The next day, as we expected, all the companies were ordered out for drill, and we exercised on the parade ground, in all known movements for infantry, for at least an hour, marching, countermarching, forward, right oblique and left oblique; now at a double quick, then at common time, marching with a full regimental front, or in column, and then wheeling front into line.

Then came the parade, where we went through the manual of arms, and at "rest," while the drums and fife marched up and down the line playing "Yankee Doodle," "Hail Columbia" or the "Star Spangled Banner."

Every day, when it was pleasant, we went through these movements. I could not see the necessity for it then, but I see now how important it all was. When it happened to be stormy, the men who were not on guard kept their tents and wrote letters home or amused themselves in reading.

Those little dog tents were anything but comfortable in wet weather. The space inside was very small, and the cloth so thin that one could scarcely touch it on the inside without getting wet. A severe rainstorm fell upon us one day. Fred and I covered both ends of our tent with rubber blankets and, sitting under the ridge- .

pole, tried to write. But the wind, which had full
sweep of the plateau, seemed to drive the water in torrents upon us. The rain beat so hard that it penetrated
the cloth and fell in a fine spray over us, wetting us,
and making the place so uncomfortable that writing.
was out of the question. We had to make the best of
it, however, and sat and smoked until the worst of the
storm was over. That was the most miserable and dis-
agreeably wet day I had passed yet. On every fairly
pleasant day we went through the same course of drilling over and over again, always for infantry—there
were no horses yet.

The colonel had come. All the officers and men had
reported for duty. Still no horses.

The team drivers who came into camp or were met
driving by were asked had they seen them on the road.
And they answered :

"No; not a sign of a hoof."

Still we looked for them. Still they did not come.
Disappointment was widespread, and grumbling grew
loud. In addition to all this, a rumor went over the
camp that we were soon to move. It did not seem possible that, in the face of the promises made to these
men, we would be asked to move without horses.

One afternoon Fred, Jake and I were sitting smoking
under a tree on the edge of the plateau, where we commanded a view of the road leading from the camp
down the slope into the valley, and for a long way up
the valley beside the river.

Jake had called our attention to a line of army wagons
on the road, saying :

"Here comes the grub train."

For lack of anything else to do, we were watching it
drawing near, one wagon after another appearing from
behind the woods.

"I wonder what that means," muttered Jake. And I looked closely to see if there was anything that had escaped my attention.

"What?" I asked.

"Why, that wagon-train. It's three times as long as usual. Let's go and meet it."

We went, Fred and Jake looking anxious, I thought.

We met the train at the entrance to the camp and found Jack Maddox on the first wagon.

"Well, boys, yer off, for sure," he shouted as soon as he caught sight of Fred. "This is the last train coming down here. I heard 'em say so in the quartermaster's office at Lebanon."

"I suppose so. But where 're the horses?" responded Fred.

"You haven't got them yet, have you? Didn't I tell you so up in Lebanon?"

Jake muttered an oath or two, turned away, and I followed him, leaving Fred and Jack together.

"So we are not to have horses after all?" I said.

"I never thought we would. But this thing won't go down. The boys 'll—well, you 'll see when they hear it. They have grumbled a heap already, 'cause they thought they were exercising too much, as if they were to be nothing but infantry. I, for one, don't propose to stand it."

We were not far from the wagons then, and looking back I saw that a crowd of twenty or thirty men had gathered about Fred and Jack and were gesticulating wildly and swearing, and some of their faces were not pleasant to look at. While we stood there looking back, Peter Grimes, a veteran of Company G—old Pete, his comrades called him—left the crowd, his face hardened into a firm, determined scowl, and his short, iron-gray beard curling with anger.

" Boys !" he shouted with an oath. " I am done."

He stripped his belt, with bayonet sheath attached, from his body, lifted them high above his head and threw them into the road, where they lay half-buried in the dust. He jerked off his cap and threw it beside them. Then, running his fingers through the thick locks of bristling hair on his head until they stood on end, and with a curse that seemed to roll up from his very bowels, he cried :

" I 've just come off guard, and by the living God, if they don't give us horses, I 'll never go back again !" and without another word, or a look to right or left, he strode away to his tent.

I looked away from him to the rest, and saw that many were preparing to follow his example, when—

" Boys, what 's the matter ?" said a quiet voice in their midst, and at the same instant Captain Hartees appeared from behind Jack's wagon.

Jake and I walked back to see what would come next.

" Where 's the horses we were to have ?" growled several who had just been relieved from guard, and stood with their accouterments on just as they had come off duty. They did not turn toward the captain ; the hard lines in their faces did not relax ; some of them even took off their belts and pitched them as determinedly and as resolutely into the dust as Grimes had done.

The captain walked up to the man who seemed most determined and, pointing to the discarded belt in the dust, said :

" Look here, my man, pick that up !"

The man looked up with a derisive smile on his face, but the smile and the look of derision faded under the piercing gaze of the captain.

" I know you are disappointed," said the captain ;

"so am I. We have done our best to keep our promises; but, because we have failed, this is no way for you to do. Pick that up!" and the man, after waiting a moment, obeyed; but his face, though the smile had vanished, was as hard and as grim as ever.

"There's yours and yours!" said the captain, turning to the other men and pointing to the belts that they had thrown away.

I was relieved to see the belts taken from the ground, although the men held them in their hands without making a motion to fasten them about their waists.

"Whose is this?" the captain asked, without addressing any one in particular.

"Pete's," growled the first man who had been spoken to.

"You take it to him then," said the captain, picking it up; "and tell him from me not to throw it away again. He will need it by and by;" then, turning to the crowd who were watching him in gloomy silence, he said:

"Boys, this war is not over. A great work still remains to be done, and it needs just such men as you to do it. When your time expired, you said that you could not and would not leave the work unfinished. You reenlisted again, and I hope you'll live in the service until the last blow is struck and the war is over.

"But you did this with the understanding that you were to have horses, you say. I grant that horses were promised to you, and that they have not come. But this is a greater disappointment to me than it possibly can be to you, for I feel in part responsible. It was I, perhaps, who urged you most, but it's too early yet to give them up. I still think the horses will come. When we go to the front it will probably be in the cars from Lebanon, and we shall, without doubt, find our horses waiting for us at the end of the route. Till then, we must be patient, and wait and walk. I know what walking is, and want you to remember that I ask no man to do what I would not do, or to go where I would not go. I shall not send you one inch nearer the enemy than I go myself. Great deeds are still to be done. This regiment has done them and will do them again. In the three years of your hard-fought service you proved yourselves men. Don't shame your record now."

He turned, and walked calmly away; but as he passed us, I saw that his face was very grave, almost anxious; and when he had gone some distance his hands met, and clasped each other behind his back. His pace became gradually slower, and his head fell forward on his chest, as if he were oppressed with the weight of serious thoughts.

The men remained standing for a few moments in the same positions. The three who had thrown away their accouterments were buckling them on again, but they all looked as morose and savage as ever. We felt that the storm had not broken after all, but was still brewing.

As the crowd separated Fred joined me, whispering as he did so:

"It is not over yet. This is only a beginning."

That night the whole camp was gloomy; no songs were heard, no laughter. The men, squatting about the fires, cooking their suppers, were silent and sullen; and when the evening meal was finished and darkness had fallen, the same feeling of uneasiness was in the air. Nothing was heard but growling and grumbling on every side.

I lay for a while on the ground, listening to the discontented mutterings of my comrades, and wondering how and when it would all end. When my pipe finally went out I put it in my pocket, arose to my feet and walked away.

Fred, who had been seated near me, sprang to his feet and followed me, saying:

"Where are you going, Dan?"

"I am going to walk," I replied. "I go on guard at eight o'clock."

When he came quite close to me he said:

"This looks bad, mighty bad, and I don't like it."

"Neither do I. But what's going to be done. The boys have been used badly; there's no use denying it, and somebody is to blame for it."

"There's one thing you can count on," said Fred. "The boys are not going to leave camp quietly without horses."

As we walked we approached the quarters of company I. Owing to the fact that this company had not been recruited, there were fewer men in it than in ours. But these men were veterans, who had fought side by side since the regiment was mustered into service. They were mostly from the same section in Kentucky, all of the same habits of life, too—all mountaineers.

When we reached them they were grouped around one fire which, uncared for, was dying slowly away.

The red embers glowed without giving much light, but occasional flashes of flame enabled us to see the scowling faces and iron frames of the men, who seemed to be gathered in council, some standing, some sitting on the logs and some lying flat on the ground, while wreaths of pipe-smoke floated away into the clear, moonless night.

They were not given to much talk, these silent, resolute men, and we stood for some time on the outskirts of the crowd before we caught the drift of what they had been saying.

"They say we're to have 'em bum-by, when we get nearer to the front," somebody on the opposite side of the fire was saying.

"It's a lie," some one else growled. "Who believes it?"

"What are we drillin' and drillin' as infantry every day for, if we're to have horses?" said another. "I tell yer, boys, it's dog-goned crooked, an' we don't stand it."

There came a deep growl of assent from the hearers assembled.

Another spoke, after a pause:

"I'll tell yer what, I'm in fer the work, if they'll use me squar', but I'll be dogged if I'm goin' to tramp another three years and tote the duds I have had to, to make me comfortable for the last three. I 'listed for mounted infantry and not for 'foot,' and if they don't give us horses I'm done."

The silence which fell then was soon broken by another harsh voice.

"'Pears to me like the only chance the reb's have for success is in our government goin' back on the soldiers that's willin' to do the fightin'. We're strong 'nough, know 'nough, and we're brave 'nough, but the men that's over us don't know 'nough 'nd they can't do the work as belongs to 'em ter do. We went through one three years, and 'pears to me a man's got no right to tell us we're goin' to have horses when he knows we ain't, just to get us to 'list over again. No Kentucky man would do so mean a thing as that."

"No Kentucky man would do it," repeated another voice.

Just then the dying fire gave out a flash, and looking toward the place whence the last voice came, I saw that Still Dick Vedder was the man who had

spoken.   He was seated on a camp-stool at the back of
the circle, a little apart from the others.

The sudden flash of light appeared to startle him,
and as he looked up I thought I saw a murderous expression just vanishing from his face.

Vedder was known as a strange man ; something
peculiar about him.   He had no chums ; did not seem
to want any, and no one cared to cross him in anything.

It was told of him that his father, mother and his
wife and children were shot by a band of guerrillas, or
driven into the woods to die, and some one said that he
had sworn a fearful oath of vengeance.

This accounted for his hatred of the rebels.   There
were strange stories told of his doings in battle.   He
was reckless, brave to a fault, and would fight as long
as there was any one to fight, and had almost to be
driven from the field.   Last of all it was told, and often
repeated, how, at Chicamauga, he walked up to a de-
fenseless prisoner and shot him dead.   He had recognized one of his father's murderers, it was claimed,
but the action was brutal.   Such was the man—silent,
determined, reckless ; not to be turned aside when once
he had made up his mind to an action.

CHAPTER VI.

It was a night of cloudless beauty that closed this most eventful and, as we learned later, last day of our camp life at Point Burnside.

When we left the camp fire of Company I, Fred and I walked together as far as the headquarters of the guard, where we parted. Here I found the corporal just about to take out the relief, so I fell into place and soon reached the post where I was left to my duty.

Alone with the cold stars staring down from above and my thoughts—which were not, on that occasion, the most pleasant companions—I tramped back and forth from a solitary tree, which was the boundary at one end of my beat, in a direct line to a big stone marking its limit at the other end.

I could think of nothing but the disturbed state of our camp and of the air of surly and defiant stubbornness in the men of Company I. But, however much my mind was occupied with a consideration of the present condition of things and of the causes which had given the boys occasion for grumbling, I still found myself trying to reason out, to my own satisfaction, what the result of this disappointment was likely to be. As may be imagined, there could be one conclusion from my point of view.

[73]

That there would be trouble was evident to all.
There was little that these men would not do if the
proper leader was at hand and had the courage to step
to the front at the right time. Recklessness certainly
had no limits to which they would not go if occasion
offered.

Again and again I came to the conclusion that we
were standing over a volcano, which might burst forth
at any time or place. And as often as I arrived at
this conclusion, and its horrible results became clear to
me, I would be aroused from my meditation, with a
shiver, to find myself standing still, grasping with both
hands the stock of my gun, the barrel resting across my
left arm, and my eyes fixed upon the ground. It may
have been the chill of the dew that affected me, or it
may have been the feeling of dejection with which I
seem to have been overcome, that was responsible for
these creeping chills; but of one thing there was no
longer a doubt in my mind—this matter was working
me up to a high state of nervous excitement, and, for a
soldier, this ought not to be.

As I stood in the darkness and listened with anxious
ears, I would catch, now and then, a vague murmuring
sound from the camp, like the moaning sometimes
heard in a forest before a storm; then the bodeful,
startling cry of some night-bird hovering over the
place would sound out upon the quiet air. Occasionally
I heard the slow and measured tread of the sentinel
whose beat adjoined my own.

The moon rose about eleven o'clock, throwing up a
delicate rosy haze at first, then mounted into a green-
ish silver, dispelling the melancholy gloom, and, as the
obscurity of the night vanished, I could look about me,
out over the vague unearthly landscape, over the hills
and dales, and up and down the shadowy, winding

river. Just then, also, a breeze sprang up, and the dewy freshness that filled the air was a thing for which to be grateful.

By the smoldering camp fires, I still could see indistinct forms of men ; few had gone to their tents, though it was long after "taps." The very air breathed suspicious wakefulness. Occasionally I heard footsteps, not of my comrades of the watch, but of some one approaching from the camp ; but those that made the noises either stopped short or turned away before I could make out who they were or what they intended doing.

At length a more hurried and more decided footstep startled me. It did not turn aside, but came straight on. My heart beat fast, and I confess to a feeling of loneliness, as if every friend had deserted me. Very distinctly do I remember also the stirring of the hair upon my head, an effect, I had thought once, was beyond the most extreme result of terror. A cold sweat started from my face, and my hands grew wet, as if they had been doused in water ; and had I tried to run away I believe my legs would have failed me. I had no time for a cool decision between the glory of death at my post of duty and shameful retreat, for the footsteps came pounding on. I was scared, and would have run, but something beyond my power to name rooted me to the spot.

Hastily summoning all the resolution at my command, and nervously bringing my rifle to a position of defense, I cried with a voice as loud as the dry and parched condition of my throat would permit :

"Halt ! Who goes there ?"

"Friend," came the response, and the dark form of a soldier stepped from the shadow of a tree into the moonlight, not ten feet away.

"Advance, friend, and give the countersign," I said, in as steady and stern a voice as I could command.

" I haven't any countersign but horses. That 's what 's the matter with me, 'nd I 'd as lief be sent to the guard house for it as not," the man said, as he came to a stop not two paces from the point of my bayonet.

"Well," I replied, gaining confidence in myself as the knowledge that I was master of the situation dawned upon me, " I don't propose to send you to the guard-house ; only don't try to cross the line here."

The man moved away, and I resumed my walk with a sigh of relief.

For a time everything was quiet. I saw nothing new —heard nothing strange. The soldiers lounging about the camp fires left one by one, until all had disappeared. The neglected fires were fast dying out, and I was just calculating that my time for duty was about up, and that I would soon be relieved and asleep, when I saw something moving among the headquarter tents.

Soon the black shadow of a man on horseback left the camp and approached the line of guards across the wagon road. It halted at command, approached the sentry, gave the countersign, probably though I was too far away to hear it, and was allowed to pass. Then I heard, indistinctly, the hoof beats of a galloping horse.

I wondered what it all meant, and watched the rider in his course down the road to the valley, and up along the river bank ; saw him pass into the shadow of the woods ; watched for him where I knew he must reappear in the moonlight, and so on, until he finally disappeared behind the woods of the valley. I turned away, for I knew I should see him no more.

A few moments later I again heard footsteps ; this time coming toward the camp from outside the line. This was the first time I had heard any sound outside

our lines, and thoughts of an enemy at once presented
themselves, only to be dispelled by the thought that we
were much too far north for that. Strange to say, I
was not nearly so scared as on the former occasion.

A steady look in the direction of the new-comer soon
revealed our orderly sergeant, walking leisurely and
unconcernedly toward me.

" Halt !" I said, when the sergeant had approached
to within a few paces of me.

" Hello, Dan !" was the response.   " Is that you ?"

I was somewhat surprised—rather pleasantly than
otherwise—at the first non-commissioned officer in the
company addressing me thus familiarly, so I replied in
a voice full of confidence in myself :

" Yes, it is I !"

" Has there been any passing the lines to-night ? "

" Not on this beat."

" Heard anything or seen any of the officers of the
other companies ?"

" No.   They haven't been this way !"

" Well, there 's lot of 'em out, and they 'll be along
soon !   We 've been out since sundown, and there isn't
a blessed one of us has the countersign.   Lucky for me
I happened to strike your post instead of that of some
of the men who came day before yesterday ; for you
happen to know who I am, and that makes it all right."

"Certainly !" I replied, repeating the last words of
his remark.   " That makes it all right."

"By the way, Dan," said the sergeant, pausing in
front of me as he crossed the line ; " I notice there 's
one thing you have either forgotten or have never been
taught.   Let me show you how to hold your gun when
you challenge an officer."

This was a new idea to me, and supposing there
might be something that I had not learned in the line

of respect due an officer from a sentinel on duty, I handed my gun to the sergeant.

"Now, sir!" said the sergeant, sternly, bringing the gun to a charge and pressing the point of the bayonet so hard and close to my breast that I was compelled, in order to prevent injury, to step back—back—back. "Now, sir, supposing I was a stranger and an enemy, who had wheedled you in giving up your gun. Where would you be? I could easily lay you out, eh?"

This was a fact, and I had to admit it.

"I have purposely done this to teach you a lesson. Always remember, when you are on duty, that until you get the countersign, there is no more respect due from you to your superior officer than there is to a private. You are not supposed to know any one. What you want, and all you want is the countersign; and that in every case you must have before you let any one pass. Another thing; don't let any one—not even a general—take your gun away from you again. Never let it go out of your hands. The safety of the army depends upon the faithfulness of those detailed to watch while others sleep. Never forget this. An unarmed soldier on guard is as useless as a cat without claws in a fight. Here, take your gun, hang on to it, and don't give yourself away to your comrades to-morrow morning. The countersign is 'Sherman.'" Saying which the sergeant left me and walked toward the camp.

I was somewhat humiliated by this experience, for the necessity of being vigilant and alert was already known to me. It had been impressed upon my mind before we went on guard; but it occurred to me that this was an emergency, an affair where circumstances seemed to alter cases—one demanding the exercise of sound judgment. I saw now that I was wrong, and was ashamed I had been so easily caught. The only bit of consolation left me was in the warning, "Not to give myself away." It was evident my instructor was one who considered only the importance of my efficiency as a soldier.

Shortly after this I heard a commotion along the guard line, and by the heavy tramp of feet knew that my neighbor had been relieved and that it was my turn next.

CHAPTER VII.

When I awoke the next morning Fred was already outside, talking with Bence and Kimball, who occupied the next tent. Kimball was saying:

"They won't dare to order us off after what happened yesterday. They know mighty well we won't leave here if we don't get them."

It was plain to me that horses formed the subject of their conversation, and that, with the rising sun, this one absorbing topic for discussion was returned to with as much passion as ever.

"And I tell you they will order us out," drawled Jake, "and they won't make any bones of it, either. The men who left last night knew what they were about." Then, after a moment of pause, he added impatiently: "I was a fool that I didn't go, too."

"Has anybody gone?" I asked, sticking my head out of the tent, and feeling, at the same time, that I could account for one absent one if I would.

"I reckon there has," responded Jake, with a flourish of the pipe-stem he had been cleaning. "Company D lost two, three gone from Company I, and when roll-call is over you 'll find a heap more missing."

And sure enough, when the roll was called, at the

name of Hiram Haines no voice answered; and so,
later on, there was no response to the name of Henry
Roberts.

The call over, we began to cook breakfast. All the
time the conversation moved upon only one subject—
horses, and the trouble sure to come if we were ordered
to leave without them.

"What are we going to do?" Fred asked.

"Do!" sneered Jake, with his arms squared firmly on
his breast, the rugged wrist of one hand showing out
past the dark, half-concealed knuckles of the other.
"Do! I don't want to be the man to give the order to
leave this place."

"You wouldn't mutiny, would you?" I asked.

"Couldn't say what a lot of men that have been im-
posed on would do," replied Bence, with a challenging
glance toward headquarters. "We're no fools, nor
cowards either, and they'll find it out."

Immediately after breakfast we were ordered to
strike tents, to roll up our blankets, and get ready to
move.

"That settles it," said Taylor. "There're no ifs about
that."

"Didn't I tell yer," muttered Jake, and both men,
from very force of habit, started to obey the order,
although they first looked around expectantly, to see
if any opposition was made. All over the camp men
were executing the command; but slowly, as though
they were doing it under protest.

Shortly after this we were marched by companies to
the supply wagons, where three days' rations were
issued to us. Then forty rounds of ammunition were
distributed. This filled our cartridge boxes and left a
handsome balance to stow away in our haversacks with
the rations.

Men were gathering in little groups, and in some instances exhibiting considerable feeling; still, there was no alarming disturbance. I was all keyed up with suppressed excitement. What could it mean? All the talk and bluster of the day before must have meant something; and that it did, indeed, mean something, I saw too plainly, as I glanced at the faces of the veterans about us.

There is a point where surly, dissatisfied obedience ends, and mutiny—defiant, reckless and often deadly mutiny—begins; and this crisis in our affairs was fast approaching.

At last the tents were all struck, divided and rolled up with the blankets. Every one had decided how many of the little things that had been collected he would want to carry in his load, and how many must be left behind.

When my accouterments were all on, my load, perhaps a fair sample of the others, was as follows: A haversack hung by a strap from my right shoulder across my body to my left side, and in it were knife, fork, spoon, plate and enough pork, hard bread, coffee and sugar for three days. In my knapsack, strapped to my back, were writing paper, pins, pens, pipe and tobacco, ink, soap, towels, underclothing, stockings, etc., etc. Hung over my left shoulder was a canteen full of water; also over the same shoulder hung my blankets and tent, rolled up tightly into a horse-collar shape, and tied at the ends. From my belt hung a dipper, a cartridge-box, which was heavy with ammunition, and over my left hip a bayonet in its sheath. This, with my gun, made load enough for one man to carry.

All that was now left for us to do was to kill time by talking, smoking and lounging around, waiting for orders. This is an experience which enters largely into every soldier's career, and, already familiar with many of the possibilities in this direction, I had seated myself and was smoking my pipe and dreaming of home when, unexpectedly, one of the teamsters arrived from Lebanon with the mail.

Thoroughly aroused by the chances of that mail-pouch containing a letter for me, I arose and, with others, followed the mail-carrier to headquarters, where the letters and papers were distributed.

There were two letters for me—one from mother, which was opened first and read where I stood. The other letter I knew, by the writing on the envelope, was from Mary. It did not take me long to find a place where it could be absorbed without disturbance.

Again and again I read it, until every word seemed to me a text from which a sermon on the loveliness of woman might be preached. I was assured that the house was now very lonely without me. That my room remained just as I had left it, and that nothing in it should be disturbed until I returned. That every evening, when it was pleasant, she had been to walk along the same road and by the paths which we had so often walked together, and that every step she took, every foot of ground passed over, reminded her of some word or look from me, which she had jealously hoarded in the treasure-house of her heart. She would wait and hope and pray for my safe return.

. By the time I had fully digested the contents of my two letters and returned to the company, the incident of the unlooked-for mail had apparently been forgotten, and horses again formed the topic for discussion.

About ten o'clock we had left the camp ground and were standing by companies in a line on the road at the foot of the slope facing the hill.

"Where 's the colonel?" Fred asked.

"He left last night, so the boys say," muttered Kimball, abstractedly.

"Yes, and I saw him leave ; he went about midnight," said I, for the rider of the horse which I had seen galloping away last night could have been none other than the colonel.

"He did well," said Jake, harshly.

"Who 'll command ?" I asked.

"Hartees, I reckon ; he 's the senior captain.   Yes, there he is now !"

I looked in the direction Jake indicated and saw the captain standing in front of the center of the line, leaning against his sword, the point of which was resting on a stone behind him.

He was waiting until we should be joined by the last of the purposely straggling squads which kept coming in sight on the brow of the hill.

At last, a party of three or four came down, followed by a lieutenant of one of the companies.   The men took their places in line, and the officer reported that the camp ground was clear.

Then the command was passed from company to company :

"Right face !   Forward !   March !"

Away off to the right of the line the drums began to beat and mechanically we obeyed the order.

Without the buoyant feelings and the excitement that change is wont to bring, for even the drums seemed to be affected by our discontent, and without other noise, except the scuff of feet in the dust and a muttered oath now and then in grim, determined silence, we began our march.

But the complaints of Company I, which was directly in front, kept coming over to us, keeping my comrades in a chronic state of discontent.   They had come into

possession of some liquor somehow, possibly from the
sutler, for he was a sympathizer in our troubles, and
that also added vehemence to their grumblings.

I think we would have gone along quietly enough if
left alone. Jake Bence was the most mutinous in our
company, and his growling was without effect, for he
was always at it; but listening to the grumbling in
Company I, which was every moment becoming louder
and more excited, we were rapidly being wrought up
to about the same state of mutiny.

Besides, the sergeant of Company I was chiming in
with the men, and was as mutinous as any one. It
seemed to me, though, it was his duty to encourage a
cheerful obedience of orders rather than to discour-
age it.

Right in the midst of it, happening to look up, I saw
the captain standing on an embankment beside the
road watching the regiment, as company after company
marched past him.

No man's actions or bearing escaped him as the lines
marched by; and although he seemed at ease, on his
face I plainly saw the same expression of anxiety that
I noticed there the day before.

Every muscle in his body was strung up to its highest tension. His face was paler than usual under its
coat of tan, and his eyes and hair never seem so black.
He saw clearly in what a demoralized condition his
command was, and knowing that something must be
done to improve it, was watching for the proper time
and place for action. Nor did he have long to wait,
for the steady marching brought Company I, with its
mutinous sergeant, directly in front of him.

The company was making its way along the road
with a shambling, devil-may-care gait for the most part,
and growling as they went.

The sergeant had not seen the captain, probably, for he was saying :

"To be cheated and gulled into re-enlistment, as we have been, and then to expect us to quietly give in like a lot of whipped dogs ! I tell you, boys, I 'm not going through this sort of thing for another three years."

"There it goes," said I to Fred ; "somebody will catch it now."

I had hardly spoken when the captain, with two steps, stood beside the orderly.

"Give me your sword," he commanded sharply, at the same moment snatching it from .the sergeant's hands. "You are under arrest ; go to the rear."

The action was so unexpected that the sergeant, dumfounded, shrank back, and for a moment looked at the captain irresolutely ; then, turning to the men, ran his eyes quickly over their faces, as though seeking some sign of encouragement.

The whole regiment had been watching the motions of the captain, and, simultaneously with the arrest of the sergeant, moved by a common impulse, broke from the order of march, fell back, and gathered in a circle around this center of interest.

In that center stood the captain, with his black eyes flashing lightning as he swept the circle of faces, watching for the first sign of what was to come next. He was playing for his life, and he knew it. He was one man at bay, and encircled by a regiment—six hundred angry, desperate, reckless men. It was a moment to try the stoutest heart.

As I followed the captain's angry glances around the circle of faces, noting the well-conveyed indifference to his peril, the extraordinary actions of Still Dick caught my eye. He was leveling his musket over the shoulder of his file leader, and had lowered his head to

HE LEVELED HIS MUSKET AT THE CAPTAIN'S BREAST.—*See Page* 86.

take sight at the captain's breast, not a dozen feet away from the muzzle of his gun.

Dick was as cool as ice. His wooden face was as vacant of expression as if he were about to fire at a target; his eyes alone revealed, in their cold, glittering, cruel glance, something of what was passing in his mind.

The two men immediately in front of Vedder, when they saw the gun barrel appear between them, stepped quickly to one side, leaving the captain thus face to face with his silent enemy, the most dangerous and deadly-sure man among us, who held a loaded musket at his breast, making preparations to fire.

It seemed as if the silence, broken only by the "click," "click," as Vedder pulled back the hammer of his gun, could be felt; and, while the crowd behind the captain separated to the right and left to be out of the way, the rest of us, paralyzed by this deliberate murderous intention, stood spellbound, and watched every motion with strained eyes, expecting to see the fire leap out, and our captain fall bleeding and dying in the road.

Yet Vedder did not fire, and those moments of hesitation seemed to our torturing suspense expanded into hours of waiting. The man's face was changing, too; taking on an ashy pallor and becoming expressive, first a black, determined scowl and tightening of the lips, then a nervous twitching of the features and the gun barrel began to waver.

Quicker than thought—so quick, in fact that none of us really saw it—the captain's sword flashed up beneath the gun-barrel, struck it a ringing blow, and the musket, knocked from Vedder's nerveless fingers, exploded harmlessly above our heads. And, in dumb, motionless astonishment, we stood staring at the two men until the captain, pointing with his sword up the road, cried :

"Now, men, to business ! Fall in !" *

The hard faces relaxed, the trouble was over. A sigh of relief parted the lips of all ; and, as we fell into line, some one in Company I waved his cap in the air and called for "Three cheers for our captain !" in a loud, clear voice. They were given with a will, and it seemed as if all the reckless desperation vanished in them, giving volume and power as it went out of the hearts of men into harmless sound, just as a heap of powder touched off in the open air bursts forth into harmless flame and clouds of smoke.

"Forward ! March !"

Was it because we were in fear that we now so cheerfully obeyed this command? Did we repent our mutinous attitude when we saw our captain standing before the muzzle of Vedder's gun ? Were we ready now to give over our grumbling and go in peace, because the officer in command had so ordered ? Were we fickle ? Were all the grumbling and threats so freely indulged in the day before all idle bluster ? With me it might have been so, but with the others it was not. A thousand times, no !

In that moment, when our captain faced Vedder, if he had betrayed the slightest movement of a muscle, if his eye had wavered from Vedder's by a hair's breadth,

---

* I often pause to wonder over this incident in our history. Why did not Vedder fire? What power rested in the eye or will of our captain to turn that man of all others from his purpose? What did the expressions of Vedder's face mean, if they were not the outward signs of the struggle in his mind? The determined scowl and tightening of the lips signifying that his resolution was wavering, and he was trying to force it to stand firm.

His mental strain must have been terrible; but, though careless and reckless of all consequences to do this one deed in the way it had to be done, he had not the nerve.

The captain did not stain his victory with any harsh measures, and Vedder, thoroughly cowed and trembling like one stricken in years, was allowed to tramp on with rest.

he would have fallen at our feet with a bullet in his heart, and a little later six hundred veteran soldiers would have been tramping away from that place, in perhaps as many directions, going back to their homes.

It was the man who could look death in the face without flinching, that had caused this revulsion of feeling, had excited the admiration of his fellows, and had conquered. Among soldiers, it is not the face nor the form, nor anything else, that is admired except the will, the indomitable will that knows no fear. Whatever sort of man our captain might turn out to be, he was at least a brave one.

All day long, up hill and down, through mud and dust, in broiling sun and cooling shade, we tramped. Though the shoulder-straps of our accouterments were cutting into the flesh, though our feet were blistered, still we did not complain.

At last, almost at night, we came into a quiet valley with pleasant fields beside the road, and fence rails for fire wood.

"Halt !" came the command from the head of the column.

Here we were to camp, and we knew it ; a tired but unanimous cheer waked the echoes of the valley.

In a trice our guns were stacked ; the load was off our backs ; fires were built and supper cooked. We were contented—almost happy ; for we were at rest.

The power of one man ; that power which had paralyzed Still Dick's finger on the trigger of the gun aimed full at his breast ; which had quelled the mutiny and kept us wearily but willingly plodding on through dust and heat, all that livelong, tedious day, was over us still : and when, at night, we gathered about the cheerful camp-fires, with our pipes well filled, we came to talk of that never-to-be-forgotten scene, as we recalled the heroism of the captain and in our minds' eye saw him again standing unflinchingly before the muzzle of Vedder's rifle, horses were forgotten, and our weariness lost sight of.

Would there be any more trouble, any more attempt at mutiny?

Never. The captain had conquered the whole regiment—made us as one man. There was not one among us who would not have faced a battalion at his command.

Did we talk of horses?

They might have been mentioned, but they were not considered of so much importance now. The captain had tried to get them, we said. The colonel was the most to blame. He had fled, leaving another to take his place and front his danger.

The veterans were loud in the captain's praise and promised themselves that their old achievements would be as nothing compared with the glory they would win under such a leader.

The sentinels pacing the watch that night looked on a different scene from the one I saw the night before. They saw no restless excited forms about the dying fires, heard no footsteps save their own.

Our regiment had, indeed, settled down to business. We were on a war footing. One man had controlled and united us into one huge machine, obedient to his will.

We slept soundly, undisturbed by dreams of home or friends or battles; only for an instant, as I slept, Mary seemed to be standing before me, and her eyes were sad with tears. I seemed to be saying: "Now I am off to the war"; and she vanished.

We awoke, footsore but refreshed. But we must "up stakes" and be off.

The distance travelled that day, however, was not nearly so great as that of the day before, but at night there was hardly one in the regiment who had not a blister to remind him of the two days' tramp ; and then we saw something of the spice and wit that flow so easily about the campfires of soldiers on the march.

At Point Burnside our life had been like a picnic, in a way. We had a few hours of drill and duty, it is true, but there was no danger and no changing scene. We had collected, besides, little conveniences—bits of comfort, as it were—but these were now left behind, and I was surprised to see how easily we got along without them. The days then were all alike, but now no one could tell what the next hour would bring forth.

For several days we marched from place to place, but no day's journey was as long as the first ; resting-places were more frequent, and the hours of camp more pleasant. Everybody seemed in excellent spirits. We were well, though simply, fed. Our blisters were disappearing, and our load was getting lighter.

We were marching in a northward direction through Somerset, Waynesburg, Stanford, Danville ; thence across to Lebanon, where we were put into cars and landed at Louisville.

Here, many were mustered in, and after a few days we were cooped up in box-cars on the road to the front.

Travelling in box-cars is not the most comfortable way of going from place to place, but we enjoyed it nevertheless.

Many were the little devices we made up to make our quarters comfortable.

By forage we collected hay and straw enough to cover the floor of our cars, and on this we lay and

dozed, or listened to such parts of the stories that were
told   as   the   rattle   of   the   train   permitted   us   to
hear.

We were hastening toward the front, covering a great
deal of ground without marching, and without having.
as Jake said, "to take our accouterments;" and for all
this we were thankful.

CHAPTER VIII.

After we had travelled thus by rail for two days or more, I awoke one morning to the consciousness that something must be wrong.

I had an idea that we should be rattling and slamming over the road as usual, but, on the contrary, the train was now stopped, and the clatter I had gone to sleep by having ceased, the silence of death seemed to have taken its place. As I lay, for some moments, on my bed of hay, drowsily pondering the situation, I became more and more aware of the fact that most of my comrades in the car had disappeared, and that the few whom I still could see standing at the door between me and the bright sunlight were talking together and pointing in various directions.

Raising myself upon one elbow, my eyes first fell upon a broad river sweeping by. There was no breeze to ruffle its surface ; no merrily dancing sunlit waves , nothing but a darkly flowing stream, smooth as a polished floor, sustaining a reflection of the opposite shore on one side, and on the side nearest me a few wavering creases of the surface marking the whirling eddies underneath.

Beyond the stream I saw the outcropping rocks and heavily-wooded hills of a very broken and mountainous country. Taking the whole scene together, it made an impression upon me that I shall not soon forget. Whether due to the wild and rugged character of the hills and mountains, standing out so bold and striking in the clear, strong light of the morning, or to the resistless rush of the river, which I instinctively felt rather than saw, or to the unwonted stillness into which I had been so unconsciously and suddenly plunged, or to a mingling of all these effects, I cannot say; but whatever it was, some time passed before I could make up my mind whether I was really awake or dreaming.

"What river is that?" I asked, throwing off my blanket and coming to my senses, at least sufficiently to ask questions.

At the sound of my voice two comrades by the car door turned around, and at the same time the heads of several others appeared from the outside. What a shout greeted me as they heard my voice, and what unflattering remarks were bestowed upon me!

"Oh, you're awake, are you?" said one.

"If you are as much of a fighter as you are a sleeper you will be a corporal before you know it," said another.

"You'll wake up some fine morning to find out that we have wound up this war business and gone home," continued a third.

By this time my connection with the regiment had taught me to take such shots at my greenness in the right spirit, and to give, now and then, a volley in reply. Begging them not to let such tender solicitude for me disturb their sweet repose, I repeated my question as to the name of the river which, now that I had come to the car door and could get a better view of it, seemed more magnificent than ever.

"That is the Tennessee," said Jake; "somethin' of a brook, ain't it?"

There did seem, indeed, to be a large body of water passing by, and I said so, which induced Bence to remark that the river was specially high this season, which may or may not have been the case; I did not know.

"But what are we stopping for, and where are we?" I asked.

"Don't get anxious, little one," said Bracebridge, a particularly quiet, unimpressionable old veteran in our party. "You know as much as the rest of us do."

Bence broke in here to remark that Fred and one other of the boys had been seen near the head of the train, with comrades from other companies, listening to our captain, who had been in conference with a lot of strange officials; and that, probably, when he (Fred) returned to our car, we would have some definite information.

"And here they come now!" cried one of our men from a position outside the car.

Shortly afterward Fred climbed in; and we plied him with questions to our heart's content. In the meanwhile "All aboard!" had been called, and the train began to move.

It seemed that we were within a few miles of Bridgeport, Alabama—that we would probably have to leave the cars at that place and go the rest of the way on foot, as the track to the rear of Sherman's army was already overcrowded with trains.

"I gathered from the conversation in general," Fred went on, "that we have about sixty miles to go, over a part of the Racoon Mountains near Shellmound, to a

place called Ringgold, where Sherman's army is, and
if we don't find him there, we 're to follow on until we
overtake him."

"Mighty poor pickings we 'll get after Sherman's
army," muttered Taylor.

"Well, we can be trusted to make up for it when we
get a chance," said Jake, sententiously.

"Yes," Fred broke in, "and it looks as if we
were going to get a chance right away, for the captain
said that he was going to take us over a road that had
not been travelled before."

"That 's the kind of talk!" we all cried, impulsively.

After this, Fred's stock of information having been
exhausted, we fell to discussing the fine prospects of
good foraging, which we might reasonably expect, if
the captain did what he hoped to do.

I felt as if walking would rest me after being cramped
up in a freight car for three days, and, not knowing
how the rest felt about it, I ventured to say as much.
This also shook down an avalanche of unflattering
remarks.

"That 's all very well, but you just poke your head out
here," cried Jake, seizing my arm and leading me to
the car-door.

We were rattling along over the road at a good rate
of speed at the time, and though there was a sameness
about the green wall of forest foliage that fronted us,
I could catch, now and then, through open spaces,
glimpses of rugged scenery and of the eternal hills
beyond.

"Yes," said I, "that is what I have been looking at
for some time."

"Well," said Jake, "those hills lie right across our
track, and by the time you have marched over them
two or three months and been in the service as long as

we have, you'll make up your mind that there's no fun in tramping up and down hill all the time."

"Besides," interrupted Kimball, feeling that the subject of walking should be tabooed, and anxious to talk of something else, "we are going to find it a trifle hotter in Alabama."

"A trifle!" cried Jake, as willing to grumble about one thing as another. "A trifle! it'll be a heap hotter; the summer's only just coming on, too."

In the midst of our good-natured chaffing, the train came to a stop, and we were all ordered out. In a few minutes more we had cleared the cars of everything that belonged to us, and were marching up the track beside the train. Afterward we passed through the town and over a bridge to where we halted, to light our fires for breakfast.

From this halting place, looking back across the river, we could see Bridgeport and the railroad for some distance, where long lines of empty cars were waiting to pass the train which had brought us, and start on their journey northward, for "more provisions and more ammunition," it was said.

We learned, later, that we had enjoyed a special favor in being transferred to the front in cars, as all other regiments joining Sherman had been required to march, because the railroad was taxed to its utmost in carrying to the front ammunition and provisions.

As soon as breakfast was over, the command to "fall in" was given and, as we stood in line, in the road, fully equipped for whatever might happen, when we had got fairly into the enemy's country, Captain Hartees stepped in front of us and, calling: "Attention!" said:

"Men, we are just on the borders of a hostile country; our previous methods of marching will now have to be changed! I want you to keep close together from this time out. No straggling, remember! I hope to pass through a country that has not been tramped over by both armies and, if we do, I believe you will enjoy it."

Smiling, good-naturedly, as he concluded, he turned away, took his place at the head of the line and, after three rousing cheers, which we gave with a will, away we went.

We followed the main road as far as Tyler, a small town which we reached early in the afternoon.

There was nothing to be begged, bought, borrowed or stolen in this place. It was literally cleaned out of everything.

The few people still living there looked peaked, half-starved and poor, indeed; the rest had gone away, leaving behind them only their houses and other immovable property.

We filled our canteens with fresh water, however, and, after thoroughly satisfying ourselves that there was nothing else worth taking, we moved on, leaving the main road, at that place, to follow one that evidently had been less traveled.

Along this new road we marched for three or four hours, without seeing signs of habitation of any kind.

There were neither fences nor clearings, nor anything but woods and breaks, and rocks, that sometimes lay close to the edge of the road, but quite as often had rolled in heaps into it, making our path the roughest kind of walking.

Late in the afternoon we came to a clearing, in the center of which stood a house. On one side the landscape was just beginning to turn green with young shoots of corn. On the other side vegetables, of various kinds, were planted and beginning to grow. At the open door stood two small white-headed boys, watching us as we turned in from the road ; and within we caught sight of a red-cheeked woman. Her sleeves were rolled up as if she had been cooking.

"Got any chicken ?" Fred asked of the woman who came to the door, as soon as she discovered our approach.

" No, I aint got no chickens, nor anything else, 'cept a duck and a drake, and those I don't want to sell."

" Sure you haven't ?" Fred insisted. " No use to hide them, you know ; if you 've got 'em we are goin' to make a search for 'em. We'll buy 'em, but we'll have 'em sure."

" I tell you I aint got no chicks, nor ducks, nor nothin' else. You'd better go on about your business. Come here robbin' people !"

"Quack, quack, quack !" came from the back of the house. The woman's face flushed as she started from the door and ran round the house to a little pen that stood behind, where we soon saw her struggling with old Grimes for the possession of her duck, which was flapping its wings violently and giving utterance to half-strangled cries in a vain effort to get away from the strong hand that had grasped its neck.

"It 's no use, mum," said Grimes ; "the duck 's a goner. I 'll give you four bits for him, but he 's my meat."

While she was fighting for one bird the other mysteriously and noiselessly disappeared, and we were about to investigate further when a beehive, that had been upset to open a way to the honey, sent out a swarm of maddened insects, and we fled before them. In spite of the bees, however, some of the boys got a little honey.

We left the young corn standing when we went, and while our actions, looking back on them now, were unquestionably mean, it seemed to me at the time that the woman, poor as she was, ought to have been grateful to us for not taking everything, whether we wanted it or not.

The next habitation that we discovered on our march was a large, fine-looking mansion, having a double row of balconies running entirely around the house, and surrounded by numerous outbuildings.

The sun was on the point of setting when we arrived; and in a moment, after we were ordered to halt, the place was swarming with our blue-coated men.

I saw a private of Company I fix his bayonet and run it through a young pig that, with several others, was following its mother at full speed away from him. A number of our company, Fred among them, joined in chasing the pigs that had not been secured.

I, however, felt too tired to go running about after pigs, and so, with others, selected the house as the scene of my explorations.

As we approached we saw a few black faces shyly peering at us from around the corners of the building, but we saw no one either to welcome us or to dispute our right to enter and make ourselves at home.

Entering, we gave attention first to the cellar where we found, among other things, a half-barrel of peach brandy, some preserves and thirty or forty pounds of honey. When we came up we found the owner of the place.

We had no particular use for him, but he was a sight that, in spite of us, claimed our attention for some little time.

He stood on the stairs cursing and calling down all sorts of maledictions on the heads of Yankee soldiers, in general, and upon us in particular; and his fingers worked as though he would have liked to have a clutch

upon each and every one of us; but he did not have it
and seeing, probably, that we were a few too many for
him, contented himself with words only. After silently enjoying his antics for a little while, we left
him, talking as loudly and as blasphemously as
ever.

Loaded down with bacon, honey, corn-meal, preserves, brandy and wheat flour, we left the house and
joined some of the boys in the road. Other comrades
were coming from all points of the compass, some with
chickens, ducks, peas, fresh pork; some with one thing
and some with another; and, while we waited, out of
the woods, away up on the other side of the road, came
perhaps a dozen others, bearing on a fence rail several
portions of a cow which they had found and killed.

There was little use in our attempting to go much
farther that night, and it was with gladdened hearts
that we received orders to bivouac where we were. In
a short time a guard had been thrown out around the
house and the regiment; rail-fences were then pulled
down, fires lighted, and in a short time a glorious feast
was preparing. We had plenty of everything that
night, and all at the expense of one man who, thus far,
had evidently not been treated to a taste of war.

There were a charm and a romance about this sort of
thing which rather pleased me, and I began to see
something of the glamour that surrounds the soldier's
life and leads him to reënlist in spite of ties of blood
and home.

Hay and straw from a well-filled barn supplied us
with comfortable roadside beds, and the next morning,
a little after sunrise, our breakfast eaten, we took to
the road again.

Since starting, we had been marching in column;
now, however, our company were deployed as skirm-

ishers on the right of the regiment which was following the road.

Fred explained to me, as we tramped along, that marching thus, something in the shape of a letter T, with a line of skirmishers thrown out each side from the head of the column, we covered more ground, and guarded more completely against surprises from the enemy.

The rest of the regiment marching in the road found no difficulty in getting along but for our company, scattered in a long line at right angles to the regiment, with about twenty or twenty-five feet between each man, this method of marching was hard work. With no road or beaten path to walk in, we were compelled to force our way up and down hill, through woods and creeks, and swamps and tangled jungles and places where it seemed as if the foot of man had never trodden before.

Sometimes we, at the further end of the line, would come in sight of the road from a clearing on the top of some hill, a quarter of a mile distant; then the road would be lost to sight for an hour, perhaps. Occasionally we were walking comfortably along over some sparsely wooded hill, where the bright sunlight poured through the branches above us, and in a moment afterward we were plunging through the tangled undergrowth of some densely wooded dell, always trying to maintain our distances, keep up with the left of the line, move when the regiment moved, and halt when it halted.

Dismal and lonely, with no other sign of life except the whir from the wings of some bird, that had been startled from its meditative solitude by our approach or the far-off sound of " H–a–l–t !" or "At-ten-tion !" as it was borne to us on the quiet air.

On one occasion, after we had been tramping for a long time over this rugged country without resting, Fred discovered a little clearing and a house hidden away off to the right. It was a spot that did not appear to ever have been visited by foragers from either army.

Just at that moment it also happened that our boys in the road were called to a halt. Here was an opportunity for our own exclusive investigation that was too good to be resisted ; and, stimulated by the same impulse, tired as we were, we started on the run for the clearing.

As we drew nearer we saw a little shanty, or curing-house, which held forth a promise of tobacco. A few steps farther, and we saw hidden in a hollow a little stone building sitting astride a brook, evidently a spring-house, where milk, butter and eggs were kept. The promise of something more than tobacco was enough to divert our attention from the shanty, and when the spring-house was reached it was but the work of a moment to remove the wooden pin from the staple, pall back the hasp, open the door and walk in.

The room we entered was not above six feet high and, perhaps, ten feet square. It was provided with a brick floor, in the middle of which, running from wall to wall, and through a stone-lined ditch about two feet wide and eight inches deep, flowed a stream of clear cold water from a neighboring spring.

A single crock of fresh milk sat cooling in the water.

"They did not hide that, did they?" said Fred. " But," reflectively, " they 've hidden the cow."

" We are not going to find fault with the milk for that," said I.

It was surprising how careless of dirt I had become after being a soldier for so short a time. I rubbed the dust from my fire-blackened tin dipper as well as I

could against a wisp of grass that grew by the door,
and scooped up a dipper full of milk.

Fred, who had filled his dipper before me, did not
even take the trouble to clean it ; just hit it against the
wall of the building.

After drinking our fill, we poured what milk was left
into our canteens and looked searchingly around for
something more.

"What's above here, I wonder?" said Fred, looking
upward.

I glanced up and saw, just over my head, a square
hole cut in the flooring. Raising myself through the
hole by my hands, I got my head above the level of the
floor and, with Fred's assistance underneath, was soon
sprawling up there in the darkness.

"Find anything?" Fred asked, expectantly.

"Yes ; here 's some tobacco."

"Throw it down."

I threw down half a dozen heads at least—all I could
find, at any rate—and continued my search.

"Here 's some beans or peas ; I don't know which
they are," said I, after a few moments' search.

"Let 's have 'em. We do not get peas or beans either
while marching."

Down went the beans.

I felt along a little further and came upon a small
barrel which seemed to be half full of something, as,
when tipped to one side, it fell back heavily into its
upright position.

"What is it?" said Fred, hearing the jar on the floor.

"I don't know. It 's heavy, like sirup."

"Perhaps it is honey—strained honey. They hide it
in that way sometimes. It takes up less room."

We were in a bee country, and had found some honey
the day before. Why should not this be honey? I

reached my hand down into the barrel until it came in contact with a soft, sticky fluid. There could be no doubt about it. My imagination swam in honey. I did not have my share of yesterday's find, and with that in mind, perhaps, my anticipation now was the more lively.

"Well," cried Fred, somewhat impatiently, "what are you going to do about it?"

"I smelt of it and imagined that it smelt very much like honey."

"Smells like it," said I.

"Taste it, or else let me," said Fred, impatiently, catching hold of the side of the floor.

I took one taste and that was enough. It was nauseating. It seemed as if I never could get that taste out of my mouth, try as hard as I might.

"Dash it, it 's soft soap!" I cried, fairly shivering with disgust, and my face, particularly the mouth part of it, went through all sorts of contortions at the same time, which were of course, lost in the darkness.

Fred who was looking up in expectation uttered a snort, half of disappointment and half of enjoyment at my ludicrous mishap and said:

"Never mind, pass me down a dipperful" — and I saw his hand with the dipper sticking up through the hole, and I heard him say, as I was filling it:

"I wish I had time to wash a shirt."

CHAPTER IX.

That night there came up a violent rainstorm that seemed to have been sent purposely to unpleasantly vary our experience. How long it had been raining before I woke I did not know; but I was fully conscious of the fact that one corner of our tent had broken away from its fastening and was flapping in the wind, that my feet were in a pool of water and that I was literally drenched.

As sleep was out of the question, I put my head through my poncho [rubber blanket] and went to a sputtering fire that some of the boys had kept well supplied with wood. To get dry was impossible. I could only keep warm.

One after another of our rain-soaked and thoroughly demoralized comrades joined us at the fire, where we spent the night feeding the blaze, rubbing our eyes, which smarted with smoke, and toasting our calves and shins.

By daylight the rain had ceased, and we were able to wring the water out of our blankets and tents and partly dry them by the fire before breakfast.

When our morning meal was finished and our damp blankets and tents were rolled up, we went trailing and sloshing along, through mud and wet, as disconsolate-and gloomy-looking a column and skirmishing line as

ever ventured into an enemy's country. Shortly after
we started a drizzling rain set in and continued throughout the day.

The boys all put on their ponchos, from the corners
of which the water flowed in streams and, in this
picturesque condition, carrying our muskets at a "secure," we plodded along hour after hour.

There was little or no comfort to be gained from the
"rests," for the ground was soaked with water, and
sometimes we went in over our shoe-tops in the soft
earth. About the only bit of pleasantry offered during
the day came from Fred, who said :

"I did hope to get time enough to wash a shirt ; but
it's all right now. All I need is to dry it."

The only encouragement we received came late in
the afternoon from "Black Lige," who, with a couple of
fat chickens in each hand, passed us, singing softly to
himself :

> " Nebber min' de wedder so de win' don' blow,
> Nebber min' de wedder so de win' don' blow,
> Nebber min' de wedder so de win' don' blow,
> Don' yer bodder 'bout yer trouble till it comes."

Here was a bit of philosophy for me ; for our situa-
ation, bad as it was, would have been infinitely worse
had there been any wind blowing. The life of a soldier,
in fine weather, had thus far possessed for me an inde-
scribable charm ; but a soaking rain was something I
had not bargained for, and but for the sentiment con-
tained in the song of Black Lige, my patriotism,
which was already at a low ebb, would have disappeared
altogether.

All day long we had marched over hills and mountains, and into valleys so deserted and lonesome that
they seemed isolated from the rest of the world ; now
threading our way along ridges so narrow that a dozen

men could scarcely walk abreast; at other times slowly
pushing through the heavy wet undergrowth in deep
defiles, with towering, perpendicular cliffs on either side.

The sun was already getting low and the prospect of
finding a good camping spot for the night was dreary
and cheerless enough, but after a while, coming to the
top of a hill, we saw, in the valley below, a small village
nestled among the trees.

A little brook, concealed here and there by bushes,
threaded its way close by the village. Along the banks
of this rivulet everything was fresh and green, while
the foliage in the country beyond looked, in the murky
atmosphere, as if it needed a week of steady rain to
redeem it.

"There's a good place for a bivouac," said I, pointing to an open field, near the village.

"Yes, looks as well as you might expect on a day
like this, but there are too many houses around. Too
many houses. You never know what to expect when
you camp near a town," Jake answered thoughtfully.

"But you don't call that a town, do you? There are
only a few houses, and they certainly look honest
enough."

"Looks don't count for much down here. It don't
take much of a town to stir up a hornet's nest, where
there's a few lively rebs living. Just give 'em a
chance, and they're like a lot of wolves; they'll sound
an alarm, and bring a whole pack down on you. I had
a taste of it once up in East Tennessee, in 'sixty-two.'"

"Come, men," said Corporal Stebbins, "we're goin' to
camp on the other side of that town below there; nice
place, heaps of rails, straw, water."

"What, water?" interrupted Jake, sarcastically.

"Yes, and everything else we want. Move along a
little faster, men. Let's get down there as soon

as the column does and have our fires started before it 's any darker."

Stimulated by this cheering bit of information, we put more vigor into our movements, and, after passing one or two houses, reached a broad, level bottom-land, where we halted and went into camp for the night. We seemed to be in a sort of basin, surrounded by woods, and only a short distance removed from the town, which consisted of a dozen or more old tumble-down houses, scattered along, at irregular intervals, by the side of the road. These houses were without paint and falling to pieces, and we would have thought them tenantless if we had not seen two or three men standing about the doorways, who acted as if they had a right there. The fences, that had formerly inclosed the yards from the road, were all down, leaving only a post here and there to mark the place they had occupied.

The road itself showed signs of having been used at some time or other, but it was now cut by deep ruts and washouts, and the grass grew rank there. Altogether, it was a sleepy, deserted place, firm in the grip of decay.

The zigzag fences in the fields gave us firewood; and, after a little patient effort, we got a fire started and went to work to cook our supper.

The two or three men we had seen at last gathered courage sufficient to satisfy their curiosity as to what sort of beings we were, and came cautiously slouching along the road through the camp, watching, with hungry, wide-open eyes and mouths, our boys cooking supper. They did not improve in looks on near view. They were thin, lank, barefooted and dressed in tattered clothes; their beards were tangled, their long hair uncombed, and their faces almost imbecile for want of expression. They were the poor whites, corresponding to what are called "Crackers" in some parts of the South.

"Hello, stranger," cried Fred to one of them. "What do you call the name of this place?"

"'Coon Bottom," drawled the man, discharging a mouthful of tobacco juice upon the ground.

"That 's for Raccoon Bottom?" I asked.

"Yes, 'Coon Bottom," he repeated, looking at me out of the corners of his yellow eyes.

"Can we get any milk here!" inquired Fred, as he blew out the blaze on a piece of bacon he had been holding in the fire.

"No cows," drawled the bushwhacker.

"Got anything at all?" Fred asked again.

"Nope."

"Seen anything of Sherman's army?"

"Nope."

"Do you belong here?"

"Yep," and he skulked off after his companions, who had gone on ahead.

"Didn't get much out of that chap, did you, Fred?" said I.

"No; he didn't seem very anxious to talk."

"I wonder if they are all like that down here in these parts?"

"Whether they are or not," Bence broke in, "there 's a devilish grin in their ugly faces that I don't like, and I can't feel easy in this place, wet or dry. Wish we were out of it."

So do I, if there is any harm in staying!" said I. "The guard will have to keep their ears open to-night."

"Of course they will," answered Bence. "But what 'll that amount to, if there 're any bushwhackers lying around here? They 'll sneak up on the best of us.

These fellows will be away to give the alarm long before we can surround the place and keep them in with a picket."

"Well, I suppose we'll stay, whatever comes!"

"Yes," he responded; then, pointing to the hill, he said: "There, what do you think of that?"

I looked in the direction indicated and saw, fading in the gloom, on the top of the hill, the dark forms of three men.

"That looks like trouble for us," Fred remarked, tersely. He, also, had followed the direction of Jake's finger. "But, perhaps not," he added. "I hope not."

Shortly after supper the storm ceased, the clouds parted, the stars came out, and the air became clear and warm. After we had partly dried our clothing the fires were allowed to die away, and the regiment, with the exception of the guard, was soon asleep.

I was suddenly startled from my dreams by a wild yell, a volley of musketry and the whistling of bullets. Every man of us was on his feet in an instant. But, by the time we had seized our weapons and rallied to repel our enemy, there was nothing to be seen in the darkness except the woods and the black outlines of the houses here and there. Neither was there a sound to be heard, save the thud and thump of horses' hoofs retreating up the road.

Replenishing our fires with more broken fence rails, we found, by the light, that Peter Baker, one of the boys in Company D, had been killed outright and perhaps a dozen others had been slightly wounded. Undoubtedly more would have been killed if the enemy had fired at us at a little shorter range.

There was nothing we could do about it except to attend the wounded and await further developments. The camp was soon as deathly still as the dead form of our comrade, lying motioness beside us, and there yet remained many dark hours of the night in which I might think it over. I was glad when I saw the day break; happier still when the sun rose above the edge of the woods.

At an early hour, and after another, and this time successful, effort to dry our blankets, and when everything was ready to resume our march, we were drawn up in line and addressed by Captain Hartees.

" Men," said he, "before we leave this place we must bury Peter Baker, who was shot last night by that gang of cowardly ruffians who fired upon us when we were asleep."

Two men detailed from Peter's company had already dug a grave at the foot of a huge butternut tree, in the bark of which a comrade had cut a large cross.

While they were bringing the body, wrapped in a blanket, to lay it in the grave, we could see the hang-dog, sulking vagabonds of the village collecting on the other side of a distant fence.

This was the first death in our regiment and, coming as it did, in a time of comparative peace, it oppressed us with a sorrow more than usually keen and, as we stood in silence about the grave, we marked well the indifferent curiosity of the people who were watching and grinning at us from behind the fence.

It was not the chance of battle, but an assasin's bullet that took a comrade from our ranks forever, and many a savage scowl came to the bronzed faces of my companions; many a muttered threat passed from mouth to mouth, against the wretches who were responsible for this thing.

When the body had been lowered to its last resting-place and the grave had been filled in, Captain Hartees, said:

" I want Comrade Baker's company to fire a volley over his grave. Fall into line, Company D, on the other side of the road."

Baker's company then fell into line as ordered, and at the word of command, faced about, bringing themselves opposite to the distant fence, with the men from the village partly concealed behind it.

" Ready !" ordered the captain.

"Captain !" cried the orderly sergeant of the company, " these guns are all loaded with ball."

" Silence ! Aim."

" But, captain—" said the sergeant, not wishing to be misunderstood.

" Fire ! Right face ! Forward march !"

We had little time and still less inclination to see what the effect of that volley had been upon the people in the vicinity of the fence, but there was evidently some excitement over there, from the appearance of things.

" Served 'em right," said Fred ; " I only hope the seed we planted fell into proper ground. This is the second time we have been served like this by trusting these people."

" It is a little rough if we 've punished the innocent for the guilty," said I.

" There hain't no innocent," muttered Jake ; "all those were gone long ago."

Resuming our order of march, we moved on without a word. I was thinking of him who had been left asleep under the butternut-tree, and wondering when my turn would come.

Nothing unusual happened to us that day. We picked up forage enough to give diversity to our meals ; enjoyed the usual number of halts, and grumbled over the same amount of tiresome marching as on the day before. At night, tired, as usual, we came to a halt in an uninhabited valley, and, after a supper from our rations and forage, we turned in and slept, undisturbed.

The next day and the next we went through the same round of changes, from rest to motion and back again, up hill and down, with nothing especially new to excite us, until the life seemed to be getting about as monotonous as our existence had been at Point Burnside.

On the evening of the second day after we left Raccoon Bottom, we marched down through Rossville, and there reached the main road. We did not halt in the village, but marched two or three miles beyond it and bivouacked for the night.

CHAPTER X.

The day following our arrival in Rossville was Sunday, the 8th of May; but, notwithstanding the sacredness of the day, we were on the march as early and we marched as far.

There was so little to attract the attention on this monotonous tramp that I kept continually thinking of the changes time brings about. In my mind's eye I could see my New England home, the village of Waytown, steeped in Sabbath stillness. The shops were closed and the roadways full of pious people, in response to the tolling bells directing their way, with sober faces, to church. I wondered if Tommy was among the number. What a difference there was between that scene and the one of which we formed a part!

I thought of old Joe; of the sounding horn, and of the scene in front of the tavern on the night he brought in the news that Fort Sumter had been fired on, and then the stranger—now our captain—reading to us in the tavern. How curiously it had all come about! I thought of the disturbance and of my father. Poor father, a rarely good man at heart and made fretful only by sickness. How it all came back to me, and how little I then realized that the war would last long enough for me to have a part in it.

This days' tramp was not as interesting as those of the few days before, because, now that we were follow-ing the main army road, those little delicacies obtained in the fresh country we had passed through were no longer to be had, even by Black Lige, the most sharp-eyed genius for foraging in the regiment. Everything eatable and drinkable, with the exception of water, had been already seized, devoured or drunk by the hordes of Confederates and Unionists that had preceded us. Indeed, the region in which we now were had been well stripped by the enemy before Sherman arrived, and our people finished that work completely.

I was now more accustomed to marching, and, realiz-ing more fully that every step was taking me nearer to the front, I did not lack food for thought and excite-ment with which to brace my nerves. Almost any-thing, I thought, would be better than tramping through that desolate and devastated country ; but the proba-bility that only a day or so more of such work would put us in the midst of action did much toward reconcil-ing me to the present.

In this day's march we passed through two or three villages, or rather groups of houses, but made no halt among them. The houses looked so empty and deserted, with windows open and doors agape and no signs of life anywhere, that none of the boys were tempted to investigate.

All along the line of march we were constantly dis-covering evidences of the wreck and waste of war, and of the myriads of men that had marched that way before us, and were then pressing hard upon the enemy behind the hills in front.

The fences had vanished from the roadside and from the fields as far as we could see. Here and there we came upon groups of blackened circular places which marked the location of camp fires. At times these blackened spots were numberless, dotting the ground for miles around. The turf was cropped short by horses, torn up by their hoofs, and scored into deep ruts by gun-carriage wheels. The lower branches of the trees also, those within reach of a horse's teeth, were stripped of leaves; the bark had been gnawed from the tree trunks, shrubs and bushes had been torn up by the roots, and skeleton twigs and branches lay scattered about.

The banks of the water-courses showed the plainest traces of the army. There, in the moist ground, as far up and down the stream as we could see, were the tracks of brogans, bare feet, hoofs and wheels, just as they had been left when the feet were drawn out or the wheels rolled on. If we had had no idea before, we learned from these tracks what it was that had ground the earth up into the fine dust that now rose about us in stifling clouds at the softest footfall or lightest breath of wind, and, floating away, covered houses, trees, grass and shrubs with a thick, dry coat of yellowish gray.

In this bed of dust we were constantly turning up all manner of things which the army had cast away: broken wheels, bits of harness, worn-out shoes, hats, under-clothing, broken canteens, battered dippers— everthing that was useless, worn out or cumbersome.

In a little rivulet stood, or rather lay, an army wagon. The forward wheels had been dished as the wagon came down the steep bank to enter the stream, and there it lay, emptied of everything except the smell of pork brine. One end of the wagon was beneath the surface of the stream, and the water rippled through and around it, while the dirty white cover flapped lazily in the breeze.

Such were some of the scenes we met in that country on that Sunday march. It seemed as if Sherman had used the country as the men did their shoes and their clothing—used it up and then dropped it in the dust.

That night we arrived at Ringgold, a town somewhat larger than any we had passed through and decidedly more populous; for, although the former inhabitants had, in great measure, disappeared, there were blue-coats enough to take their places. Here was another new and striking scene for me. In the place of white tents scattered through the fields, there were the yellow-white covers of army wagons, drawn up on the lawns beside the road. They were the baggage and supply wagons of Sherman's army, which could not now be far in advance of us. In these wagons, also, I found most positive proof that we were not advancing alone into the enemy's country, but that not far away, though hidden now by intervening hills, we should find the encampment of friends. I even went so far as to carefully scan the country in front of me, to see if I could catch the gleam of a tent.

While some of the boys were building a fire, I started, coffee-pot in hand, for a well that stood near and, while waiting among a crowd of others for my turn at the bucket, I noticed, a short distance away, a pretentious-looking mansion, which must have belonged to the village magnate. The air of former grandeur and present desolation that pervaded it attracted me so strongly that I approached it to get a better view.

No noise broke the stillness surrounding the place, nothing was heard except the rumble of some distant wagon or the low growls of the tired and foot-sore soldiers about the well. The doors to the house were gone; the windows were open, and without shutters or curtains; everything wide open and staring, like the eyes of a dead man. Tastefully laid-out flower beds were trampled out of all shape ; urns had been over-turned and broken, and the contents, roots and mold, scattered over the trodden turf. All around lay broken pieces of crockery and of furniture. The marble steps and the floor of the veranda were covered with dust and dented with musket butts. Inside, I saw what had once been a piano ; the cover off, the strings all broken and snarled, and a jagged hole in the sounding board, where a musket butt had been smashed down through it, shredding it into splinters ; and as if this were not enough, the keys of the piano had been broken and some of them were sticking straight up into the air.

If the house and its contents had been fired and consumed, I should have passed the place without thought ; but, standing, as it did, in desolation and ruin, with that unmusical ghost of luxury in the parlor, it left a picture in my mind that I would gladly be freed from ; a picture which is like a lasting reproach. .

But little time was left me for gloomy reflections as I was soon startled into consciousness of myself and my duties on that occasion, by the voice of one of our company who, in language more emphatic than choice, demanded what I was doing there with the family coffee-pot ?

That evening I hurried through supper, that I might use the fading daylight to add a few more lines to the letter that, at every opportunity for several days, I had been writing to Mary. Not an hour slipped by without some thought of her ; not a day without some addition to this letter, which I had carried in my knapsack. At Point Burnside the mail had arrived regularly ; but, since the day of our leaving that place, I had received no letter, and, compelled to be satisfied with the ones I already had, I lived in anticipation of the one that must

be waiting for me with the army in front.   This evening, not knowing how long it might be before our regiment would be plunged into the very heart of strife, I
was especially anxious to improve the opportunity for
writing.

I had now determined to bring my letter to a close,
so as to post it in Ringgold, but it was a hard thing for
me to do ; there were so many little things to be said,
so many pledges to be repeated, that I lingered over
the epistle until the daylight was all spent ; then, under
the shadow of the rapidly approaching night, I folded
up the letter, and, almost with a wish that I might carry
it myself, placed it in the bag with other mail for the
north.

After this I joined Fred, Jake and others of our company, who were just starting out to find the provost
guard, and from this source learn the latest news.

We did not find the provost guard, but discovered a
group of wagoners, which answered our purpose quite
as well.

The wagons were standing on the turf of an unfenced
yard beside the road, and in their order of arrangement
formed a crescent, between the arms of which brightly
blazed a most extravagant fire, that lighted up a picture
of camp-life comfort which left nothing to be desired.
The men looked contented, fresh and must have been
supremely happy in the knowledge that, when ordered
to move forward, they could either ride or walk, as best
suited them ; and they seemed to be experts in the art
of "taking things easy."   There were men reclining on
wagon tongues, others seated by the fire, and others
luxuriously stretched at full length on wagon seats,
lazily watching the play of light and shadow on the
scene in front.

They were evidently just finishing supper, as some of

them still held half-emptied dippers of coffee; while others, with pipes already lighted, were enjoying a quiet smoke. Somebody was saying as we came up:

"It 's surprising how well they do feed us!"

"I tell you," said another, "there 's many a poor chap in the army, doing garrison duty at some fort, struggling with salt horse and smacking his lips over it; while we, always on the move, get fresh beef," and the speaker jerked the coffee dregs out of his dipper under the wagon behind me. "But, hello! Who comes here?"

All eyes were instantly turned toward us, and one man, while he gazed at us inquiringly, said, in reply to the last speaker:

"Yes, and we are goin' to have it right along! The old man" [meaning Sherman] "knows enough to keep communication with his base of supplies and good food coming forward all the time." Then to us, while he puffed hard at a short clay pipe: "Reckon you belong to that new regiment, don't you?"

It occurred to me at that moment that I had never before heard so harsh a voice.

"Yes," I answered.

"What may it be?"

"Twelfth Kentucky."

"What division?"

"Cox's," said Fred.

"That 's the Twenty-third Corps, Scofield's!"

"You 're right," we answered.

"Have some coffee?"

"No, been to supper," responded Fred.

We advanced to the fire, took positions that suited us best, and opened on the mule drivers with our questions, Jake being the first to speak,

"What 's goin' on ? Why are you all here ?" he asked with his usual drawl, addressing no one in particular.

Two or three made ready to reply, but he of the harsh voice and the obstinate pipe, anticipating the others, replied :

"You see, the old man's got things about right to begin work, and he 's begun. Ain't he, boys ?"

"Yes," one or two voices replied, and one pleasant-voiced fellow near me continued, this time getting the start of the harsh voice :

"One fine morning, two days ago, the boys got orders to lay in ten days' rations, and started off ; they left all the baggage wagons here."

"They 'll be back in about four days," interrupted the harsh voice.

"Don't you believe it," said the pleasant voice. "They won't be back here for some time. Old Sherman is goin' to push the Johnnies, as they were never pushed before."

"How many men are there with Sherman ?" asked Fred.

"Some say one figure, and some another, but they all fix it about one hundred thousand."

"Is this all the baggage there is ?" I asked with a surprised look at the little groups of wagons.

"That 's what it is, baggages for the whole army, 'cept what the company mules took."

"How is that ?" I asked ; but, feeling immediately that this was a question calculated to show my ignorance, I glanced at Fred's face to see if he disapproved of it. Judge of my silent relief when I saw plainly that he was as much in the dark as I had been.

"You see," said our pleasant friend in explanation, "each company has a mule and a darkey to drive it, and between the two they carry all the cooking things."

" Oh, I tell you," said the harsh voice, " the old man knows how to save lugging, and they do say that the boys have better fixin's than the general officers."

" But where 's our division ?" asked Fred of a soldier between him and me.

" Let me see," said the man addressed ; then, taking his pipe out of his mouth, cried :

" Say, Bill, where 's Scofield and the Twenty-third Corps ? Down at the Roost ?"

" Yes," answered Bill, from the other side of the fire.

" Well, Bill, you are wrong for once," said somebody at my elbow, who up to this time had taken no part in the conversation. Noticing how the others stopped to listen to what more this quiet man might say, I concluded that he must be the wagonmaster, as he was looked upon as an authority.

" Wrong, am I ?" cried Bill. " What did that darkey say who came in last night ? Didn't he say that the rebs held the Gap and our boys were marching up to it ?"

" Certainly," the quiet man assented.

" Then what 's the matter with what I said ?" asked Bill in an aggrieved tone.

" Oh, dry up, Bill," cried several voices in a chorus.

" The boys want to find their division. Let the boss tell 'em where it is. He knows more about it than you do."

" What is this Buzzard's Roost, and where is it ?" asked Fred of the wagonmaster, to change the conversation.

" The Roost is a cliff, and overlooks a deep gap which divides the ridge of Rocky Face, and lies away off down yonder to the southeast " [pointing in that direction] " about fifteen miles or such a matter. The Rocky Face Ridge is a chain of break-neck hills several miles long,

and running north and south. Dalton, which I make
out is Sherman's present objective point, is just in
behind the south end of this ridge. The rebels are
now using this ridge as a fort, and they are spread out
along the top of it the whole length ; and at the north
end they turn off to the east at right angles and spread
out across a railroad that runs into Dalton on the other
side of Rocky Face. They have centered in one or two
places, and the Roost is one of them."

"That's all right enough," cried Bill, "but to get at
Dalton without leaving the railroad, we 've got to drive
the rebs away from Buzzard's Roost so that we can
follow the other railroad through the Gap."

"That's what Thomas is trying to do. You see,"
said the wagonmaster turning to us, "this railroad, that
runs through Ringgold, enters Dalton through the Gap
in Rocky Face, under Buzzard's Roost, and Thomas is
down there with the Army of the Cumberland, the
Fourth, Fourteenth and Twentieth Army Corps, trying
his prettiest to get through, judging by the firing we
heard this morning."

"But isn't the Army of the Ohio there, too ?" questioned Bill.

"Of course not. You ought to know that. We 've
not seen anything of that corps yet, and we would
have had sight of it if it had gone down. Besides, two
days ago, which was before Thomas's army left here,
Scofield, with the Twenty-third Corps, was at Red Clay,
a long stretch off to the northeast ; but I heard them
say that when Thomas moved from here to Tunnel ·
Hill—a hill between the Ridge and the Roost, so called
because the railroad tunneled it—Scofield came just over
the hills yonder" [pointing behind him to the north-
east] "to Catoosa Springs. Now, I reckon, he 's spread
out in line about east of here, facing the south, and

trying to force that wing of the rebs, which I told you runs out east from Rocky Face."

"Then, to reach our corps," said Fred, "we must leave the railroad and start off across the country to the east?"

"That's about it," the quiet man assented, "if you want to go right away; but, in my opinion, you'll meet them in an easier way. McPherson, with the Army of the Tennessee, is far away to the south, a long piece beyond Thomas's, and you may be sure he is there for a purpose. If you start off down the railroad to-morrow, I shouldn't wonder if, by the time you arrive near the Roost, you should find that Thomas had already pushed through. In that case you'll be pretty sure to meet your corps somewhere on the road; either on this or the other side of Buzzard's Roost Gap. According as they march into Dalton direct from where they are now or come around to this side of Rocky Face and follow this railroad in."

"Well," drawled Jake, with a yawn and a stare of amazement at the wagonmaster, "it is pretty evident that there is something goin' on, and I guess we'll get our share of it; but I am dead tired, and going to turn in."

"Oh, you'll be in the thick of it before long, make no mistake," some one cried laughingly after him as he went away.

Fred and I stayed but a short time to finish our pipes, and then we also turned in.

It was very strange how all my ideas of war had changed since my joining the regiment. This was due to the fact that my companions were veterans. Hearing them talk so much of their battles, a feeling of contempt for danger began to pervade me; then, too, when I first joined the regiment, I had an indefinite idea that there

would be firing and bloodshed right away. I lived in
daily expectation of it ; but, as days passed, and, much
to my surprise, nothing of the kind occurred, this feeling of suspense gradually yielded to one of indifference.

I had been wearing the blue for three months, and no
sign of the enemy had I seen or heard, except the hurried shots in the dark at Raccoon Bottom. And now I
half expected to be cheated out of my glory, or that,
when it did come, it would not realize my expecta-
tions.

I do not remember that I ever slept more soundly than
I did that night, under the little five-by-six tent in Ringgold, by the side of the baggage of Sherman's whole
army, on the eve of the campaign against Atlanta.

CHAPTER XI.

Monday morning dawned fair. Our little camp was broken early and, after several hours consumed in serving out rations, we were again in marching trim. From this time forth we were going forward like other regiments, prepared for days of hard fighting and forced marches, and where the opportunities for foraging would be few and far between. The cool part of the forenoon had passed before we were able to move, so that when we did leave Ringgold and the baggage-wagons the sun was high and shining hot upon our heads.

Beside the heat of the sun there were added to our other discomforts the extra rations, which were a load in themselves, and the fact that we were hurried along without the usual frequent halts. Under these conditions we had put miles behind us before we saw the head of the column break and scatter to rest by the roadside.

"Here," cried Fred, when the halt was called, and running, as fast as his weary legs could carry him, to a little grass-covered knoll about one hundred feet from the road—"here's a good place."

But I was already at his side, throwing off my accouterments previous to stretching myself at length on the dusty but welcome grass.

"This has been the worst day yet," I said, throwing myself down by the side of my cousin and pillowing my head on my blankets.

"Boom!"

"Hello! what 's that—thunder?" asked Fred, excitedly, scanning the sky as he raised himself with a jerk to his elbow and listened intently.

"It sounded to me like a salute being fired from a gun, far away," I replied.

"Boom! Boom!"

"That 's a fight for sure, and at Buzzard's Roost," said Jake, eagerly, who had also raised himself on his elbow to listen.

"Reckon you 're right," responded Fred, as he resumed a prostrate position. "Well, we 'll be into it soon enough. It 's so long since I 've heard a gun that thunder was the first idea which that firing put into my head."

I lay for a few moments listening to this distant booming of cannon and then sat up to see what the veterans thought of it. But they seemed quiet and, for the most part, indifferent; many of them, indeed, were already asleep. Only a few, here and there, gave the incident special attention and then, merely, to shout to some particular comrade that it sounded like old times or to make some similar remark.

"Boom! Boom! Boom!"

I listened earnestly, vainly trying to interpret those voices of war; as if perchance they might tell me which side was speaking at that moment and with what effect. The sound was low-toned and drawn out by the distance, lonesome, and like a note of warning; but it seemed innocent enough to me, and try as I would I could not connect it with battle or bloodshed.

There was an air of excitement and threatening in

it, but to me it awakened no personal experience, presented no picture of men falling dead in heaps. It was to me the beginning of a new experience; the first few drops of a protracted storm into which I was about to enter. Who could predict how I should come out of it?

For some time we lay and listened to the sounds which came to us—sometimes singly, then in groups, and again in confusion—until the cry, "Fall in!" brought us once more to a sense of the present.

Hour after hour we plodded on, the sounds of battle becoming louder and more and more distinct, until Fred said he thought he could hear infantry.

I could not tell, although I stopped to listen. For me there was only a confused roar of sounds, some louder than others, but I did not know enough at that time to distinguish the different reports; later, however, as we lessened the distance to the conflict, I was aware that the intervals between the roar of cannon were filled with lesser noises, which the initiated recognized and pronounced musketry.

At last we reached an elevation not far from Tunnel Hill, and from this point saw, rising like a wall before us, but still far away across the valley, the rugged, precipitous sides of Rocky Face Ridge, full of such lights and shadows as are made by ravines and jutting ledges. There was also a lofty, darkly-frowning wall, with a crest cut out in rugged peaks and hollows that stood out in clear relief against the blue and white sky beyond.

To the left, directly across the valley from where we stood, the ridge came to an end, sinking rapidly to a much lower level; but away to the right there seemed to be no limit, and the ridge in this direction extended away off until it met the sky. Even the gateway in the Gap, under Buzzard's Roost, was not visible, as we were not in a position to see through it.

We could determine, from what the wagonmaster had told us, where it should be, by a little sharper indentation in the outline, by heavier shadows, and because, in this neighborhood, the smoke of the battle seemed to be the thickest. But we were still too far away to distinguish individuals. Masses of men, when not concealed in the shadows of trees, were, however, distinctly visible. We could see, also, the flash of guns and the lasting color of flags moving hither and thither, sometimes shining brightly in the sunlight, at others almost vanishing in shadow or in smoke.

The crest of the ridge occupied by the Confederates, from the north end, nearest us, and away to the south, as far as we could see, was alive with men and sparkling with fire, while from every shadowy ravine that scarred the sides of Rocky Face our troops were sending out flashes in reply; and from the whole surface thin wreaths of smoke were rising and drifting off among the leaves and blasted tree-tops, just as I have seen the steam creeping up from the shingles of our cottage roof, wet from melted snow.

As we have been told, the Roost was the center of attack. There was the meeting-place and crash of battle. Heavy banks of smoke were floating away from this section, and the air above was dotted with fleecy puffs of smoke from bursting shell.

It was a sight full of grandeur, and terrible—to me, at least—was its import.

My heart for a moment stood still, but the intoxication of such excitement was not to be resisted, and it resumed its beating with such force that the blood surged to my finger-tips. I would have rushed wildly to take part in the struggle had not the distance and the calmer actions of others restrained me.

I looked in the faces of my companions; there was

fire in every eye, buoyant firmness in every step, as steadily, surely, but not one second faster, they marched on and on. Despite the impatience burning in their hearts, their movements were as orderly and methodical, and their bearing as unchanged, as if the battle smoke were harmless mist and the roar of guns but the wind moaning among the trees.

But as we advance with eyes fixed on the scene of strife, the sun sets, the firing gradually slackens, ceases, and the battle is over; and when, as night fell, we reached the rear of our lines, instead of fitful flashes, the steady blaze of numberless camp-fires lit up the scene.

About these fires thousands and thousands of tired soldiers were gathered, each telling his own story of the battle.

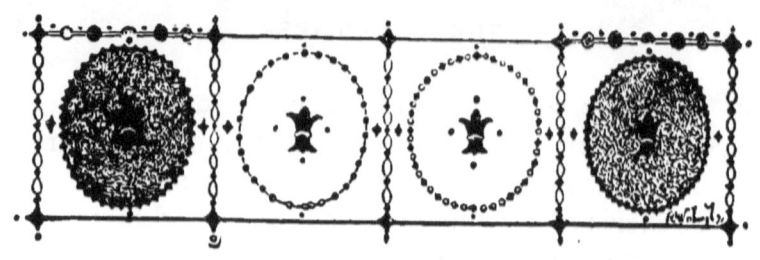

CHAPTER XII.

There are those ever ready with brilliant pens and standing far enough removed from any corporeal interest, if such expression be permitted concerning the strife of those two great armies camped so near together, who might have grasped the scene on that first night we pitched our tents with Sherman's army, and from their serene point of view have given a lucid bird's-eye view of the whole situation. I saw what was in my neighborhood only.

They would have painted in well-chosen phrases the picture of that long valley, lying to the west along the base of Rocky Face, all sparkling with union camp fires, in the light of which were to be seen horses, caissons, cannon and tents and men, everywhere. Men hard at work as were the surgeons about the blazing fires of the field hospitals; men as couriers hurrying with dispatches from camp to camp; men at rest, as most of them were, grouped about the fires or dozing far apart beneath the trees.

Mill creek would have been sketched as a muddy little stream, hedged on either side by a thicket of bush and creeping gloomily, stealthily along by the side of our camp to pass beneath Buzzard's Roost into the

Confederate lines, unseen, except where in a few places our fires extended to its bank, and reddened it with their reflection.

Beyond this, it would have been noted that Rocky Face Ridge reared its ponderous mass, blacker than the night itself, until the eye of the observer reached the top, which sparkled and scintillated with hostile fires—all in striking contrast to the blinking stars and slowly-drifting clouds above.

But the enemy did not have all of that long ridge to themselves. Our boys had fought that day to some purpose. They had won their way a little distance, at least, up its craggy sides, among the rocks and stunted trees. The northern slopes were ours, and we, camping near this upper end while eating supper, cast many wondering, curious glances along that line of friendly fires, following it away up the slope to where it stopped and a broad belt of darkness separated it from the enemy.

These fires seemed to beckon us ; and when our meal was over, and it was arranged that some of us might leave camp, my fatigue vanished and I joined Fred and two or three others who were going on a tour of investigation.

As we climbed the hill our attention was attracted by one especially brilliant fire. We found about it the usual camp scene, men lounging about, sipping coffee, smoking and chatting, while some were cleaning their weapons. The excitement of the late struggle seemed to have disappeared with its smoke and grime, for these men conversed in low, quiet tones.

The hands that poured the coffee or lit the pipes were steady enough ; it was only in the nervous, restrained laugh that they betrayed any trace of the excitement of the day.

As we advanced into the light and drew near the fire we were greeted with :

" In the advance to-day ?"

" No," we answered.

" What regiment ?"

" Twelfth Kentucky."

" That's a fightin' regiment. Part of Reilly's old brigade ?"

" Yes," Fred remarked in a quiet way, in answer.

" S'pose you had a taste of tumblin' over the rocks like the rest of us ?"

" No," said Fred ; " we 're only just from Ringgold."

" What !" exclaimed our interrogator. " The Twelfth Kentucky, and not in a fight ?"

" This is the time we missed it. We veteranized a couple of months ago, had a furlough, and have only just now turned up for another three years."

" Well, that beats me ! The Twelfth Kentucky and not— Oh, well, you 're here early enough. Been to supper ? Have ? Well, take some coffee with us, any-how. Here you, Fattie " [to a veteran, who seemed to have the coffee-pot under his special charge], "pass these comrades some coffee."

Fattie, who was tall and as thin as a rail, duly obeyed, handing us the boiling-hot, inky, aromatic fluid in blackened, dented cups.

We sat down by the fire, sipped the coffee and soon learned that the regiment to which this group belonged was part of Newton's Division of the Fourth Army Corps, and that they had been in a skirmishing line all day.

In answer to a question as to what they had done that day, one emphatic man they called Sandy cried :

" What have we done ? Look you ! You see those camp fires down there ?" pointing to the valley. " Well, they have not moved. They were there in the same place last night; but here, last night the rebs slept. We drove 'em out to-day, we did. It cost us heavy, but we did it."

"You're right, it cost us heavy," said another voice. "How they picked us off! But what a charge that was over such a mass of loose rock, and in the face of such a fire. Pratt and Sager fell first, away down in the bottom yonder, just after we started. While we were running up Magoun, just to the left of me, stumbled on a tilting rock. I had to laugh to see him run along on all fours before he could recover. But he had only just got straightened up, poor fellow, when over he went for good. That brought Ripley next to me in the line, but we hadn't gone a dozen rods together when he cried out: 'Oh, Bill!' and dropped. Clark, Kelley and Booth fell at the same time just about here; and just on the edge of the ridge out yonder, we left the orderly and Tom Cranford—and I know there was a heap more from some of the other companies dropped in the same place."

"What, did you get much further up?" asked Fred.

"You bet we did," he replied, "and our pickets are out there now, I reckon, but it costs, it costs, just as Sandy says. They dropped us along here pretty thick, and it got to be mighty lonesome before we came to the end of the race."

"Lonesome," echoed the deep-toned voice of a gray-bearded Illinoisan. "You were all together when you started out of the woods below, on that double quick up the hill, a-dodging from stump to rock, and from rock to tree, but I was away out on the left of the line and, somehow, in spite of all I could do, I kept getting farther and farther away from you, and edging toward the gulley which separated us from Company H. No mistake about it, the Johnnies were too many for me. Shot and shell were falling like rain out there, and the ground was getting a terrible sweeping." He paused as though to put back the thoughts that were crowding upon him, but as the rest of us waited for him to continue, he took up the story again.

"While I tried to get back into my old spot, a piece of shell struck my gunstock, knocked it into splinters, and laid me flat as a pancake. I thought I was done for. Oh, you needn't smile, you fellows, you have been through the same thing yourselves, but I soon found out what the trouble was, and that I was not hurt much. Of course, I was no good without a gun, and so I held back until I could get one. In a few minutes a fellow just ahead of me, threw up his hands and fell backward. This was my chance and I soon had the gun he dropped. 'T was barber Jim," [falteringly] "you all know him—of Company H—Jim, when I reached him, was trying to cover with his hand a hole in his breast that looked almost large enough to put your fist in. The blood was running out between his fingers, and such a pitiful look as poor Jim gave me, as I took up his rifle and hurried away. I tell you what, boys," [and the bronzed face of the speaker beamed on the upturned faces around him] "I'm right glad to get back to the company again. I've been in a good many skirmish lines before, but never in one when I was so blamed lonesome as to-day."

"Begorra, and its meself that's always lonesome in a skirmish," observed one of the listeners. "Sure, there's no fun in it at all, at all; a man's always alone in such work, wid divil a sowl near him. I always feel as if every Johnnie had his murtherin' eye on me. By the same token, it's Pat Cragin that would rather be at home carrying the hod, than standing up and stoppin' bullets for the rebs. Holy Mother, there's the liftinint, and him we left on the crust up yonder wid a hole in his head."

"Only stunned a little, that's all," quietly observed the officer, who at this moment emerged from the darkness beyond, and was passing near enough to be seen by the light of the fire.

"Sure it's meself that's glad to hear you say so," answered Pat; and, as our little group watched the officer until he disappeared in the darkness, he continued, speaking lower: "There goes a foine officer; divil a better ever drew a sword or led a charge. If he ever gets his min into trouble, bedad, but he's the boy that can get them out. I like him better 'n I did the cap'n, poor felly."

After this there was a moment of silence, for Cragin's homely words had struck responsive chords in many breasts, and afterward the talk became general. While many little dialogues were passing among the boys who had come up with me and the soldiers about the camp-fire, I turned to Cragin, who was sitting just at my left, and asked if he thought there would be any fighting the next day.

"Fittin', is it? Faith, 'nd ye may just count on that same. We'll skirmish to-morrow, just as we did to-day. Sure, we're only keepin' the Johnnies busy till McPherson has a chance to get in his work; that's him down there," said Cragin, in explanation, pointing away out over the landscape into the darkness.

"Where?" I asked, trying to follow the direction indicated.

"The light from the fire's too glaring to see it well. Just shade your eyes at the side a bit and look down there. Do you see a red glare in the sky?"

"I think I do."

"Well, that's him, and them's McPherson's camp-fires that 's reddenin' the clouds! The old man wants McPherson or some of 'em to get round into the rear of the rebs. The divil fly away wid 'em. It takes a power of marching to satisfy Sherman ; but, begorra, it is the kind of marching that counts and makes the inimy skedaddle all the same !"

It was a comfort for me to hear that tramping paid, and that it was bringing about the desired result. But what did that result signify to those who had that day fallen? This was the question I pondered. However great the importance of this movement might be to Sherman and to the country, my mind refused to leave my individual prospects. I could see myself an actor in just such scenes as had been described. Henceforth, until the end, I was to be one of those who must do not only the marching but the skirmishing.

How long would it be before I should find myself enveloped in that leaden storm? How much time might there be left me to think of home and of those I loved? How long would it be before Fred or Jake or some others of my company about their camp-fires might speak of me as these soldiers spoke of poor Tom Cranford?" We left him just out on the ridge yonder."

"Where were you to-day ?" asked Cragin, interrupting my melancholy dreaming. "What part of the line were yon **in** ?" and he looked at me from cap to shoes, as if it had just occurred to him that not only was I a stranger, but that my uniform was in pretty good condition for a veteran.

I did not care to admit that I had never been under fire, at least where I could stand up and face it, and so replied that we were not in the engagement but had been marching all day.

"Well," replied Cragin, "that 's just the same wid

Sherman—some's fightin' and some's marchin', but it all counts."

Before a second opportunity occurred to question me, Fred and I walked away and approached another fire, where another group were listening to a soldier describing his experience.

He was saying:

"We kept a mighty good line, though I never saw men fight harder than those fellows did on the right. Every time I looked in that direction I saw their ramrods twirling above their heads. They were regular killers; at work by the day; just as if the boss was standing over them. And then the charge! Boys, they put such things down in history." Then, after a pause, during which his companions sat staring at the burning logs, trying to realize the glory of it after the fire had left their blood, he added: "But I do not believe it was ever intended. It looked to me, then, and I think so now, that sombody lost his head when he ordered both the first and second charge. The idea of charging in a place like this, with the chances all in favor of the other side. Sherman don't do business in that way. I tell you, somebody blundered, and this is not the first time, either. I hope there won't be any more mistakes to-morrow."*

I fervently echoed this wish, and we went back to our own camp. I had seen something of the day's fight, had heard the booming of the guns and the rattle of musketry, and there was an awful, fascinating realism in these simple stories.

As I rolled myself up in my blankets on the ground

---

* "The orders were not to waste life in serious assault upon intrenchments, but the zeal of the troops and subordinate commanders turned the intended skirmish into something very like a ranged battle, and the Confederate reports state that five separate and regular assaults were made on their lines."—*Cox's Atlanta.*

and tried to sleep, my brain was in a whirl. I seemed
to hear the heavy tramp of armies, the ringing cheers
of charging infantry, the roar of artillery, the shriek of
shell, the groans of wounded, dying men; and then I
thought myself all that was left of an unsupported line
of skirmishers. The army to which I belonged had
fallen back; the enemy were advancing; my companions had been picked off, one by one, until I stood
alone, a target for a thousand rifles. Unable to move,
and realizing I was dreaming, yet powerless to break
the spell, I stood and waited for the end that I knew
must come, when I was roused to consciousness by
Fred, who said:

"Seems to me you dropped to sleep mighty quick.
The colonel has come. I got it from Black Lige. He
says the colonel's all broke up about the horses; that
he tried to get 'em, and tried hard; that he left Point
Burnside for that purpose; but it's no go. He couldn't
make it win. Sherman's sorry; but the change in the
plans for the movement of the army makes it impossible. The boys are satisfied it's all straight, and don't
care now."

I was too tired, too sleepy, to exhibit much interest
in that almost forgotten subject, and dozed again. The
silence and darkness deepened, the camp-fires burned
low, and yet lower; the forms that had been moving
about me in the gloom disappeared, one by one. I
listened a moment to the breeze as it freshened and
died away, moaning and sighing through the tree-tops,
and fell asleep.

CHAPTER XIII.

Waking shortly after daylight, there came wafted to me, on the soft, dewy air of the morning, the warbling notes from some far-off bugle, sounding the reveille. An instant later, another bugle repeated the call more clearly. Another and yet another brazen throat responded, nearer and nearer ; and now, as the piping of shrill-toned fifes and the heavy rolling of drums catch up and interpret the theme, the frowning cliffs of Rocky Face repeat and echo the medley of sounds until the air vibrates in all directions with martial music.

The sputtering crack of rifle shots from along the summit of the ridge and the thundering of artillery—which had again opened on the enemy—now burst in upon the chorus and, with emphatic accompaniment, announced the day's work fairly begun.

The previous evening had given me a glimpse of what one phase of my experience with Sherman's army was to be. The sounds and scenes of this morning presented the prospect to me from another point of view.

Everything was new, strange and interesting ; so different from the quiet camp life from which we had come.

Our position commanded a fine view of the plain,

the open country to the south and of that section where
a part of our army was concealed in the thick
forest.

The camps before us were springing into life. Thousands of smoke columns arose from plain and hill,
mounted, until, caught by some passing current of air,
they bent sidewise and floated out in waving pennants
to a vanishing point.

Thousands of soldier-cooks were preparing breakfast
for myriads of hungry soldiers.

Men were forming into companies and regiments and
brigades, and marching, some in one direction, some in
another.

Batteries of artillery were hurrying off, sometimes
along the roads, then across the fields, to disappear
beneath the thatch of distant woods.

Cavalrymen passed and repassed, leading riderless
horses to and from the waters of Mill Creek.

Locomotive whistles announced the frequent arrival
of provision trains, from which supply wagons, moving
every whither, were distributing hard tack, pork, coffee
and ammunition.

Occasionally a bit of color danced and waved in the
sunlight on the heights above us, as a signal-flag com-
municated a message to the officers below.

We caught, now and then, glimpses of our troops and
of the enemy, struggling away up among the trees and
rocks of the ridge, while over all thin patches of light-
blue smoke rose from the woods into the air and mingling with the white puffs from bursting shell drifted
away into the space beyond.

It was a scene and a morning not easily to be forgotten.

It seemed hardly possible that all this stir and bustle
could be the result of one general's planning, or that

one general could successfully control the movements of so many men ; but the boys, who knew, said :

"The old man can win more battles, keep the enemy more continually on the retreat and lose fewer men than any other general in the army."

"But how is it done?" I asked Fred. "How does Sherman manage to keep control of his army? How bring order out of this confusion?"

"Well, you see, Sherman plans the campaign. Through his engineers he gets the lay of the land and knows how to take advantage of it. The generals under Sherman are only his executives, who have care of the details. They are told where to go and what to do, and upon their careful obedience depends our success. Generals are born, not made. Shoulder straps never planned a campaign nor won a battle."

The arrival of the colonel was, naturally, the first subject for discussion ; but this event, aside from the letters he brought from headquarters, created no stir, awoke no feeling of resentment. The boys seemed to be satisfied that he had done all that man could do to redeem the promise he had made, and some even went so far as to say that the less we said about horses the better. Even Jake, now we were at the front, was content without horses, and so expressed himself.

Breakfast eaten, tents and blankets rolled up and guns carefully cleaned and made ready for use, we awaited orders. While we were waiting, taking in the surrounding scenery, "Black Lige" happened to pass, and Jake hailed him with :

"Ho, Lige ! Has the colonel got his orders?"

"Yes ; he's got 'em fer sure. I done heered de cap'n say dis mawnin' dat we's a goine ter jine Scofield ter-day."

"Did he say where Schofield was, Lige?" I asked.

"No, maws' Dan. He done say nuffin 'bout it 'cept wut I tell yer."

"Fall in men, fall in," called the voice of our orderly.

"That 's the talk," said Jake. "We 'll get our share now, and when we get a chance, we 'll give the Johnnies the best we 've got in the shop."

In a few moments we were in line, facing the south and quickly after, at the tap of the drum, amid rumble and rattle on every hand, we marched along the plain about two miles until near Rays Gap; then, turning east, crossed Mill Creek, and climbed to the crest of the ridge, fully seven hundred feet above the base of the mountain.

What a climb that was! Scarcely a breath of air stirred in the woods; the atmosphere was hot and stifling, and the ascent both difficult and hazardous. We were all in high spirits, however, notwithstanding the heat, and it mattered little to us that the battle was not far away.

Up the side of this natural fortification, which continually impressed us with a sense of its magnitude, over the rocks, now to the left, turning and winding, on, up and through a forest of stunted pines and a tangled undergrowth that filled the narrow clefts and crevices in this well named rocky ridge, we climbed, tumbled, slipped, scrambled and forced our way until late in the afternoon when we came to a halt near some of the Ohio regiments of Schofield's Division.

What a country was spread out before us! To the west of the open plain below were to be seen only deep valleys, densely wooded forests and the rugged chains of rock which ribbed and intersected this region in every direction.

To the south the corrugated surfaces of Rocky Face

stretched away until it's identity was lost in a background of distant hills beyond.

Eastward the scene was of panoramic beauty. Dalton lay below us, close to the railroad, and not more than two miles distant.

Nature had done much to make Dalton defensible, but added to it was the ingenuity of Southern engineers. For miles around the town we could see a series of ridges, which, with jutting spurs, stretched out in every direction; lower than Rocky Face, but much more valuable to the enemy, on account of their nearness to the town and the ease with which they might be occupied and converted into strong defensive outposts.

Creeks and rivers threaded the landscape, which was dotted here and there with houses, while away to the south and east we saw the blue summits of the hills that curtained Resaca.

The air was better on the ridge; and while we rested there, eating our dinner, and enjoying it, too, Kimball, who had been quietly taking stock of our surroundings, said, as if to himself:

"What a place for defense! The whole army of the North couldn't storm this ridge and capture it. See the chances here for sharpshooters! Why, they could pick off skirmishers as easy as you 'd pick blackberries from a well-filled vine, and not stand in fear of a scratch."

"'Nd just look at the loose rock lyin' around here," interrupted Jake, who had been listening; "'s almost as good as ammunition itself."

"Sherman don't mean to give the enemy any such advantage as this over him, I know," continued Kimball. "He 'll drive him out of here, and he won't do it in the way Johnston wants him to, either. After this comes Dalton ; just look at it ! But that 'll go in the same way as Rocky Face."

"That 's right," responded Jake ; "but, as one of those Illinois men said last night, it 's going to take a heap of marching to do it. Well, let it come; I 'm ready, and want to be moving, seeing and doing something. I reckon the colonel 's gone to report to Schofield, ain't he, sergeant ?" speaking to the orderly who was standing near.

"Yes," replied the sergeant ; "and we'll lie here until we hear from him."

Here was an opportunity to read my letters, of which I had three—two from Mary and one from mother. To be sure, I was occasionally interrupted by the booming notes of artillery, the crash of bursting shell, the crack of rifles and the "zip" or "ping" of bullets as they passed by ; but though all of these sounds were new to me and caused me no little nervousness, my interest in the letters never flagged, and I read them through to the end.

Mother inclosed in her letter a pressing invitation from Edith Miller, the deacon's daughter, to visit Way- town.

"Come to Waytown again," she said, "and come to stay. I need your kindly advice so much in my trouble. Father died shortly after you left, and mother died scarcely a month since, and you will see that I am alone, with no one to advise me. Won't you please come ? There are matters here of very great importance to you, and you must come and see to them. I cannot take 'no' for an answer."

Of course, my mother wondered what it could all mean, and referring to her reply, said she would have accepted the invitation if it had not been for my absence, but that under the circumstances she could not, for the present, think of it.

Mary's letters—ah, well, no language can describe

the comfort and encouragement I derived from these outpourings of a loving heart. They were all that could be hoped for from the pen of a true-hearted woman, and were read and reread for days and weeks afterward—the same old story, but always appealing, always new.

The rest of the day was spent in listening to sounds of the conflict still raging at Buzzard's Roost, watching the movements of the troops below us, the plain being gradually deserted, and chatting with some of the Ohio boys. From this source of information we learned that thus far the Twenty-third Corps had been used as a flanking corps, and that Sherman's movements were based on this part of his army as a pivot, swinging to the right or left as occasion demanded.

"How long he'll keep this thing up's hard to say," said one of our informants, speculatively; "but I allow he's goin' to keep at it, for we've already heard we're goin' to git out o' this in the morning."

After supper, consisting of salt pork, hard tack and cold water, for we were not permitted to build fires on the Ridge, we put in the time as best we could, chatting, observing the lights in Dalton as they flashed out one by one in the darkness settling on the rapidly fading landscape, and then curled up under our blankets as comfortably as the rocky nature of the ground would permit, and went to sleep.

I expected that the next day would certainly bring me face to face with the enemy, but in this I was disappointed, for when the day broke we were marched back over about the same stony ground we had struggled over the day before.

The whole of the Twenty-third Corps was with us this time, for to the right or left, as the openings in the trees or between the hills permitted, we saw the whole

landscape was full of bluecoats, all marching in a direction parallel to our own. Away off to the south we
heard the roar of battle. Behind us, far to the rear, a
stray shot or two, perhaps, but nearer us only the usual
sounds of the march, the clatter of tinware at our belts,
the restless tap of a drum here and there, the profane
clamor of artillerymen struggling to extricate a gun or
wagon from some muddy creek. If we were retreating
what were we retreating from ? There was not a gray-
coat to be seen, and no sounds that I called alarming
in our rear, and our movements, though somewhat
guarded, did not resemble what I imagined a retreat
must be. Nor did the talk of those about me give me
any suggestion. There were the usual growls at the
roughness of the way, but aside from that no one
seemed to care whither we were marched or what the
reason of the movement was.

When one sees hundreds of others doing the same
thing he is doing, and without a sign of anxiety as to
the result or of criticism as to the method pursued, it
soon becomes difficult to maintain even a small amount
of private worry.

Wednesday was spent in camp or in lines of battle.
We did not move much, and reports that the enemy
were advancing on us under cover of some woods at no
great distance from our lines, kept my nerves always at
a tension. Shortly after dinner we were called again
to the front, and it seemed, by the look of expectation in our officers' eyes, that this time the graycoats
must be certainly advancing. We stood and waited,
hearing and seeing nothing.

Suddenly there was a great cheering, away off to the
left of the line ; other regiments near us took up the
cry.

"What is it ?" I asked, somewhat anxiously.

" Look ! Look ! There 's Stoneman's cavalry. Hurrah, hurrah !" cried Jake at my elbow, pointing to the left.

A body of horsemen were charging out of the woods into the open ground.

It was an inspiring sight, and I swung my cap and shouted with the rest : " Hurrah ! Hurrah !" On they went, line after line coming into view, a dense mass flying over the green earth like the black shadow of a cloud.

There were but two or three thousand of them, a drop in the bucket in comparison with the hundred thousand hid away in the miles of woods between us and the place far away to the south where McPherson's guns were booming. Yet it seemed as if nothing but the cold hard rocks of mother earth, nothing of flesh and blood could withstand that onward rush of men and horses. They looked all that has ever been said of them, daring, reckless, confident. There was an easy swing and rhythm about their motion that almost set me dancing. I gazed at them admiringly.

A wild yell pierced the air, sabers flashed in the sunlight and I saw Wheeler's cavalry debouching swiftly from the opposite woods.

Nearer and nearer they came together—these two ponderous masses. My breath came in gasps with excitement, in expectation of the conflict. I imagined that when they came together I would hear a crash like the crash of an avalanche when it reaches the valley. I braced myself for the shock as if, when those two masses met, a heavy weight would strike me also in the chest. But when they had charged—to within a rod of each other I should think—a shrill bugle sounded the retreat, and the enemy turned and rode swiftly away.

"That was just a scare," said Kimball. "They only

wanted to find out whether we were in force or not."

I thought of the old saw, " A man might as well be killed as be scared to death," but simply looked wise, smiled and said nothing.

" A cavalry charge 's a grand sight," continued Kimball, encouraged by my attention. A grand sight! It 's like a living ram, to batter down or scatter everything. Cavalry like Stoneman's 's like a hurricane in a city of paper houses. They 'll break up infantry every time, and 'll silence a battery by hacking the cannoneers to pieces. Why, a cavalryman on the dead run, 's these fellows were just now, 'll split a man from head to waist, with his saber, 's easy 's a butcher 'd split a spring lamb !"

" Don't they use their Spencers ?" I asked.

" Neither rifles nor revolvers are any good to cavalry in a charge. The saber 's the thing for the rush."

The enemy made no further demonstration, and we held our position, unmolested, during the rest of the day. At night a picket was set, and our regiment came in for its share of duty.

Fred and I were assigned to the same post; and there, by a big tree, we stood and listened. That about sums up the duty of a night picket. You stand by some big tree or stump or rock, while all around you is a darkness that almost may be felt. And how you do listen ! How keenly sensitive are the ears, and how vivid the imagination at such times ! You fancy somebody is moving toward you ; the breaking of twigs and rustling of leaves settle this to your satisfaction ; the sound ceases, and the cold chills creep over you as you think the cause of your alarm may be standing on the other side of your tree, and if you but stretch your arm around it you may touch him.

I realized that the Confederate Army was only a short distance away, and, at times, strained my ears until it seemed as if the nerves and muscles of my face would crack with the tension in the effort to discover some evidence of their nearness. But the stillness was unbroken, with the exception, perhaps, of the piping of frogs and the low, far-off rumbling sound of some moving train.

At daylight we were again on the move to the southwest. This time no regiments marched in front with us. Two days before we had swept round from east to west like a long, blue tidal-wave, regardless of road or broken ground ; to-day, a long, blue serpent-line of men drew its sinuous folds. To the left of us, the gloomy, unbroken wall of forest, hiding the ridge of Rocky Face from us and us from the eyes of our enemy along its crest ; to the right, a broken country ; ahead, long lines of soldiers marching on ; behind us, lines of soldiers coming after.

"Looks as if the whole army was on the move," said Jake. "There'll be fun soon, and we'll have a chance to try these guns of ours."

"Don't be in a hurry, Jake. Our guns won't rust," said Kimball. "We'll catch it soon enough. I've had all the square meals of that kind I want. I'd rather march than fight any day. It's better to get tired than it is to get killed, and a heap better to suffer with blistered feet than to lose an arm or a leg."

"It's skeery business," replied Jake ; "but we never got killed yet, and we've been under fire a good many times."

"Some of us have been mighty lucky ; but you can't tell, you can't tell," said Kimball, as he gave his heavy cartridge-box a hitch into a more comfortable position and walked away.

We entered Snake Creek Gap and crowded on, sometimes in the stony road, sometimes over the shingle beside the creek or along its sloping banks.

Overhead the interlacing branches of the trees on either side of this narrow defile formed a thatch which for long distances shrouded us in gloom. Occasionally a break in the dense foliage let in the sunlight, and we could see the wild and picturesque scenery surrounding us.

We came through the gap at last and camped in flank with McPherson's army before the outworks of Resaca. We saw the light of rebel campfires reflected on the clouds drifting over Rocky Face far to the north of us, whence we had come, and we looked to our muskets— at least I did—expecting sharp work on the morrow ; but it did not come. The roar of McPherson's batteries and the ceaseless fire of musketry from his line, still snarling like an eager but wary watchdog before the intrenchments of Resaca, were now in our ears. We were not drawn into it, but were cautiously extending our lines and resting on our arms. That night again we saw the firelight of our enemy still in its old position to the north. But the next day a report spread like wildfire along our line that Johnston had left Dalton and was concentrating on our front. This was great news. Our marching had countered them.

We saw the smoke of a burning house or two along the railroad. We heard the shouts of our comrades of the Fourth Corps driving the enemy toward us along the ridge of Rocky Face and through Buzzard's Roost Gap, and we perceived that the fire in our front was much increased, betokening a stronger force there. Johnston and his whole army were there.

It was the thirteenth of May. I had been a soldier three months, and I had not fired a shot.

CHAPTER XIV.

The Twenty-third Corps marched two and a half miles, in a northeasterly direction, on the Rome and Dalton Road; then left it, and, regardless of roads or fences, pursued an easterly course straight across the country.

Shortly after leaving the road, we forded three or four tributaries of Blue Spring Creek. There was no time to stop and remove shoes and stockings at these places; it was simply walk in, regardless of water or its depth, just as a horse or a mule would do. Fortunately, the water was not more than half way up to my knees, and all I had to do, on reaching the other side, was to squeeze my trousers as dry as possible, and depend for the rest upon the movement of my feet, which, when I walked, worked up and down in my shoes like a pump-plunger, throwing out water at every stroke.

Our line of march seemed to be so planned that we passed no houses on this tramp, though we could not have been far removed from them, as we frequently saw fences surrounding lands under cultivation.

At Line Creek we did not fare so well, as the water was quite deep in places, and the steep bank leading to the hill on the opposite side made it difficult to continue in a straight line; but we forded the stream, and in zigzag order, with the water in our shoes chugging and crunching at every step as we ascended the hill and pressed on.

We had heard more or less firing since daybreak; but, after leaving the wagon road, the sound became more continuous, and rapidly increased in volume. When we gained the crest of the hill, close to Line Creek, the noise of battle grew more distinct, and we could with ease distinguish the booming of artillery from the rattle of musketry.

It was nearly noon when we descended to the valley and came into line on the left of Thomas, facing Camp Creek, which separated us from the strongly intrenched hills occupied by the enemy north of Resaca.

To the right and left the rattle of musketry from our skirmish lines, which were pressing the enemy toward the creek, was continuous. From still farther to the right and south, where McPherson was engaged, came the deep-toned thunder of artillery; in our immediate front the silence was absolute. We knew the enemy was there, however—perhaps felt it, rather than knew it.

Between us and the enemy there stretched a broad, green valley down to the harmless creek, which rippled peacefully along as if there were no such thing as war. The sky was clear as crystal. The sun shone brightly, as if to gladden our hearts and induce us to abandon our wretched business. But the birds among the trees near by flitted nervously from branch to branch, discontented, fearful, silent.

I had hardly taken in the beauties of the scene when an order was given for our deployment as a skirmish line. It came unexpectedly, and, it seemed to me, was given without the careful deliberation it merited, and wholly regardless of whether we were ready or not.

I felt my face become pale and my strength suddenly leave me. The least push, or, it seemed to me then, breath of air, would have tumbled me headlong to the earth.

I would, at that moment, have given all I had, or ever expected to have, for a place of safety. The idea of being ordered like that, to stand between two opposing armies. That any human being should have it given into his power to say:

"You go to the front and die!"

I looked at my comrades for a sign that all was not right. There seemed to be no spirit of concern or question either in their faces or in their actions.

Fred, on my left, was walking with his gun at the "trail," looking straight ahead. Jake, on my right, and Kimball next to him, were doing the same thing; in fact, the whole line was steadily advancing.

It seemed to me that the silence before us was awful. It did not matter that there was firing either to the right or left; my ears were closed to that, and both eyes and ears were strained to catch a glimpse or hear a sound of the enemy in front.

Of course, I was in position all this time; spurred on by pride, absence of will-power to do other than what I was bid or what you will, I kept pace with the line as it advanced.

At last a little break in the woods revealed the breast-works of the enemy.

"Forward! Double quick!" shouted a voice in our rear.

I threw one glance behind me to see if the main line were advancing.

They had not moved. Could it be that this order was meant for us alone. It seemed to me the faces of the men in our rear were cold, cruel and grim, and I wondered if it was usual to order a line of men, separated so widely as we were, to charge upon an enemy of unknown strength. It was unreasonable to expect anything like success from such a movement.

Would the silence before us never be broken? That awful hush was wearing upon me! I nervously raised my gun, looked it over to make sure it was all right, then again lowered it to a "trail," clinging tightly to it all the while.

But look! A puff of white smoke and a red blaze suddenly sprang out from the trees beyond the creek. Scarcely had I seen it, when a loud report reached my ears and then from the same spot a dozen or more fiery throats belched forth their wrath and passion.

I heard, for the first time in my life, the shrill whistle made by flying shell, and as I ducked my head, now this way, now that, the sharp, quick shots of musketry followed and bullets went by my ears with a "zip, zip" or rattled like hail on the ground around me, or drove into the earth at my feet, throwing up pieces of dirt into my face. It seemed as if we were rushing into the very jaws of death.

The artillery were getting our range now, and bursting shell were flinging their iron fragments far and wide.

A sudden tug at the strap holding my canteen caused me to look down. My canteen had been struck on the side, just tearing its cloth covering. "Whew, that was a close one!" I thought, for I did a vast amount of thinking in that scrambling dash.

"FIRE AT WILL!"—*See Page* 157.

"Forward, double quick !"

But we were going then, to my mind, at breakneck speed. What need for another order? I was running and trembling, when, suddenly, almost in our faces, a blaze of fire and the whistling of bullets nearly robbed me of what little strength remained. My heart seemed to stand still, waiting for my body to be struck. For a moment I didn't think I knew anything—not even my own name, but I pulled down the visor to my cap and bent my head forward as I ran, like one breasting a stinging hailstorm.

"Steady, boys, steady !" shouted our captain. "Drive 'em into the creek."

The veterans set their teeth, grasped their guns more firmly and sprang forward, I dreamily rushing onward with the rest, without a definite thought save that of danger and an enemy that must be forced to retreat.

"Fire at will !"

Aha ! With the first discharge of my gun fear vanished, and a proud feeling of ability to take care of myself intoxicated me after I had fired some half-dozen rounds, when I again looked to the right and left. Fred and Jake and Kimball and Taylor and all the others were there, not a man missing, all intent on the work before them, loading and firing as they advanced.

Again and again, not in volleys, but as fast as guns could be loaded and fired, the enemy's artillery from the woods across the creek blazed and thundered, filling the air with screaming, bursting shell.

But high above it all now rose a prolonged cheer from the main line in our rear. Then the quick tread of many feet encouraged us, for we knew that the army was coming on. Cheer upon cheer, in which I joined as lustily as any one, rolled like a wave along the line, and as I took place in the front rank and touched elbows with the veterans of that advancing line, a thrill of enthusiasm shot through me which I shall always remember.

The transition from weakness and fear to excitement and strength was brief but positive. I loaded and fired and cheered, loaded and fired and yelled like a madman, it seems to me, as I think of it now.

Whether I ever hit anybody I don't know, as the smoke settled down upon us and we could only aim low and trust to chance for results.

Several times in my haste I came near not with-drawing my ramrod before firing, and shooting that useful implement into the enemy's camp.

On, on, through a deadly cross-fire of shot and shell that whistled and screeched and howled above us and around us, striking trees, cutting through branches, bounding along, plunging, ricocheting, tearing up the ground and throwing clouds of loose earth over us, we hurried to the finish.

Men were now falling about me but I only loaded and fired the faster. Presently the artillery ceased firing, and almost at the same instant from out of the woods in front flashed a red line of musketry.

"Charge !"

Forward, we sprang, rushing at full speed, stumbling, scrambling through briers and leaping over such ob-stacles as lay in our path. The enemy turned and fled into the creek, we pursuing close after them, firing as we ran. Across the creek, waist deep with water, and up the steep bank on the other side we followed, lessen-ing the interval between the lines at every step.

At the top of the hill the enemy, gathering courage from the presence of fresh troops behind intrenchments, stopped long enough to fire another volley at us, then retreated to other intrenchments still further to the rear and left the outer line of defense in our possession.

And now, as the enemy's artillery from another point directed their fire upon us, a new element of confusion was added to the pandemonium of sounds about us. A battery or a number of gunners from our own side had come to our relief and began to blaze away at the enemy.

For awhile it seemed as if shot and shell met in the air and fought for right of way, such a bellowing, bursting, roaring, echoing sound throbbed and beat upon the air. It did not last long, as the enemy soon retired to other intrenchments still further to the rear.

We advanced again, occupied the second line of works, strengthened the reverse side as much as possible, and waited in silence. There were few of us who cared to talk much. I had just time enough to eat a small piece of bacon and a couple of hard tack when some one shouted:

"Look out, boys! They're going to try and take this line back again! They're coming up the hill!"

This was followed by a rattle of musketry from the enemy at the foot of the hill. They are coming in huge, dust-covered masses, loading and firing as they advance, without stop, determined to drive us out of our position or die.

When they were within a hundred yards of us we leveled our guns over the breastworks and let them have it. They did not waver, though their lines were broken and disordered, but came on faster and nearer. Bullets were flying about my head with a nearness that was exasperating.

We were standing two or three deep, with just enough space between to allow room for loading. The rear lines were firing between and over the heads of the men in front of them.

There was something maddening in the flashing and explosion of the rear rank guns, their muzzles almost on a line with our faces. The sharp report that was continuously ringing in our ears; the sulphurous odor of burned powder, and the "zip, zip" of the enemy's bullets above us, around us and between us—when they did not strike—may fairly be said to have constituted my baptism of fire.

In camp, each movement in the operation of loading and firing was anticipated by an order. Now we were loading and firing independently of each other without word of command; the man who loaded quickest firing oftenest.

I went through the process of loading and firing mechanically, and without giving any special thought as to what I was about.

The noise in my ears was so deafening that I could not tell whether my gun had been discharged or not, and I did not even feel it kick, although my shoulder was sore for days afterward.

My ammunition was fast disappearing. My cartridge-box had been emptied long ago, and I was then using cartridges from my haversack; these, too, were nearly gone, yet the enemy were coming on. Men are falling in all directions. We saw them a moment advancing through the smoke; they disappear like specters and others glide into their places; yet always the same blackened faces, flashing eyes, clenched teeth and grip- ing hands. It is hard to see men fall like that, yet the sickening work went on. But they could not long en- dure our terrible fire, that had already told fearfully on their ranks; and, at last, they doubted, hesitated, then turned and broke for the bottom of the hill, leaving their dead and wounded behind them, covering the sides of the slope.

At this moment we were relieved by other troops and marched to the rear, over the ground we had just passed. Dead and wounded were scattered in all directions, and men were continually dropping out of line to look at this one or that, and to offer such assistance as was possible. While I was looking at the faces of the different men we passed, I heard Kimball say :

"Hello! There 's Eli Norcross, and he 's been hit, too; hit hard, I reckon. Perhaps we can help him ;" saying which, Kimball, Fred and I started toward a form lying on the ground, some distance away.

Reaching the spot where the wounded man lay, Kimball kneeled beside him and said :

"Are you hurt, Eli ?"

"Yes."

"Where ?"

"Through the body. I 'm 'most gone. Can't last long. Hand me my haversack."

Kimball reached for the haversack, which lay a short distance away, and drew it toward him.

Open it, Kimball, and take out the things that are in there."

Kimball did as directed, and spread the contents of the bag on the ground, where they could be easily seen.

"Kimball," said Eli, "stand the four photographs so I can see them."

The pictures of his wife and three children were placed so he could look at them. After a moment's pause, during which the dying man gazed earnestly at the pictures, he spoke, falteringly, and with labored effort:

"Kimball, I want my wife—to have my watch—and the—little money I 've got—in my pocket. I—I—ain't got—much else—nothin' fer the—children, God bless

'em ! Give my writin'-kit ter my oldest girl. To Katie—
give my sewin'-gear. To my boy—my baby—what can
I send ter him ?"

After pondering a moment, he continued, huskily :

" Kimball, give me a drink from my canteen."

The canteen was produced, and placed to the parched
and whitening lips. After drinking, Eli said :

" Kimball, send the canteen, just as it is, to my boy.
Write to his mother and tell her that I drank from it
just before I died. Tell her—to explain to my boy—
when he gets old enough, that I was killed in defending the flag of my country. Tell her I want my son
to know all about the wrong done by the men who have
tried to ruin this country, and that, whenever he looks
at this battered old canteen, to remember that his
father drank from it just before he died on the battle-
field. Kimball, you take my blanket; it's better than
yours. My poncho—give—it—to—to— Hold the pictures nearer, Kimball ; there, that's better. Ah, Kate—
we did not think, as you stood in the lane holding baby
in your arms, the day we parted, that I should never see
you again. By-by, baby ; by-by, darling."

And a smile hovered around the lips of the husband
and father, as he closed his eyes and passed peacefully
away.

Taking the few things which had been intrusted to
his care Kimball arose, and together we left the spot,
hurrying on to our company, where we were loaded
down with a hundred rounds of ammunition.

While we were resting—waiting to be called into
action—the firing continued along the whole line, and
was kept up far into the night, when it gradually died
away, and finally ceased altogether.

At sundown the company was mustered into line and
the roll called.

" Alfred Abbot !" cried the orderly, repeating the first name on the list.

No response.

" Alfred Abbot !" the sergeant called again, this time falteringly, as, lowering his book, he fixed his eyes upon the ground ; for Abbot and the orderly were like brothers.

" Alfred Abbot was shot as we were crossing the valley, and before we reached the creek," replied a trembling voice to the right. " He was by my side when he fell."

The sergeant coughed, as if to control his voice, raised the book, and then called :

" Ezra Armstrong !"

" Here !"

" Thomas Bennett."

" Here !"

" Erastus Brown."

No response. The sergeant repeats the name, raises his eyes from the book and looks inquiringly up and down the line.

" Does any one know about Brown ?" he asks.

" We jumped into the creek together," replied Taylor, " but I missed him before we got to the other side."

" John Butterworth !"

" Here !"

" Charles Carroll."

" Here !"

And so on down the list, the response " Here " was given, without break, until the name of Eli Norcross was reached. When this name was called Kimball spoke.

" Eli is dead, sergeant. He went down in the valley yonder. Just as the order was given to charge. A piece of shell hit him in the side."

"Poor Eli!" said Fred, who was standing at my side. "It was he who hesitated so long when we veteranized. His family will miss him."

"Enoch Norton."

"Here, sergeant, all but the tip of my little finger," replied Norton holding up his left hand and showing the bandage around that member.

Altogether, we lost from our company, in missing and killed, about a dozen men, and some half dozen more that were disabled by reason of wounds. My own messmates were all present, and had passed through the fire, unharmed.

A cup of coffee, the first I had tasted since leaving the camp at Mill Creek, a piece of bacon, toasted in the fire, and a quantity of hard tack, for I was ravenously hungry, constituted my bill of fare for supper, after which I enjoyed a quiet smoke and then slept.

I tried to write to Mary that night, for I had much to tell her. I got so far as to tell her that I had passed through my first fire test unharmed when I caught my hand making unintelligible lines on the paper and myself nodding over it. My eyes would not stay open. I tore up the paper and rolled myself in my blanket. The rugged bosom of Mother Earth was softer than down to me that night and the occasional booming of artillery a soothing lullaby.

Monday morning Sherman entered Resaca and another town was scored to our credit.

CHAPTER XV.

From this time onward our movements to the south were through a country more open, less broken up by hills and valleys and much easier to travel over. The excitement was so continuous that I soon became accustomed to it, finding time to take interest in affairs beyond my own neighborhood, and to watch, as much as possible, the movements of our army.

We never saw a tenth part of our whole force at one time; rarely a battle in which any considerable number of men were engaged. But we did see any amount of skirmishing and had our share in it—enough to satisfy even Jake; at least, we heard no grumbling from him on this subject.

For the most part, after we left Cassville, we were under fire night and day, and the feeling of fright at the sound of the bullets changed to one of indifference. I listened to their bodeful whistle with respectful attention, but not with so much anxiety and dread as at first.

While we were away off on the left, watching the flank of Johnston's army and trying to turn it, we kept ourselves well informed as to the movements of the rest of the army.

Our information was always recent and very seldom erroneous, though I am sure most of it originated in the practiced judgment of my veteran comrades and their ability to interpret the sounds of distant strife rather than in definite news. We seldom had time for visiting with other regiments. Word would come galloping up from headquarters, somewhere away off to the right, or be "ticked" out in spasmodic jerks on the telegraph key, and before the sound of the hoofbeats or the click of the instrument had died away drums would be beating and a regiment or two, or perhaps our whole corps, would have gathered up its belongings and be on the move.

The boys, with Thomas at the center, had an easy time of it comparatively. It was their business to push the enemy back and to hammer away until he was driven out of his stronghold. It was on the Army of the Tennessee at the right and on us at the left that the hard work fell, and in this hard work the Army of the Ohio had more than its share. Day and night we were on the move, marching, countermarching, crossing creeks and rivers, sometimes on bridges, oftener in the water, throwing up earthworks, fighting, skirmishing, continually harassing and threatening the enemy's flank.

A forced march is a horror to the best soldier that ever carried a rifle. It means torture of mind and body; a dull aching of bones to the very marrow; intense weariness and pain, and complete prostration of the physical powers. It means to fall asleep before you touch the ground in an attempt to lie down. Ten minutes' rest at such times is only an aggravation. It is easier to keep moving than to again rise at the command, "Fall in, men!" and find yourself stiffer and sorer than before—if that were possible; but one thing encourages us through it all—the fact that the enemy were always retreating and that our pains and aches had not been needless, and when an objective point was once reached long rests were the rule rather than the exception. But whenever we started, with a long distance to cover and a clear road before us, we pressed on and on, halting rarely, and then only for five or ten minutes, just long enough to snatch a bite of something to eat and to find out how tired we really were.[*]

The country through which we passed was deserted by its inhabitants; in some places scarcely a family was left, and the males, if there were any, were either too young or too old to handle a musket or·were prevented from so doing by reason of sickness.

The slaves, also, were mostly too old to be of any use; the others had been run off to the south, where they could be of service to the Confederates.

Over the hills which had been so stubbornly defended, passing intrenchments and retrenchments, passing the enemy's dead, lying just as they had fallen, down the slope, out of the woods, to the plain we marched in a southeasterly direction and toward the Connasauga.

Reaching the river, we followed down its right bank to Fites Ferry, where we crossed. As the water was more than waist deep at this point, and as there was no bridge, the artillery was ferried over on flatboats; we were allowed to strip before crossing. A comical sight it must have been to see us with clothes, haversacks, ammunition and rifles rolled up in blankets and carried above our heads. Shouts of laughter greeted the unlucky fellow who slipped and wet his bundle, and they were not a few who fell. Whether the cool water and the opportunity for a bath presented a temptation too strong to be resisted or whether it was accidental, only

[*] "We marched and fought during the day and fortified under cover of the night. This was characteristic of the Atlanta campaign."—*Diary of O. L. Overly, 16th Ky.*

the ludicrous side of the situation was noticed, and a spectator might have easily imagined us a lot of jolly school-boys out for a frolic, instead of an army of veteran soldiers in pursuit of a hostile force. But the bath was refreshing and answered better than a rest.

Dressed and once more in line, we moved on in high spirits toward Field's Mill. At the Coosawatee River, four miles from Field's Mill, we found the road block-aded by Hooker's troops, who had preceded us. Here we halted, ate our supper, spread our blankets and were soon asleep.

The next day, the 17th, was devoted to rest for us, and bridge building for others. That bridge building was a realized ideal in mechanics, which, to the con-tractor in times of peace, would have seemed an impos-sibility. From out of the woods in all directions, along the river's bank, came soldiers, bearing timbers cut in proper lengths, and all prepared to be placed in posi-tion. While the work of 'preparation was going on in the woods, the process of construction seemed like a work of magic ; the trestle work rapidly reared its sub-stantial height to the required level, and increased in length, yards at a time. At ten o'clock that night, when the bridge was finished, we marched over it and headed for Big Springs, which we reached at three o'clock next morning.

Here we found temporary barricades of rails and logs, and were welcomed with volleys of musketry from the enemy's skirmish line.

We speedily settled it in our minds that there would be a battle at daylight, but when the day broke the enemy had abandoned their position.

Early in the morning of the 18th we marched by way of Cassville to Cartersville, skirmishing nearly all the way with the enemy's rear guard, who were driven back without serious loss.

At Cartersville there was some show of force, but the enemy gracefully retired on the night of the 19th, without offering serious opposition to our progress. From this point a detachment of the Twenty-third Corps, followed up the left bank of the Etowah to the Etowah Iron Works and destroyed them on the 20th.

From Cartersville we crossed the Etowah River, at Gillem's Bridge, and marched over the Alatoona road toward Burnt Hickory. Stoneman's cavalry were in the advance, skirmishing as they went. We were generally in sight of the enemy's intrenched lines, and subjected at all times to more or less firing from skirmishers, yet we lost but few men from the whole corps.

At Burnt Hickory we rested for three days, and most thoroughly enjoyed it, although at no time was the air free from the sounds of battle or skirmish.

Here I was initiated into the mystery of baking beans. Boiled beans or bean soup was a dish familiar enough in camp, but we never had them served to us in any other way. The feast at this place was provided by Kimball, who had captured a couple of quarts of white beans at Cartersville and shared his treasure with Fred, Jake and myself, saying as he gave them to us:

"Let 's hang on to these until we find a chance to bake them, somewhere."

At Burnt Hickory, Kimball obtained from a deserted cabin, an iron pot, which he jubilantly held aloft as he came toward us after supper, remarking:

"I 've got the thing we need, boys. We 'll have our baked beans now, for sure; and they 'll be all the better by putting what we have together."

"That 's business," said Jake, and he at once began

to dig a hole with his bayonet using his hands to remove the loosened earth.

After the hole was made large enough to accom-
modate the pot, a fire was built over it and allowed to
burn out. The pot with its precious contents of beans,
water and pork and a little salt for seasoning was then
carefully rested on the earth at the bottom of the hole,
and the glowing coals filled in around it. A flat stone
then covered the pot and a fire was built on top of the
stone, spreading out so as to heat the earth about it.

"We are not to do guard duty to-night," said Kimball ; "so we can take 'turn about' watching the beans."

"Watching them ?" said I.

"Yes," said Jake. "There 're other people who like
beans, and they know when they 're cooked long enough,
as well as we do. Besides, you 've got to keep a little
fire agoin', or they won't be cooked enough."

That settled it with me. I could have watched all
night, if it had been necessary, for the sake of the beans;
but four of us made easy work of it, and when breakfast time came, in the morning, the coals were brushed
away, the flat stone removed, and there was a sight
which would have delighted the eyes and the heart of
the most fastidious epicure in New England.

A pot of beans, cooked to perfection ; a piece of pork
on the top, with the rind brown and crisp. The water
had boiled away, leaving just enough to make them
juicy and appetizing. And then the odor from the
smoking mass as we ladled them out on our plates !—
it makes me hungry, even now, to think of it. We had
abundance for ourselves, for Taylor and for the orderly,
who happened along as we were taking them out of the
pot.

Late in the afternoon of the 25th, we heard sharp
firing to the south, where there seemed to be a deter-

mined effort on the part of one army to advance, and
equally as obstinate a disposition displayed by the
other army to prevent the advancement. Which was
the attacking party we were unable to learn. We could
tell only by the firing, which crept nearer and nearer
until the lines in front were engaged, that the movement was general.

"There 's something up, sure 's you live," said Jake.
" Just hear the artillery !"

" That 's all right," said Kimball, pointing westward.
" But just look at that for a sunset ! And look at those
clouds, will you !"

We turned and saw the sun, looking like a great drop
of blood, just ready to sink behind the western hills,
while to the south we saw heavy rolls and masses of
angry, inky clouds rising rapidly.

" We 'd better get ready for a thunder-storm," said
Fred. " It 's coming up fast, and a storm of that kind,
down here, means a drenching unless you 're housed."

"And mighty well housed, too," added Kimball.

While we were watching the sunset and the storm, as
it came sweeping across the sky, orders were received
to prepare for immediate departure. An hour later,
with arms at a "secure" and covered with our ponchos,
we fell into line and marched along the west side of
Pumpkin Vine Creek toward Owen's Mills.

Directly above us, and to the north, was a starry
space in the sky ; to the south rose the many-headed
crest of the stars, around the edge of which the lightning played continually, while to the east the night shut
in, black and dense.

Onward, mile after mile, we marched, with the boom
of artillery and the rattle of musketry behind us and
to the right of us ; on, through the darkness and desolation, the way becoming more difficult at every step.

Now and then we caught a glimpse of flashing guns and of exploding shell; and as we were not far from our intrenched lines an occasional flight of bullets whistled around and above us.

The roar of battle was unceasing, but now was added to it the distant growling of thunder, echoing solemnly down and through the vast dome of night.

"It 's going to be an awful night for a march," said Jake. "Look at the rain and wind in those clouds!"

Great masses of brass-colored clouds, led by vapory monsters, were hurrying across the heavens toward us, seemingly borne along without wind for the air was hot and stifling. The flashing lightning threw a weird distorted light upon the blackness, revealing for an instant the dark line of our column in front and rear, and the long series of rifle pits to our right, then disappearing leaving the darkness more intense than before. On rolled the brass-colored clouds, and on, above them, came the muttering storm.

"Hark, Dan!" said Fred. "Did you hear that?"

"You mean the cheering!"

"Yes. Look, Dan, look quick!" said Fred, hurriedly, as a continuous chain of lightning shot out from the clouds and illumined the scene for miles around. I looked and saw a body of men charging across a field on our right; just in front of them, separated by only a short interval of space, was another body of men running at full speed.

Immediately following this protracted flash of lightning came a peal of thunder so terrific that the roar of artillery could not be heard. Flash followed flash, crash succeeded crash, now from the heavens, then, feebly, from the guns of the contending forces.

And now, with the wind which came tearing along, filling the air with leaves and limbs of trees, the storm broke upon us. Behind the wind swung in the curtain of the rain, sparkling in the flashing light like a heavy shower of polished silver beads, and wrapping us so closely in its density that we were unable to see anything.

For a time the majesty of the storm was upon us, but we stumbled and plodded along through pools of mud and water, fearing more from the lightning which flashed and twisted and writhed and hissed through the air, driving into the ground right and left, than from the fragments of bursting shell which, notwithstanding the storm, the enemy still continued to throw toward us.

After the fury of the storm abated, though the rain continued until near midnight, we left the road and took to the fields, throwing down fences as we advanced.

Our whole course was determined by the irregular line of the enemy's intrenchments, along the front of which we marched, trying to reach the end or flank and turn it.

At midnight we came upon the mule teams belonging to Hooker's army and the Army of the Cumberland. Passing these obstacles was slow work and vexatious and delayed our progress for an hour or more.

At Brown's Mill we crossed the little Pumpkin Vine, and an hour later came in on the right of Howard's Fourth Corps, on the hills facing the Dallas and Alatoona road, with the Sixteenth Kentucky in the post of honor.

Friday's sun rose bright and hot, and with it again the spiteful sounds of battle up and down the line ; not in volleys, as when charging troops are repulsed, but the isolated, irregular fire of skirmishers and sharpshooters and the boom of occasional cannons. But we held our position quietly, with nothing to especially interest us until in the afternoon troops* were massed in our rear. From this they marched out along our division line, crossed the Alatoona road and at length stirred up a hornet's nest of rebels. They came back again and passed out of sight to the northward behind our lines.

The noise they stirred up soon died away, but this marching meant something. Soon we got news of it in the tumult that arose far away to our left, where the two armies quit worrying each other with skirmish firing and sprang at each other's throats.

We advanced our line a little without opposition, and did not see much of the sharp fighting that took place beyond. But it was practically useless. We got no real advantage and our loss was severe, so they said. Our boys were attacking an intrenched line, and the enemy hurt them sadly.

The next day and the next the enemy tried our plan on the right of our line, and they were made to suffer as they had made us. And every day the battle became more general, until on the last day of May we were included in the tempest.

Early in the day a sharper sputtering of rifles in our front warned us of the coming storm, and then our skirmishers came hurrying in ; after them, the gray backs.

"Steady, men, steady !" said Captain Hartees, in a low, quieting voice.

He was on one knee at the foot of a tree ; his face was set ; a naked sword was in his hand, and his black eyes, just raised above the level of our head log, were flashing up and down the slope in our front.

---

* General Woods's Division.

"Steady!" he kept muttering between his teeth. "Steady! Wait till you see the whites of their eyes; then give them h——! Steady!"

I felt that our time was coming.

"Aim!" There was a grunt, that expressed both discontent and satisfaction, from Jake, at my elbow, as we leveled our muskets at the line of men.

It is strange what little things fix one's attention in such instants of suspended breath. I saw our captain crouching behind the tree stump, like a panther balancing himself for a spring. I saw Fred shrug his shoulder, as though a strap was chafing him. I heard Jake grunt, and saw one clean-cut, yellow face in the advancing crowd, and—"Fire!" The yellow face was hidden in the smoke. At it we went, hammer and tongs.

They tried to break the line of an Illinois regiment at our right, but they did not succeed. We drove them back at last, and they left their dead and wounded in our hands. As they hurried away, one man stopped, and, turning to a fallen comrade, lifted him and was bearing him away. I sighted him, but Kimball stopped my finger on the trigger. "A man like that deserves better 'n to be shot in the back," he said; and I woke up feeling quite ashamed of myself; for, to tell the truth, I was still so green in this business that I didn't know rightly what I was doing, and would have kept on firing at any moving thing in range or out of it, for that matter, until brought up with a short turn. And one rebel that I know of was spared, for, though I did not realize what I was doing, my muscles were iron, my point-blank aim was sure and my musket carried true. I am glad he got away, for he was a "white" man, as my boy's slang phrase now puts it.

From this place we pushed on toward Burnt Church,

oftentimes in line of battle, slowly and surely forcing the enemy back, for they contested stubbornly every foot of ground we tried to cover.

Well do I remember our charge through Alatoma Creek in the midst of a terrible thunderstorm, the roar of heaven's artillery mingling with the boom of guns in our face and the rain falling in torrents. But we crossed the creek and drove the enemy up a densely wooded slope, where the timber was so thick you couldn't see the skirmish line back upon their reserve, who opened on us a galling fire and sent us back to the shelter of the timber along the creek. Here we fortified, for we could go no farther, as the rain had swollen the creek to an unfordable torrent.

"We're in for it now," grumbled Jake, casting an anxious glance back toward the angry river. "Our support's safe over yonder, and can't back us if they want to."

"Looks as though we were at the mercy of the rebs," Fred murmured.

"Suppose they charge us? Where'd we be?" asked Jake, sententiously.

"I guess we'd hold 'em an argument, but they won't," drawled Kimball. "We'll get a free bath, that's all. The Johnnies can't do us much harm from behind their works, and they won't leave them to-night."

Kimball's idea of the situation proved to be correct, as the enemy contented themselves with playing upon us with their artillery and musketry, by which we suffered little.

As we lay there that night, sleepless, in our intrenchments, we could hear the minie balls or the heavier iron shot, as they went sputtering through the leaves above us; but more to be feared than minie ball or shrapnel, were the shrill-whistling shells, which came hurtling through the air or pounding against the tree trunks, that turned them from their course. Sometimes they burst above our heads, showering their fragments upon us. More frequently, however, they passed over and wasted their fury among the trees in our rear.

June 3d the enemy withdrew from our immediate front, falling to intrenchments parallel with those above Picket's Mill, facing north, while we spread out all the time, I suppose, for Johnston, at last, found his flank turned; and on the night of June 4th, pulled up his tent pegs and fell back to a point between Lost and Brush Mountains, some distance north of Kenesaw.

As soon as it was discovered that Johnston had abandoned his position, Sherman lost no time in securing the railroad at Acworth. Our whole front was changed. Up to this time our corps had been on the left of the line; but now, while we stood fast to our position, the other corps were marched by us, until Thomas, with the Army of the Cumberland following one of his own corps, the 20th, that had been for a short time to our left, and McPherson, with the Army of the Tennessee following both, we were left in McPherson's old position, on the extreme right.

It was a jolly time, full of good wit and good jokes flying between us and our friends, as company after company went marching past our position toward the east. We did not see the whole army by any means, as all did not travel by the same road; but what we did see gave me a better idea of the vast number of men it had taken to bring us thus far. We were driving the enemy back, and that made every face pleasant.

While we rested there Fred and I wrote home.

CHAPTER XVI.

Much has been written concerning the Atlanta campaign, and from a broader, more comprehensive point of view than mine. Our company—our regiment, even—was but a drop in the bucket, compared with the sum-total of Sherman's great army. Though rumors flew thick and fast along our line, so that we at the extreme left knew what was going on perhaps twenty or thirty miles to the right of us, yet, from the fact that so many thousands of men were engaged and so little depended, apparently, on the acts of a single regiment, those elements were wanting which were necessary to make it seem a personal struggle.

To tell the story of our experiences, from New Hope Church to the fall of Atlanta, would be but to repeat, with slightly different scenic settings, the tale of the skirmishes, flank movements and constant pushing forward by the left, which I have already described. Of these the reader would soon weary, and that which is to come would seem to be only the ringing of another change in the same line of experience.

Of the events to be described, little, if anything, has ever been written. They occurred at a time when every man was of the utmost importance ; when our numbers were greatly reduced, and when the conditions were the reverse of those we had just passed over, as we were retreating before a vastly outnumbering foe. Therefore, as the object of this story is more to give the personal experiences of a soldier than to compile a regimental history, I hurry over the weeks and months preceding the fall of Atlanta, to take up the details of our struggles with Hood in Central Tennessee.

The purpose of describing our experience thus far will have been accomplished if the reader is enabled thereby to see in what a school for soldiers we were. On the move from morning till night, nay, even liable to be roused from our sky-covered beds at midnight to march through trackless woods, over rocky ridges, through creeks and streams and mud and dust and swamp, in rain or wind or scorching heat, often without fire, and always under the enemy's guns.

Such was our service for months, with now and then a sharp engagement, in which our number was greatly reduced by killed and wounded.

We were well fed and hearty ; sickness seemed to have vanished from us in that clear mountain air, above all, we were full of courage. We felt that the great mind of our general was directing all our movements and we saw that he had made no mistakes.

I must not forget the grim smile of satisfaction which spread over the composite face of the army when we learned that Hood had succeeded Johnston, who had so well managed his command as to win our respect. Johnston had been giving us the hardest kind of work, and it was with absolute satisfaction, therefore, that we heard of the change. Certainly Hood

could be no worse for us. Then, too, we heard that
Johnston's careful but safe policy was not the one to be
pursued by his successor; that "now there would be
something done." All of which was very amusing, to
say the least, and provoked a smile of gratification. It
was right into our hand, and just what we wanted.

But somehow those fights never came off, and there
was no radical change of policy. We continued to push
and the enemy continued to retreat, just as before.

Wherever we planted our feet that ground was ours.
It would have taken legions to dislodge us.

We speedily learned the use of the ax and shovel.
As soon as we found the enemy holding a strong position in front of us we set to work throwing up intrenchments. That this work was almost always performed
under fire did not matter. The ax was swung just as
steadily, and pick and shovel were just as unceasingly
handled until the work was complete.

Our breastworks usually consisted of a continuous
trench, about two or three feet deep. The earth was
thrown forward and sloped so as to give the greatest
height next the trench. Logs were frequently placed
along the edge of the trench as we began to dig; these
logs formed a sill. Cross timbers were then laid on
these sills and another line of logs parallel with and
above the first line were laid on the binders. The ex-
cavated earth was then thrown forward of and banked
against the logs, and the work continued until the top
log was about breast high.

In front of this intrenchment small trees were laid
together, with the branches toward the enemy. The
small limbs were trimmed away and the larger limbs
sharpened, so that thousands of wooden points were
presented—an obstacle through which the enemy must
pass in order to reach us.

Behind a fortification like this one feels comparatively safe ; before it, however, the case is different, as
any soldier of experience can testify. Many a time
have I seen some unlucky graycoated soldier caught by
the sharp-pointed abatis and shot before he could extricate himself.

In a short time after the enemy disappeared from
before our breastworks, perhaps within an hour, we left
our position and advanced to a new one, always with
the same round of work and excitement.

This constant spreading out and building intrenchments, together with the fact that we were never
attacked with our own numbers, never had a chance at
the enemy except when we found them in superior
force or behind strong intrenchments, so worked upon
us that we were all "spoiling for a fight."

If we could only get a chance at the enemy in the
open ground. But the country around New Hope
Church, Kenesaw Mountain and Alatoona was so
broken into hills and irregular ridges and ravines
and valleys that it was impossible to get the vantage
ground we longed for.

However strong the intrenchments of the enemy
might be, we could find high places enough in their
immediate vicinity from which to make an attack,
and sometimes to overlook and command their positions, but that was all. Then, too, the thick cover of
the forests so completely veiled our movements that
we were frequently enabled to get into the rear of the
enemy and make the attack from that side. But Hood,
whenever he found there was a possibility of his being
cut off from Atlanta, rapidly abandoned his positions
and fell back, and the actual contact, the pitched battle,
never came.

This round of duty became more or less monotonous

as the days grew into weeks, and the weeks into months. Of course, our talk of narrow escapes, on picket or in the skirmish, was often relieved by some extraordinary event, which gave variety to our after battle talk ; but for the most part, as we were having things very much our own way, we gave but little thought to passing events.

While we were at the battle around Pine Mountain an incident occurred to which many of us owed our lives.

Early in the morning of the 13th of June we were advanced as skirmishers up the side of the mountain, and in front of the line of battle formed by our army. The skirmish line was well extended, the men being separated from each other by a distance of perhaps three paces.

Our movements were in plain sight of the enemy, and a continual popping was heard from their sharpshooters' pits, while over our heads whirred and screamed the shell thrown at the line in our rear.

Up the hill we went, from tree to tree, from stump to stump, and from rock to rock, one eye on the line of rifle-pits, in front and above us ; the other eye on our own line, the next stopping place, or on the ground over which we were travelling.

There was a quality of excitement in this running and jumping, and darting from cover to cover—daring, challenging the markmanship of sharpshooters—that provoked a spirit of recklessness which increased with every successful advance we made. I appreciated the protection of a big tree trunk, or rock, and cannot describe the combined feelings of confidence and doubt which possessed me as I stood for an instant in a place of comparative safety selecting my next goal, and then took the plunge from security into danger, not knowing but I should fall by the way.

My interest in this method of advance so absorbed me, that I took little note of anything else, until Fred shouted :

" Keep your eye on the line, Dan ! Don't get too far ahead of it !"

It was hard for the individual to regulate his motions by the movement of the line, as the chances for success seemed to be lessened by being thus handicapped. Sometimes the firing in my immediate front was so heavy that I waited an instant before starting.

To be sure, we had now been under fire for a month, but somehow there had never before appeared to be so much danger. Heretofore, we had been screened by dense woods and a heavy undergrowth, and so, with one exception, had never been brought so clearly face to face with what we had to encounter. In previous engagements we had touched elbows, and had felt the thrill and encouragement of companionship. Now we were as individuals, a mark for sharpshooters, toward whose pits we were pressing on and on.

A small house stood almost in our path as we advanced up the slope. There was little or no protection between that point and the first line of the enemy's intrenchments. A good number of our men were shaping their course to get behind that ; but Captain Hartees, noting the movement, shouted :

" Keep your distances, men ; and whatever you do keep away from that house !"

Pressing on, we turned farther to the left, avoiding the house. Company A, however, determined to take advantage of the shelter.

" Keep away from that house," I heard Hartees shout to the captain of Company A, but no attention was paid to the warning.

Up, up we went, until we were close upon the enemy's

works. Here every man, behind the best shelter he
could find, halted for breath. I turned for a look at
the main line and when I saw, perhaps a hundred
yards below us, those solid ranks of men who were
used to this sort of thing, who had made war and battle
a business for the last three years, when I saw those
men moving hurriedly yet steadily forward, a feeling
of security came over me that whistling bullets and
shrieking shell could not dissipate.

I looked over our skirmish line to the right and left;
every man was at his post, eager, expectant, waiting for
the word to go. I saw besides that we were in direct
line with the house and that Company A had huddled
in behind it.

We were waiting for breath and the word to charge
upon this outer work in front. The enemy were in
good position and would make it warm for us. There
was no doubt of that. We might succeed in getting
force enough into their works to drive them out, but if
we didn't—what? It would be a hand-to-hand fight—
and if it should come to that—

"Forward!" yelled the captain, and as we sprang
out with the order to advance, the guns of the enemy
were opened furiously upon us.

"Quick, my men!" shouted Hartees, who was in advance of us. "Now's your chance!"

With a sort of scared hurrah which was caught up
and echoed by the line behind us, we broke for the
works, passed the rifle pits, with the sharpshooters still
in them, and into the line of intrenchments, where we
took a few prisoners. Why the force opposing us was
not larger was quickly explained by one of the captured men, who said to Hartees:

"Captain, nobody here. They've gone 'nd are tryin'
ter lead yer on. Yer 'd better not try 'nd go any furder

ter-day. I 'm a prisoner now, 'nd it don't make no difference ter me what I says, but we 've got a right smart
work back o' this; been at it fer a month. 'F yer try
it on ther men 'll git cut up purty bad 'nd the rest 'll
git gobbled."

Captain Hartees sent the man to the general, and
while awaiting developments we lay down under cover
on the reverse side of the works we had captured, safe
from the action of the artillery beyond.

Looking backward over the ground we had just
passed we saw in the prostrate forms, lying just as they
had fallen, the wretched work made by the enemy's
guns. We also saw why it was that we were ordered
to keep away from the house. The fire of the artillery,
at the moment of our advance, had been concentrated
on this house and had riddled it, the enemy knowing
that men would naturally seek shelter behind it.

The result was disastrous to Company A, and many
were killed and wounded with shot and shell and flying
splinters, while we escaped almost without losing a
man.

The works we captured were of great strength, built
of logs and stone and covered with loose earth.

CHAPTER XVII.

From the time we were within twenty miles of Atlanta we were kept constantly informed of the cruelties practiced on our men who were prisoners at Andersonville—a place about one hundred miles from our camp.

Every day or two one or more escaped prisoners would be picked up by some portion of Sherman's army, and the story of their sufferings passed from camp to camp. There was one story that came home to us.

One day we had settled into position at the siege of Atlanta. Kimball, who had been out with a squad from Company I, brought back with him a poor fellow who had escaped from Andersonville.

"I found him in the brush, asleep," said Kimball, "and I thought he was dead at first."

To describe the half-crazed starving stranger, and do justice to the appearance he presented, would be to fill the page with sickening details ; suffice it to say, that soap and water were vigorously applied ; his tangled, matted hair and beard were trimmed ; his clothes were all removed, thrown into the fire, and he was dressed in another outfit, worn and old to be sure, but clean, and contributed by the boys.

After this he devoured all we dared give him, and slept by the fire during the rest of the day. At sundown, he awoke apparently much refreshed, and we placed before him a piece of broiled beef, a cup of coffee and a half dozen hard tack. And, while sitting with his back against a tree, still eating, he told the story of his imprisonment and his suffering; and a feverish glow arose to his pallid cheeks, and his eye glittered with a wild, demented light, as he talked.

"Boys," he said, as we gathered around him to eat our own supper, "you want to know how they treated us down there?" lifting his bony finger in the direction of Andersonville. "Look at me. I'm the kind of work they turn out. A few months ago, and I was the equal of the best of you. And now—"

His eyes filled with tears, and his voice grew husky, as he continued, tremblingly :

"Boys, it unmans me to think of sitting here, eating and drinking, while thousands of our poor fellows over there have nothing fit to eat ; not a drop of pure water to drink ; not even a bone to gnaw ; nothing but a little measure of thin ham broth every day ; hundreds dying of starvation, and hundreds going mad every day."

He carefully set down the dipper of weak coffee from which he had been drinking. His head sank on his breast, and he was silent for a moment, while great drops of sweat rolled down his face. But we waited patiently, in full sympathy with his emotion, and in time the story was resumed.

"What is it like? It is a pen; a slaughter-house yard ; an open field surrounded by a high log fence, perhaps a quarter of a mile long each way. Into this place last June twenty-six thousand men were crowded. 'T is true ; the fiends themselves said so. Hot ? Not a breath of wind sifted through the pine forest outside the tall stockade. All night as well as throughout the day the heat was intense—something we never have north. The brook which flowed through the pen was filthy with the offal from the rebel camp and cook-houses before it reached us ; but we had to drink it ; 't was all there was."

" What did they feed you on ?" asked Kimball.

"Feed? A bit of moldy bacon and musty meal. That's what they gave us. 'Twas just enough to keep us alive to suffer—no more. Our strength soon failed, and our hope, too. Our clothes, what we had, were in tatters or had been torn up for bandages, and we were covered with vermin from head to foot. Still the rebs were afraid of us, weak and helpless as we were, for they shot us down like dogs if we dared cross the dead-line near the stockade.

" And then the new comers. Every morning brought them, sometimes by the hundreds, and yet the pen never grew any fatter. There were as many dead carted away next day. Stand in any part of that place to look about you, the same scenes met your eye ; groups of men sitting or standing and looking toward something in the center ; men walking or crawling between these groups ; everybody dirty, ragged and starving. No sound of voices, except in oaths or yells of the mad or in the groans of the dying. Conversation, such as there was, was carried on in low tones or in a whisper. It would break your heart to look in there. Men, as well as I, watched by the sick ; while those who were only able to move watched by the . dying.

" Hard sights those. They would turn your hair white as mine is, to see all that misery and cruelty."

" What about the wounded ?" I asked, after the stranger had rested for a time.

"The wounded were treated like the rest. They could get no attendance. The surgeons never came to our relief. Hundreds of men were lying about that lot, only a quarter-mile square, dying of gangrene and mortification, without relief, except what we well ones could give them. We, who had nothing ourselves, not even shirts with which to make bandages, and no water anywhere, except what we drank, and that was not fit to wash a wound with.

"I remember one poor fellow—'t was just after I was thrown into the pen that I met him. Such sights were new to me then, and I could not look at them calmly. He was a smart young fellow, good looking, or had been, and was well educated. Anybody could have seen that. He had a nice home in Kentucky, and he used to tell us about it, that is before he lost his head. He went to the war at the first boom of cannon, like the rest of us, and they caught him early in the game.

"At that time the rebs didn't have so many prisoners, and what they did have fared pretty well. Then this young fellow was strong and healthy; but when more men came and were crowded into the same inclosure, things got rapidly worse, till he thought he couldn't stand it any longer; then he made up his mind to escape, and he did.

"He only got as far as northern Tennessee, when he was captured by a band of guerrillas. They wouldn't have got him, but they first wounded him in the knee, and he couldn't get away. He was sent back to the pen and thrown in with others, and there I found him, lying on the ground, without shelter, without food, without medicine and fast going into the fever.

"For days we watched beside him, two or three others and myself, bringing him dirty water, moldy bacon and musty meal—queer food, for a dying man—

and standing up that he might have the benefit of our spare shadows when the sun was hottest.

"I tell you boys, 't was hard. I raved and swore and begged the guard to send somebody, to do something; but they wouldn't listen. 'T was no use; but I was new to the place and didn't know men could be so inhuman.

"The night following the second day after I found him—I think it was the second day—it was sweltering hot and the air was terrible. It seemed to settle down upon us like an invisible blanket, about to smother us out of misery. Is it any wonder that men went mad? To lie there on such nights and see the moon rise bright and full over the tops of the dark, motionless pines! Many a poor fellow stood as I did, watching the great shining ball roll higher and higher, and groaned in his misery. It seemed as if I could feel the sweet, cool breezes of the night, away off among the hills where that moon was shining; see the soft mist steal up from the brooks and rivers, and—let me see— where was I? It was the second night, and after the sun had been down about two hours I went for some water.

"When I came back there were half a dozen men squatting around my young friend. They motioned me to stop as I came up. I looked at the face of the dying man. The moonlight was shining in his eyes and they glistened like diamonds. He had caught sight of me and called me in a loud whisper, seeming to take me for his brother:

"'Look, Fred, look! See! See!'"

Fred left my side at the fire and drew closer, so that not a syllable of the stranger's weak voice should escape him. The stranger continued:

"What he saw we did not know. Most likely 't was

home, poor boy ; but death came and took him. The next day he was carted off among the usual morning load of those that went out feet foremost."

The stranger ceased, and a silence which we could almost feel fell upon us. I looked around me. The stranger was leaning forward, his face covered with his hands, his elbows resting on his sharp, pointed knees. He was exhausted with his story.

Our fire had mostly burned out, but it still gave light enough for me to see, behind the circle of our own mess, seated on the ground or standing, bending forward in strained attitudes, a deep circle of men from other messes, who had, unperceived, come up to listen.

Fred, who was half kneeling beside the stranger, watched him earnestly, as if waiting for him to speak again. At last he said, in a husky whisper :

"What was his name ?"

"Charles Nichols," replied the stranger. "He told me he had a brother in a Ken—"

But Fred waited to hear no more. He arose and hurried away into the darkness of the woods, whither I followed him.

Fred was a surer shot with his rifle after that.

CHAPTER XVIII.

When Atlanta fell into our hands, in August, there was a work of reorganization to be done. This great manufacturing center of the South must become a military post and nothing more. As a means to this end, all the civil inhabitants were forced to leave; they could go South or North as best suited them, but go they must.

The majority, clinging to the Confederate cause, went South, taking with them, in long wagon trains, all their belongings. In a short time there was not a family left in Atlanta.

The streets were filled with marching troops and rumbling wagon trains. The largest buildings groaned under the weight of provisions stored there. The post-office was opened and run by soldier clerks. Bakeries, blacksmith shops, machine and carpenter shops, operated by soldier mechanics, were running night and day, and the city at once became a workshop, in which the wants of Sherman's army were promptly and satisfactorily supplied.

Meanwhile we were resting on our arms at Decatur, in Northern Alabama, and in the midst of plenty.

In the second half of September rumors of Confederate activity spread through our camp. We learned that Hood had met and conferred with Jefferson Davis at Palmetto, and that Forrest, the Confederate cavalry leader, was disturbing our friends in east Tennessee

Soon it became apparent that an attempt would be made to break up the railroad, which was our line of communication with the north. The whole army was immediately in motion, and leaving the Twentieth Corps as a guard to Atlanta, we started on the back track to Marietta.

When in the neighborhood of Kenesaw, we heard sounds of heavy firing away to the north in the direction of Alatoona, a railroad point of the utmost importance to keep in our possession. If the enemy captured this place our line of communication would not only be broken but a million rations, which were stored there, would also be lost.

At Kenesaw, our corps branched off, marching along the Burnt Hickory turnpike to the west, burning bushes and hayricks as we went, to show Sherman, who was watching from the side of Kenesaw, what progress we were making.

We did not meet the enemy, and to us it seemed that the movement had been of little use, as the next day we learned that Alatoona was perfectly safe. Hood had threatened Rome, then Resaca, and we followed him closely. From Resaca we marched southwest along the Coosa River, reconnoitering and foraging and on the 20th or 21st of October pitched our camp near Cedar Bluffs.

Hood had departed from the railroad, and we next heard of him before Decatur and still later that he was concentrating his forces near Florence, also in Alabama, on the north bank of the Tennessee River.

Sherman's army was scattered all the way from Chattanooga, which General Thomas held, down the railroad to Atlanta. Every exposed point was fortified with blockhouses or redoubts and strongly garrisoned.

Hood was not our equal in strength and showed no disposition to attack us, but was quietly concentrating and organizing at Florence. Just what his purpose was, we did not know, but it was rumored that he had in view an advance into Eastern Tennessee.

We, in the heart of Georgia, with one hand on the the main artery of the South, knowing that Hood was not strong enough to drive us out, felt that his object was to entice us away. If he succeeded and lured us back to Tennessee our toil for the summer was thrown away. What would grow out of the situation was a puzzling question.

As a rule, soldiers, especially veterans, if they are well-fed and officered by men whom they respect, rarely bother their heads about plans for the future. The only time when they departed from this rule, to any extent, was at this crisis, when Sherman himself seemed in doubt. At this time the possibilities of and projects for the future were being thoroughly canvassed.

By the 1st of November Sherman had reached a determination in regard to the Twenty-third Corps, at least. The Fourth Corps [Stanley's], 15,000 men, had been sent to reinforce Thomas, at Nashville. On the 31st of October we, the Twenty-third Corps, under Schofield, 12,000 men, were ordered in the same direction. At Resaca, Cooper's division halted; but Cox's division pushed on.

We entered again into the outlying spurs and well-constructed earth-works of Dalton, and, halting near the railroad, waited for transportation, northward, through Buzzard's Roost Gap, to Nashville.

There was hardly a moment of the day or night

when we did not hear the "puff-puff" of locomotives drawing heavily loaded trains through the town or the shrill whistle of others dashing through the Gap to the north and around the curves and spurs of Rocky Face Ridge.

Sherman was sending back all his stores in Atlanta, all his sick, wounded and disabled and all his baggage. There was life enough along the railroad in these hurrying days, when endless trains went rattling and slamming by, headed for the North, trailing behind them banners of smoke and steam ; and when trains returning from the North brought recruits, ammunition and returning furloughed men.

While waiting, we often went to the road to watch this constant flowing stream of war. And when a train of wounded men stopped near us we offered what assistance we could. Many a sad sight we saw. In box-cars, half full of straw or brush, lay sick and wounded, some with arms or legs or heads tied up, pale and sunken faces distorted with pain. Here and there lay one raving with fever. There were always water to be brought and little things to be done, which were works of mercy, and which we could do well enough to assist the tired, overworked surgeons and nurses.

And what a change was there when, perhaps, the same train returned with recruits and furloughed men. The open doors of the box-cars would be filled with eager faces of green recruits, sturdy but inexperienced, looking far away before them, as if they expected to see the surrounding hills sparkling with fire.

On the 3d or 4th of November a train ran in bound north, bearing soldiers looking hale and hearty. They were Cooper's division of our corps, who had taken the cars at Resaca. It was four days after they disappeared through the Gap before we procured transportation and followed them, through Buzzard's Roost and Ringgold, travelling over the old ground.

As we rattled and jolted slowly northward, it seemed to us that the war was drawing to a close. We had read of the Confederate army penned in around Petersburg, and we knew that the authorities at Richmond would not permit Atlanta to fall into our hands without sending assistance, if assistance could be spared.

We read, too, of Sheridan flying up and down the valley of the Shenandoah. The stories of his exploits reminded us of our Fitzpatrick, and we enjoyed them.

Mobile had fallen. No troops on the other side of the Mississippi were available to the enemy. Their forts on the sea-coast had also been mostly taken. Fort Fisher alone was hostile.

We had left General Sherman behind us, making preparations for a grand undertaking, which we knew would not be long delayed. He was going to the sea, If he succeeded—and not a man among us doubted it— a broad road of ruin would be laid from border to border, directly through the heart of the would-be Southern nation. What could there be left for the Confederacy? The stars and bars were floating now over a disheartened but desperate country—a nation whose actual possessions were rapidly melting away—a nation on paper only.

In due time we were landed in Pulaski, Tennessee. With us there were Stanley's Fourth Corps. To the south of us our cavalry, under Hatch, Croxton and Capron, was scouring the country and watching Hood, who was still in Florence, organizing and preparing. Strickland's brigade of our division of the Twenty-third Corps was in camp at Columbia, a town behind us, on the road to Nashville, where General Thomas was drilling recruits. There, too, was Wilson's dismounted cavalry [10,000 men], and thither General A J. Smith was hastening from Missouri, with perhaps 10,000 more.

Hood, meanwhile, showed no decided signs of moving. He had, no doubt, intended to be on the march before, but all his preparations were delayed by the wretched condition of the single track railroad over which his provisions and stores had to be transported, and by the state of the country, which was softened by rains and flooded by swollen rivers.

CHAPTER XIX.

Sherman had, at last, gone south and east, without a foe in his path. Hood, with fifty thousand men, had left Alabama, was slowly working his way north, aiming toward Pulaski and, just now, was making demonstrations on Lawrenceburg and Waynesboro, in middle Tennessee. We, perhaps ten thousand strong, were expected, so it afterward appeared, to oppose this advancement, and give General Thomas an opportunity to still further recruit and increase his army at Nashville.

The storms, which had delayed Hood for so long a time, were still raging; and, while they had been fortunate obstacles to his movements, they had also proved equally discouraging to us.

A shower, or even a rainy day, now and then, was only a disagreeable incident, common to a soldier's life, and to be expected; but these cold, continuous storms of rain, sleet, snow, hail and wind were a lasting misery and very demoralizing.

If the weather had been all we had to contend with, however, we might have endured our hardships much better than we did, but we were sadly in need of clothing. Mine was worn and thin. The skirts of my over-

coat had been burned in a dozen places by coming
too near the fire. A goodly number of us, also, were
without blankets. Many a night, in stormy weather,
we went into camp, wet and muddy, and without fire or
blankets passed the night in sleepless misery.

When we were at a safe distance from the enemy far
enough away to indulge in a fire, I have stood half the
night smoking my pipe, scorching, burning and drying
my clothes, trying to warm myself and, at last, lie
down on a pile of green boughs, with no other covering
than a rubber blanket, and shivered myself to sleep.

Rations, too, were not always plenty, and while, as
yet, we had not been compelled to do without, we were
far from being well fed, and sometimes had to eke out
our supply of food with such forage as we could pick
up from the already well plundered farmers along the
road.

The few families, who yet remained in Pulaski, had
endured the hardships of war with a half-starved,
heroic patience, born of necessity. This town had
alternately been visited and robbed by both Union and
Confederate soldiers, so that there were at best only
small pickings for us; but though the people were
poor, and had scarcely provisions enough for themselves, when any of our boys called on them for something to eat, they were always given such as the house
afforded, and as much as could be spared.

Women who had hitherto been waited upon were
compelled to learn the art of serving themselves, and
much of the bitterness reported of these people in the
early part of the war had disappeared; their pride had
been humbled, and in its place had sprung up a more
respectful, if not a kindlier feeling toward the Union
soldiers.

We were well informed as to the movements of the

enemy, our information coming, for the most part, from scouts, deserters from Hood's army—who occasionally came into our lines—or from cavalrymen, who were continually scouring the woods in front of us.

The most positive knowledge concerning Hood's movements that we were able to get was obtained from an old negro, who came into our lines on the night of the 21st of November.

Fred and Jake and I were on picket, and stationed by a clump of bushes, near the Lawrenceburg Road. The hour was hardly later than ten, when our attention was attracted by a low, rumbling noise, away up the road, coming from the direction of the enemy.

The sound became louder and more distinct as it approached us. At times we fancied we heard voices. Was it possible the enemy were so near? And were they moving toward us in such force as to set aside all thought of a surprise? were questions we asked ourselves.

We strained our ears to listen more carefully before sounding an alarm, and finally convinced ourselves that the noise proceeded from a rickety wagon. Later we were satisfied there was but one voice, and shortly after our fears were allayed by seeing, in the dim starlight, a man standing in a wagon, belaboring a mule with a stick, and calling out, at the top of his voice:

"Git along dar, you mule! Git along dar, git!"

"Reckon I'd better stop that fellow where he is," said Fred, as soon as the team came within hailing distance.

"No, no!" I responded. "Let him come a little nearer. Let's see who the fellow is."

"Whack, whack, whack!" resounded the stick as it struck the "cast-iron back" of the mule, while the wagon rattled its way toward us. Finally, Fred, who was unable to restrain his impatience longer, cried out, in a tone unusually severe for him :

" Halt !"

"Golly! Who dar? Wha–what 's dat? What 's de matter? What 's de matter?" replied the startled darkey, as he gave a sudden jerk to the reins which brought his animal to a standstill.

"Who goes there ?"

" Nuffin' but a pore ol' nigga, who 's a-tryin' ter get away from de rebels and to jine de Yankees !"

" What do you want to join the Yankees for?" asked Fred.

" Kaze I does! I done got a heap tired ob de rebs, and I 's a gwine ter jine de odder side, I is !"

" Well, what have you got in your wagon ; anything to eat ?"

" Ain't got nuffin', marse boss, but a few ol' fings, what ain't no good ter nobody but a pore ol' nigga !"

" Drive up this way. Let 's see who you are."

" All right, marse ! I 's a comin', sho ! Git along dar, you mule ! Git along dar !"

Again the stick was brought into service upon the back of the unimpressionable mule and again every bolt and rivet in the old wagon clattered and rattled as it moved toward us.

" There," said Fred, " stop where you are."

" All right, marse ! Tell me ; is you de Yankee soldiers ?"

" Yes," replied Fred. " Where are you from ?"

" 'Bout two miles from Lawrenceburg."

" What are you running away for ? Don't you know the Johnnies are not within nine miles of you ?"

" Gollies, marse, I knows dat ; but dis chile 's power-ful afraid of a flank movemant. Dat 's what 's de matter wid me."

" Where are the Johnnies now."

" Dey was in de 'burg this morning, and I jest got up an' skedaddled 'fo' dey had de time ter flank me."

" Do you know how much of an army Hood has ?"

" I don' know, Marse, but dey has a heap o' men, and dey's jist a gwine ter do a heap o' flanking, so I heerd de white people sayin', but dey don' flank this chicken— not much."

" Where did you hear the rebs were going ?"

" Dey's a gwine ter git in the raar of de Yankees, an' is a makin' for Duck Ribber."

" Was Hood's army moving when you left."

" Yes, an' dey was on deir road to Pulaski."

" Was the whole of Hood's army moving or only a portion of it ?"

" I heerd dey was all amovin'."

" Think I'll take this fellow in," said Fred.

" Drive this way a bit, uncle, and I'll go with you. Perhaps the captain would like to ask a few questions."

" All, right, marse, I'll do all I kin, de Lawd knows. I dunno much, but I'll tell de cap'n dat sho. Git along dar, you mule ; git along dar, git !" shouted the darkey to his mule as Fred got into the wagon, which soon disappeared in the darkness, down the road toward camp.

Shortly after Fred returned to his post, and, with his welcome presence, brought the information that our wagon trains had already begun to leave Pulaski, were on the road to Columbia, and that we would probably shake the mud of that place from our feet before long.

A little after daylight next morning we were called in, to find that orders had been given for the entire force to fall back to Lynnville, a little place, about half way between Pulaski and Columbia. Here we were joined by Wagner's Division of the Fourth Corps, and with them intrenched ourselves in positions covering the road leading from Lawrenceburg. We remained at this point two or three days, and it was while we were here that Black Lige disappeared. Captain Hartees seemed to take the matter philosophically enough, and said that he would see him again before long; that his wife and children lived not far from Columbia.

On the night of the 23d we left our intrenchments and fell back to Hurricane, which is ten miles farther north, and toward Columbia.

Jake, who was one of the first to get the news of this movement, came up to the fire, where a little group of us were making preparations for breakfast, and said:

"We've got to move again, boys. I tell you what, we ain't got nothing to say about Hood not being smart. He's turning the tables on us with a vengeance. We don't no sooner get settled in a place than we have to get. Just the same as Johnston did before Sherman."

"Where are we going now?" I asked, as soon as I could get a word in.

"To Hurricane. Hood's a chasin' us up mighty sharp, you bet. He's a-getting over the roads after us about as fast as we can get out of his way. If we keep on at this rate we'll see Nashville soon, I'm thinking."

"Yes; but we're not going to see it without first having a fight that'll be a bad one for Hood," interrupted Kimball, as he calmly blew the ashes off a roasted potato, which he very mysteriously produced from the hot ashes near the edge of the fire.

"Fight!" repeated Jake, abstractedly, as his eye fastened on the potato. "Fight! Where'd you get that potato?"

Here everybody laughed at the sudden change in Jake's manner—from a grumbling tone of voice to that

of a person intensely interested in something to eat.
But he recovered quickly, and resumed :

"If we are ever going to do any more fighting, it 's
about time we were at it. It 's mighty discouraging—
this weather, not enough to eat, and a running away
from a lot of graybacks, that haven't known in a long
time what it was to win a fight. No wonder we haven't
seen the sun since the day we left Pulaski. I 'm dogged
if I don't believe he 's ashamed to shine on us for sneak-
ing away from the enemy all the time."

"Keep cool, Jake ; keep cool, my boy," replied Kimball, breaking the roasted potato in half, and handing
one of the pieces to his grumbling comrade.

"'Nebber min' de wedder so de win' don' blow;
Don' yer bodder 'bout yer trouble till it comes.'

"We 'll get all the fighting we want before we reach
Nashville, don't you worry."

CHAPTER XX.

We started early in the afternoon for Hurricane, which we reached late that night. A little before daybreak, on the following morning, we were aroused by musketry firing, west of us and immediately were in rapid motion toward it. After marching a little more than two miles through the woods, we came in full view of an engagement between Forrest's cavalry and a part of Stanley's command.

"It 's a cavalry fight," said Jake; "and we ain't here any too quick for 'em either. Our boys are backing out. See !"

We had hardly discovered this fact when we heard firing from the right of our own line. Simultaneously came the order :

"Column, front into line !"

"Now Mr. Johnnie, look out," said Kimball.

"Fix bayonets !"

"That 's business," said Jake, as the click and clatter which immediately followed this order, ran up and down the line. "If we can't make Johnnie Reb skeedadle, this time, we 'd better go home."

"Forward, double quick, march !"

There were no laggards at that command; every man was in his place, all anxious to make the most of an opportunity to drive the enemy back. **After** reaching easy range, came the command :

"Halt !   Load and fire at will !   Load !"

"Now then !" said Fred, as he tore away the flap of a cartridge with his teeth. "We 'll show 'em what 's what !"

By this time a rapidly increasing fire, from the whole length of our line, was being poured into the ranks of the enemy ; who, dismayed and bewildered at the sudden appearance of a force they evidently had not counted on, speedily fell back in great confusion. The punishment inflicted being so severe that they did not again trouble us.

Later we fell back to Columbia, where we threw up breastworks and otherwise strongly intrenched ourselves south of the town.

Most of us were heartily sick of Hood's flank movements. To make ready for an enemy and then not have him do as you want him to is vexatious enough when it occurs only once in a while ; but when it happens right along, without any change whatever, the life of a soldier becomes monotonous in the extreme.

We were all anxious to bring matters to a crisis ; to force a condition of things where our position would, in a measure, balance Hood's greater numerical strength and where he would be compelled to fight. The work we had just completed at this place seemed to me all that could be desired for this purpose, and I suggested the probability of meeting the enemy and having our trial with him here.

"You wait !" responded Jake. "Wait till Hood comes up with his force and sees what we 've been doing. There 's nothing to prevent him from flanking us here, same as he 's done in other places. We 'll have to get out here in a hurry before long, I 'm thinking ; then all this dirt digging goes for nothing."

"Well," said Fred in reply, "we can't help it, if we do have to get out. I hope, though, we 'll reach a place before long where we can give Hood a warming. He 's stronger than we, to be sure, and 't would be foolish enough to try and break him up until we have Thomas's army to help us. We can punish him badly, though, if we are well intrenched and he ever gives us the chance."

Jake gave a grunt of disapproval and turned away. He did not "take stock" in Hood's ever giving us that chance ; but Kimball did and quickly responded :

"He 'll give us all the chance we want, sure 's my name 's Kimball, and that, too, before we reach Thomas. He won't content himself by doing as Sherman did. He 'll try and do better—be smarter, like."

Our well-defended front kept the enemy quiet for a long time ; but on the night of the 25th there were whisperings of a flank movement. Shortly after, in company with another brigade we left our intrench-ments and marched through Columbia to Duck River, which we crossed on the pontoons.

The stream at this place describes a sharp curve, and the point upon which we were halted and expected to defend, if need be, was partly surrounded by the frowning bluffs on the Columbia side. The next morning we were again called up to handle the pick and shovel.

Breastworks were thrown up a little way from the river bank, but the position was one of the worst that could have been selected. Do what we might, there was absolutely no protection for us. We were on nothing like an even footing with the enemy.

I never had found a great deal of fault with places that had heretofore been selected as best suited for defense, because, for one good reason, I did not, for a long time, know much about these things ; and, secondly, I was never much of a faultfinder on any occasion ; but I could not help ventilating my opinion as to this position.

I had learned something in my past six months of active army life—something of movements and defensible positions, and was thereby enabled to talk understandingly at this time and on this particular subject. A man, without any special knowledge of such matters, could have seen, at a glance, the position we then occupied could not be held. In reply to what I had to say on the subject, Fred said :

"It 's a fact, Dan, it 's not much of a place for intrenchments ; and, for the life of me, I can't see the use of wasting labor here when we might do better farther on. Orders are orders, though ; and whether they 're for good or for bad, we 've got to obey them."

" I reckon Hood 'll make mincemeat of us if he catches us in this fix," remarked Jake, who had been listening to our conversation. "Just see what a chance for a cross-fire of artillery," pointing to the hight bluff on the other side of the river. " Why, they can just toss percussion shell on to our heads if they want to, and we can't help ourselves. Just after breakfast I heard that the whole of our army was going to leave the works on the other side to-night, and come over here."

"What else can they do ?" responded Fred. " They can't hold out against Hood's whole army."

"No," I don't expect they can," answered Jake. " Neither do I expect Hood's army is going to give 'em much of a chance, if they wanted to fight ever so bad. I 'll tell you what, boys. I 'm getting sick of this. I 'd a heap rather fight than dig dirt."

"Well, Jake, you 'll soon have a chance," said Kimball, "they 're having a little skirmish now, along the line, outside the town. Don't you hear them? That sounds as if Hood was drawing in on our front, don't it?"

"Yes, I hear 'em," said Jake, as he rested his foot on his spade, a moment, "but that don't signify anything. He 's just thrown out a few skirmishers to hold our attention while the balance of his army is working around in our rear. I 'm afraid it 's only another signal for us to fall back again."

"Well, I don't care if it is," said Fred. "This is a little the worst place for a stand that I ever got into." Every one echoed this sentiment, but, as usual, we kept at our work until it was finished.

Late that night, I awoke shivering with the cold, and had to get up and move around to warm myself, for we dare not have any fires now. The river and the high bank on the opposite side were shrouded in gloom. I could see nothing in this inky blackness, but on one side, I could hear the tramp, tramp, tramp of infantry, crossing the railroad bridge, and on the other side, the scuffle of many feet on the pontoons.

As I stood listening to the various sounds of the night, I heard a familiar voice singing, softly—

> "I 'll be dar,
> I 'll be dar,
> W'en de judgmen' roll is call,
> I 'll be dar."

"Ho, Lige!" I called. "Is that you?"

"Yes, Maws Dan."

"Where 've you been?"

"Been home ter see my wife."

"See her?"

"Yes. She 's dar still. Hed a powerful good time, Maws Dan! Powerful good time!"

" Where 's Hood ?"

" He 's a gwine ter work around in our raar. Gwine ter cross de ribber above here a piece and git in 'tween us an' Nashville. Here, Maws Dan, take dis! Dinah bake dat dis mawnin'."

I held out my hand in the darkness and received a spongy substance, which proved to be a most delicious corn pone.

" They 've got us in a box here, Lige !" I said ; but he was gone, and I heard him, as he vanished in the darkness, singing, as usual, to himself :

" Nebber min' de wedder so de win' don' blow."

There was a peculiar philosophy for me in that song, and, as I ate my corn pone before going to sleep, I determined not to bother about trouble until it came.

In the gray of the early morning, while moving farther down the stream, we discovered that the whole of our little army had crossed the river in the night and that the bridges, over which they had passed, had disappeared.

We reached our new position and had intrenched ourselves in it by sunrise. The sky was dark and cloudy, and the deep shadows of night still lingered in the chill mists that clung to the trees on both sides of the river. Fred and I stood on the edge of the bank, gazing up and down the stream ; everything was so quiet on the opposite side that we had no thought of danger here. Just at this moment, however, Captain Hartees, who had come up, unobserved, behind us, shouted :

" Look out, boys—down !"

We three dropped to earth, instantly ; and almost at the same instant two reports from the thick woods above us, on the other side, followed by the "zip, zip " of two bullets passing harmlessly over our heads, explained the importance of the caution.

"Close rub that, cap'n," said Fred.

"Got to keep your eyes open sharp," replied Hartees, as he arose and quickly disappeared through the woods in our rear.

"Queer," said Fred, as he turned and looked after the captain, "queer; that man's always around when we're in danger. Come, we can't follow his advice any too quickly; let's get out of this. There's another." A flash, a little puff of smoke, a report, and another whistling evidence that the enemy were watching hurried us back to the shelter of our rifle pits, where we were content to await further developments.

Later in the forenoon a succession of brighter flashes, from the woods skirting the edge of the bluff, followed by clouds of smoke, the roar of cannon and the shrill piping shell, announced that the enemy had his artillery in position and was disposed to use it. Still later, our own artillery behind us, replied to the enemy's fire, and kept it up at intervals throughout the day.

It was an artillery duel, with a stream of water separating the combatants; but with the exception of making a deafening roar, neither side enjoyed any peculiar advantage over the other.

Late in the afternoon, during a lull in the firing, some one shouted:

"Look, the Johnnies are coming out of the woods! They are running down the bank and are going to cross."

"Fact!" said Fred, peering through the bushes in front of us. "And they're bringing their pontoons with them."

"How many are there?" I asked.

"Perhaps two or three regiments," answered Fred.

"May be there are more. Look out! There goes the artillery again, to cover 'em. Let 'em fire if they want to; it won't do 'em any good."

"What 's the matter with our own batteries?" I asked, noting that the firing was all from one side.

"Oh they 'll get 'round to it later—but what 's that going on there over on the other side?"

"Why, what do you see?"

"I don't know as I see anything now, but I thought I saw a—a—yes and by Jove I did see it too;" said Fred, excitedly pulling back the hammer to his rifle which he raised to a level with the earth in front of us. "See there, will you, over there by that little open space in the woods, and on a line with that chimney above; see 'em, the Johnnies, they 're coming down the hill, and, as sure 's you live, they 're going to cross. Now 's our time, Dan, let 's put in some good work, my boy, while we have a chance. There 's one of 'em now. Just keep your eye on that fellow in the lead; the one with the pole on his shoulder, I mean."

Looking in the direction indicated, I saw, among a lot of stalwart fellows coming down the hill and struggling through the thick underbrush, which at that point reached the water's edge, the head and shoulders of a man, made more conspicuous than his comrades by a stout pole he carried on his shoulder. While watching, I heard the crack of my companion's rifle, and instantly saw this man stumble and fall.

"How was that, Dan? Did I hit him?"

"Think you did," I replied; "he fell over as soon as you fired, and those who were with him disappeared at the same time."

We 'll just lay for those fellows, now, and give 'em a warming. They will break cover directly, and we 'll have a good whack at 'em before they get away."

Presently the enemy appeared near the water's edge with their pontoons, which were quickly launched, loaded, pushed off and started in an oblique line for our side of the river. Fred and I fired again and again, but with what effect we could not see, the enemy working hurriedly, paying no regard to us.

"Well," said Fred, speculatively, as he eyed the crossing boats, "they 're not going to land here, at all events. They 'll bring up somewhere below us, I 'm thinking."

I confessed I was not sorry; for, with our scattered line in the pits, we could not hold out against any body of men. It was true there was not more than a brigade of the enemy, at most; but they were together.

The boats soon passed from sight, under cover of the bank, and it was not until toward dusk that we heard anything more of them. Then a rapid succession of shots gave signal for "the rebel yell," which was answered by loud shouts from the heights on the opposite side, supplemented, in turn, by a roar of artillery and small arms.

"That 's business," said Fred, "and if there were more of them it might be just as well for us if we got out of this; but they can't spread, they 'll lose their grip if they do."

"Sounds as if our skirmishers were on the run."

"Of course they are. They 'll fall back until they reach the main line, and then, Mister Johnnie, look out."

At this moment the enemy's battery ceased firing, and we could hear our men contesting every inch of the way in their retreat. Later, the tone of the shouting was changed, and we heard the welcome shouts of the reinforced skirmishers, who were now returning and driving the Confederates before them.

As the noise of the conflict drew nearer, some of the boys began to leave their pits, when Hartees shouted :

"Down, every mother's son of you ! Don't let a man leave his post until he gets orders !"

"That's the thing to do always," said Fred. "Better be in the reserve all day and stay there until you 're wanted, than rush into a fight when you 're not needed. Rosseau 's got all the help he wants to run the Johnnies into the river."

More and more distinct became the tramp of feet ; louder and nearer grew the rattle of musketry, as pursuers and pursued approached the bank of the river. Finally the tramping ceased, and a line of flashes from the rifles of our troops seemed to say :

"The enemy have reached the water and we 're doing our level best to drive them into it."

Almost immediately the artillery from the other side again opened on us, and we were compelled to lie low and keep out of the way. This time, too, our guns responded to the fire and, I fancied, with rather more spirit than before.

It is tedious business to be compelled to fold your hands and submit to inactivity in a rifle pit, but there 's no help for it when a battery, stationed a short distance in your rear, is keeping up an incessant firing over your heads. The roar of cannon, the scream and hiss and shriek of flying lead and iron, the uncontrollable feeling of dread and doubt, intensified by every bursting shell, maddens and keeps the nerves strained to their utmost. But we had no choice in the matter, and there we lay, smoked our pipes and listened and shivered and waited.

After a while our fire slackened considerably and finally ceased altogether. Still later we heard a few orders given, which were quickly followed by the movements of "limbering up," then the familiar cluck of gun-carriage wheels, growing fainter and fainter as the battery moved away.

"Thank heaven, they're gone!" said Fred, a few moments after their departure. "I'm tired of artillery fighting, and don't want to hear any more of it in a hurry. There's always so much bluster and smoke and bellowing about it. It's all well enough to be backed up by a battery or to know you can have one when you want it, but it's a mighty noisy helper."

"Nothing like it for shrapnel or for grape or canister, just when the enemy are bearing down on you a little too hard, eh?"

"Oh, yes; artillery's a mighty good thing then, but too noisy for steady work at short range. Great Scott, how my head aches! Fit to burst, and my ears fairly ring with the infernal noise they made. Well, they're gone and we can straighten up once more. But we've got to keep our eyes open. I wonder what's going on in the rear?"

Looking in that direction I saw, in the fading light, the shadowy forms of orderlies flitting to and fro among the trees.

"What's up?" asked Fred.

"Looks as if we were getting ready to move again," I replied. "Do you think we are?"

"Hard to tell. There's Jake, just coming out of the woods and crawling toward his pit. Hail him and see what he has to say about it."

"Ho, Jake!" I cried. "What's the matter back there?"

"Matter enough," responded Jake. "Forrest's cavalry has crossed the river below us, and they're to swing around on our flank so as to strike our left and rear."

"Where's Hood?"

"Crossed the river farther up, and is coming down the other way."

"What have we got to do?"

" Stay where we are. The entire force, with the exception of the Twelfth and Sixteenth Kentucky, are going to fall back to Franklin."

" What are we to be left behind for?"

" We 've got to do skirmish duty until midnight, then we 'll git too. By that time, though, Hood 'll be between us and Franklin, and we 'll not only have to frog it ten or fifteen miles, but we 'll also have to do some mighty sharp work, I 'm thinking, to git by the rebs without being seen. They 'll gobble us, sure 's you live, if they only catch sight of us. It 's always the way. Whenever there 's any dirty work to do the Twelfth and Sixteenth have got to do it."

" Our forces start soon, then?"

" Start? They 've already started. There 's going to be some awful close work in the next forty-eight hours," muttered Jake to himself, as he turned and crawled back his post.

" Gad, Dan!" said Fred. " This is a bad business—a mighty bad business, whether it 's orders or not! This gives us no chance at all, and leaves us completely at the mercy of the enemy. We 're only a handful of men, at best, and we 've been left here to be taken prisoners, to be slaughtered or anything else, so long as an appearance is kept up that our whole force has not stepped out."

" It seems as if it wouldn't have been any more than fair to have put some one else down for this work," said I. " Hardly the right thing to make two regiments do this kind of work all the time."

" That 's just what 's the matter," assented Fred, his face suddenly assuming a thoughtful expression. Then rousing himself, he asked, in a voice which had not a trace of discouragement in it:

"What have you got to eat?"

"Only half a dozen hard tack. Why?"

"Nothing much. Only that's six more than I've got, and it seems to me that it's about time that we were eating something. I'm as hungry as a wolf, and have only a small piece of bacon."

"No pork?"

"No. Pork's been a mighty scarce article lately. What with Forrest's Cavalry flying here and there all the time, being always on the move ourselves, and the bad roads, it's a wonder to me that we get anything to eat."

"Trot out your bacon then, if that's all you've got, and we'll divide! Here's three hard tack for you!"

"Hark!" interrupted Fred, suddenly, standing up and assuming a listening attitude. "What's that? Skirmishers to the rear? Hello there, sergeant, what's the matter now?"

"Orders to leave here," replied the sergeant, hurriedly. "Got to take position farther down the river—just beyond the bend. Better get over there lively; the rest of the boys have started."

"Here's some of our boys now," said Fred. "Let's go along with them. Here is Jake and Kimball and Taylor—"

"Well, Fred, they're bound to do us up this time, sure," said Jake, not giving Fred an opportunity to finish his sentence. "This is what I call rough—to make a fellow leave trenches like these for a place where, I'll bet, there ain't no cover at all."

"Rough or not, we've got to make the best of it," replied Fred. "It's all in 'three years or during the war.' What's troubling me now, more than anything else, is something to eat." Then to me : "We 'll have to postpone our supper until later, Dan ; guess we might as well divide those hard tack now, and the bacon when we stop. Come !"

Leaving our narrow quarters, we followed on after our comrades. Almost perfect silence was observed during the half hour we were changing positions. Only the muffled tramp of feet, the cracking of twigs or the rustling of leaves gave any indication of our movement.

CHAPTER XXI.

I had no desire to talk, for my mind was filled with the gloomiest forebodings. We were only a handful of men, and I had no doubt that Hood's army was at that moment cutting off all hope of retreat to Franklin.

A little beyond the bend we found men, belonging to other companies, stationed at regular intervals along the bank, and, just as Jake predicted, where there was little or no protection from the enemy's fire, in case they should open on us.

Fred and I were assigned to one post and, after the sergeant with the rest of the company had left us, we endeavored in the darkness to take in our new position. As near as we could make out, we were near a ford. Directly in front of us were two small trees standing close together. A little beyond this, we heard the river with its whirling and plashing current of black waters. The night air was heavy with moisture, which hung over us like a pall, and made the darkness, shrouding both sides of the river, more intense, more impenetrable.

We immediately set to work with our bayonets and hands, and soon had piled the earth high enough, between the two trees, to make a comparatively safe shelter for ourselves. The enemy's picket, which lined

the opposite side of the river, at this point, seemed determined to make our position as uncomfortable as
possible, and opened fire on us occasionally. This made
it necessary for us to lie flat on the earth most of the
time.

During the intervals of firing, with the exception of
some far-away echo or the sound of the stream as it
flowed lapsing and sucking by the banks or rippled
over the shallows at the ford, the silence, after the roar
of artillery through the day, was startling. After lying
in this position some moments I felt something touch me.

"What is it?" I asked nervously.

"Bacon," answered the reassuring voice of Fred.
"It ain't much of a supper, Dan, but it's all we've got,
and we'd better eat it now."

Neither of us had a drop of water in our canteens,
and we were both chilled to the marrow; but I cannot
remember when I ever enjoyed a meal more thoroughly
than I did my share of the last six crackers and an
equal part of Fred's bacon.

For fully a quarter of an hour the solemn stillness
reigned. Then suddenly, as if in obedience to a given
signal, a line of fire blazed out from the woods on the
opposite bank, and the whistle and zip of a shower of
bullets struck among the leaves around us or flew harmlessly over our heads.

Word was quietly passed from post to post along the
line that our safety depended on silence and hugging
the earth as closely as possible. We made ourselves as
comfortable as we could, and listened to a sound, like
the noise made by an army crossing a pontoon bridge,
somewhere below us.

"Our line can't be a very long one," I said. "The
enemy don't seem to have any opposition in crossing."

"Sound travels a good bit on the water. Then our

heads are close to the earth, and we can hear a noise like that made below a long way off."

"This sort of thing can't last long," said I. "Hood is close upon us, and it seems to me he's going to force a fight soon."

"That's what he's after, you may depend. Well, some of our boys have been aching for a fight for a long time. As if one fight would settle anything!"

"There's one thing we've learned, and that is to appreciate the feelings of Johnston's army when it was being pressed by Sherman. It isn't the fight the boys want so much as it is to be doing something. Action is better than freezing."

"I'd rather get warm some other way. There they go again!"

Once more the enemy opened fire upon us; this time a little heavier than usual. Almost simultaneously a voice on my right cried out in agony:

"Oh! Oh! Oh!"

"God!" said Fred. "Who's that?"

"Oh, help!"

"Careful!" said Fred, loud enough to be heard by the wounded man. "Don't let 'em hear you on the other side. They'll fire again if they do."

"Oh—I—can't—help—it! Oh! Oh! Help me! Help!"

"I can't stand this," I said to Fred, and started to relieve the sufferer; but Fred pulled me back, saying:

"Be careful, Dan, you can't do him any good, and the rebs will fire again as soon as they hear him."

"I don't care if they do. I'm—"

"H-e-l-p!" shrieked the poor unfortunate, with all the strength at his command.

As this cry of distress echoed up and down the river, another blaze from the enemy's rifles, and another

shower of bullets whistled through the air uncomfort-
ably near us. One of these missiles struck the tree
nearest us and burst.

"My God !" exclaimed Fred, who had observed this
fact. "They 're firing explosive bullets at us. There 's
no help for a fellow if he ever gets hit with one of those
things."

An instant of silence and another agonized voice cried
out :

"Come here, somebody, quick !"

"Who 's that ?" I asked of Fred, thinking I knew the
voice.

"Oh, hurry, some one—quick ! For God's sake, help
me, quick ! I can't do anything alone. Jake ! Fred !
Dan !"

"Yes," said Fred, who had located the voice, and was
now, regardless of his caution to me, moving quickly
toward the spot whence it came. I also started, but
in the other direction, to aid the first comrade who
called. I found him only a short distance away. He
was lying on his side, dead. I felt of his face ; it was
beardless, and covered with a cold sweat. I could not
tell, in the pitchy darkness, who he was, and I crawled
back to my post, where I was soon joined by my companion.

"Who was it, Fred ?" I asked.

"It was—was—ah, how can I say it ! How can I
believe that he is dead !"

Then, after a pause, he continued :

"It was—Kimball, poor fellow. He was shot in the
shoulder, and, when I got there, was trying to prevent
himself from bleeding to death. He had pulled up the
cape of his overcoat, and was trying to press it into the
wound. He told me what he had done, and that his
entire shoulder seemed to have been shattered by an

explosive bullet. I took out my big red handkerchief to help him, but 't was no use; before I could think of what I ought to do, he said : ' Give me some water, Fred,' and fell over dead."

" He is the first of our mess to go," I said.

"Yes; we 've been together a long time, Dan, and to think this is the end. Kimball was a brave soldier, Dan ; he never shirked his duty. Many a time, when he 's been as much used up as any of us, he has helped you and me and others over hard places. Then, he was always ready to divide rations with his comrades. Poor Kimball! God help us all! Common bullets are bad enough, but these infernal machines—they 're only fit to be used by cowards and assassins."

" It 's too bad !" I said. " The other one on the right is also dead."

" Did you go to him ?"

" Yes."

" Who was he ?"

" I don't know. No one I could think of in our company. This has been a bad night for us, so far. I wonder how much longer they intend to keep us here?"

"Oh, I don't know what to think ! If you 'd been over there with Kimball when he was hopelessly struggling for his life and been made to feel as I did, that only a few minutes were left in which to do anything, and then to know you were powerless and unable to save him, you would feel as dazed as I do. I 've left many a good man behind me in a charge and, in the excitement of the moment, thought nothing of it ; at least, it never made the impression on me this has. There is only one thought uppermost in my mind, and that 's Kimball. I wish we were out of this. In all the time I 've been in the service, I never felt as I do now."

"Oh, pshaw !" I said, trying to make light of Fred's melancholy mood. "There's no use getting blue over what can't be helped. You're only cold and nervous."

"I feel as if something were going to happen." Then, as if he had suddenly realized he was getting to be a trifle childish, he added : "This day's work has been too much for me. Look out, there they go again !"

Once more the rifles of the enemy flash out in the darkness on the opposite bank, and this time a shower of bullets whistled harmlessly over our heads. After an instant of silence, the clear ringing voice of Hartees, echoed up and down the river :

"At–ten–tion !"

Absolute silence was preserved along the line, on both sides. It seemed as if the river had ceased to flow ; that the leaves had stopped their rustling ; that even the winds, with bated breath, had paused for what might follow. Again the commanding voice of our captain pierced the chilly night air :

"Men," he said, "if another shot is fired from the other side to-night, open every gun on them."

"That ought to fix them," said Fred, in a low tone.

Fix them it did, for they had not forgotten the shelling of the afternoon, and must have been in doubt whether our artillery was still before them or not. However that may have been, the picket on the other side did no more shooting that night.

An hour later I took Fred's canteen and my own and crept out from behind our shelter, toward the river bank, where I dropped silently down. There, on hands and knees, through mud and ooze, to the water's edge, I felt my way, filled both canteens, and returned to my post.

Once I heard the breaking of a twig, not far from me ; then came a hurried rustle of leaves, quickly followed by a furtive intermittent noise, as of an animal moving through the woods. "It is the wind," thought I, "or, perchance, some of my comrades who, like myself, have been to the river for water."

Whatever it was that occasioned the noise, nothing further occurred until midnight, when I heard a slight movement in our rear, as if some one was cautiously approaching. I listened intently, and fixed my eyes in the direction from which the noise came. The darkness was impenetrable. I could discern nothing.

Suddenly a sound, as of a musket-stock striking a stone or stump, and then :

"Who goes there?" from Fred, in a quick, low tone.

"Co'p'l o' the guard," came a suppressed reply.

"Oh, it's you, Dick, is it? What's up?"

"Goin' to git out o' this at once. Goin' to fall back to Franklin. Fall in on the Pike's the orders."

"Thank God for that! Did you know Kimball was gone?"

"What? Dead?"

"Dead."

"That's bad. Where is he?"

"Next post. Can't a few of us bury him?"

"No; we've got no time to do that. It's mighty hard to leave him to be stripped by the rebs, but there's no help for it now. Did he have any valuables with him—a watch or anything?"

"I know he had a watch, but I didn't have the heart to look for it or for anything else?"

"His friends would like 'em, mebbe. Where does he lay?"

"About a dozen rods, in a straight line, below us."

"I'll take a look. Hurry back to the road. We've got no time to lose. Rebs are already between us and Franklin. Ought to have been out of this an hour ago."

As the corporal hurried away we started for the road from which we had been separated by a narrow belt of woods. Here we groped and stumbled and fell, being compelled at times to almost feel our way, the darkness was so intense. Once Fred took hold of my arm and said:

"Stop a bit. Didn't somebody call me?"

"No," I replied.

"Thought I heard my name."

"Imagination," I said.

"Perhaps so, but somehow the sound of Kimball's voice keeps ringing in my ears. I fancied I heard some one calling for help."

"Come," I said, "let's get out of this. We've a long tramp ahead of us, and but little time to do it in."

After pausing a moment or two longer, and satisfying himself that the sounds he heard were only the product of his imaginings, Fred let go of my arm, saying, as he did so:

"Well, we can do no good here." Then, with a sigh: "I hate to leave a man like Kimball was lying there like a dog. We may as well go, though."

Again we groped our way through the woods, Fred occupied with his thoughts, I with mine, and neither of us speaking. Just before reaching the road I kicked along a small object which aroused my curiosity.

Stooping down, I picked up what proved to be a soldier's cap. It was just what I wanted, for mine was worn and old and the visor was twisted out of shape. The cap I had just found was apparently new. I could tell that by feeling the nap on the cloth. The visor was also straight.

Passing my hand mechanically around the lining, my fingers suddenly slipped through a ragged hole in front and above the visor strap. The inside band was also wet and stuck to my fingers.

With a thrill of horror I dropped the cap, satisfied that the owner had been shot through the head, and if it were now day instead of night I should see him lying dead within a few feet of me. As a full sense of the picture filled me, I could not help the thought, "If a soldier must yield his life for his country, better die a swift death like that than die as Kimball did."

A few steps farther on I reached the road, but was surprised to hear none of our men passing, nothing but the far-off sound of footsteps hurrying on their way to Franklin. Here I also discovered that my companion was not with me. This startled me into a realizing sense of my loneliness, and I waited and wondered. Where was Fred?

Had I loitered? I was not conscious of it. Had Fred retraced his steps? He surely would not do that? He was with me just before I picked up the cap; since that time I had heard nothing of him; there could be only one reasonable solution to my perplexity. Fred had passed me, joined those who had gone ahead, and if I would overtake him I must follow him quickly. This I did.

Once I fancied my name was spoken by some one. I ran in the direction of the voice and shouted: "Fred! Fred!" but obtained no reply. There was no one to answer me. Not even the sound of footsteps now. I was alone. The deep silence which brooded over the earth seemed ominous of evil. Should I go on or wait?

I could travel this road alone, and perhaps remain undiscovered as long as the night lasted. But what would the daylight bring? A night bird flapped his wings above my head and uttered a cry of warning. Fearful of further delay, I pressed forward.

A mile was passed without a sound other than my own footsteps. What wonder was it that a deep-toned voice, speaking out in the darkness, almost at my side, caused my heart to bound and set my pulses throbbing ?

"Say thar !" said the voice. "What 's yer hurry ?"

I stopped instantly.

"Hello ! Have yer seen any 'f ther Sixteenth Kentucky ?"

"No," I replied, in a scarcely audible voice, though with a feeling of relief that I had not met an enemy. "Belong to the Twelfth myself."

"Glad ter know it, dogged 'f I ain't. Heerd yer comin' 'nd thought p'rhaps 't was one 'f our crowd, so I waited fer yer. Reckon 't ain't no use huntin' fer any more 'f ther stragglers, such a night 's this."

"You 're right," I responded, glad to know I had met one of my own brigade. " I left my partner back there by the river an hour ago, and have been waiting and hunting for him ever since, thinking he would turn up."

"P'rhaps he 'll turn up after awhile ; but I 'm thinkin' yer 'll see ther rebs first. They 're thicker 'n bees in swarmin' time 'tween us 'nd Franklin, 'nd 'f we don't keep tergether 'nd hurry along right sharp we 'll git snapped up, fer sure."

"Come on, then. I 'm with you."

" Thar 's whar yer right. Better a blamed sight look out fer yerself ; yer partner 'll turn up all right at Franklin."

" If we ever get there," I interrupted.

" Oh, we 'll git thar, 'f we only stick ter it long enough. Say, pard, what 's yer name ?"

I told him.

"And what 's yours ?" I asked.

" Nicholas Searle. Ther boys call me Nick fer short. I say, Dan, we 'd better double-quick it fer a while 'nd see 'f we can't catch up with ther rest 'f ther boys. It 's gittin' a little skeery 'round these parts, 'nd we 'll stand

a heap better show er gittin' through 'f we 're all tergether."

"Double-quick it is, then," I responded.

After running and walking for half an hour or more,
I saw, a short distance in front of us, a small point of
light—now glowing, now disappearing, as a firefly light.
I knew it could not be produced by an insect at this
season of the year ; and, becoming puzzled to explain
it to my own satisfaction, I took hold of Nick's arm and
stopped him.

"What 's ther matter ?" asked Nick.

"A light," I said. "See it ?"

"What ? Where ? I don't see no light."

"Wait a moment, and you 'll see it ; it 's only a small
speck of light, but it 's over there on the left."

At brief intervals the light appeared and disappeared.

"See it ?" I asked.

"Yes," replied Nick, after a moment of hesitation,
"it 's some Johnnie smokin' ; 'nd yer kin bet yer shoes
they 're mighty thick 'round here ter be so car'less 's
that. We might 's well jog along ; they 've heerd us
'fore this. Come on. I 'll do ther talkin'."

In a few moments we were hailed with :

"Halt ! Whar yer gwine ?"

"Lookin' fer ther boys," replied Nick.

"What regiment d' yer b'long ter ?"

"Georgy Tigers."

"Which-a-way 'd yer come ?"

"'Long ther Pike Road, from Columby."

"Seen any 'f ther Yanks ?"

"No. Why ?"

"Thought mebbe yer mought 've seen some 'f 'em."

"Who be you uns ?" asked Nick.

"Twenty-ninth North Car'liny."

"Whar 's Hood all?"

"Spring Hill, 'nd a right good jog ahead it is too."

"Wall, here 's arter 'em," and Nick grasped me nervously by the arm, saying as he did so, "come on boys!"

"Hold on thar! How many d' yer count?"

"Lively Dan, lively my boy," whispered Nick, increasing his speed, "we 've got to leg it ter git er this, 't won't do ter let 'em scratch a match on us. Thought they was lettin' us off easy-like."

"Halt thar! D' yer hear?" demanded the voice.

"Quick, Dan," said Nick, "let 's leave ther road. We 'll do better on ther side 'nd won't make so much noise."

We scarce had time to reach the roadside when a shot was fired after us. Another and yet another rifle flared out in the darkness, but the bullets, while we heard them whistle by, did us no harm. Our inquisitors were evidently too tired to pursue us, for they contented themselves with these three shots and we heard nothing more of them.

We ran at full speed some distance and then slackened our pace to a rapid walk. It seemed to me I never was so tired, that the roads were never in a worse condition, and that we would never overtake our men.

CHAPTER XXII.

Several times we heard firing ahead, but this only stimulated us to greater exertion. We knew the importance of making the most of our time and reaching the main body of our detail while it was yet dark. At last we found them walking, rapidly and silently, on the right of the turpike. Nick was first to discover the progress we had made, and encouraged us with :

" Here they are, Dan. Take it easy, now, my boy We 've got along so fur all right, thank God ! Hard work, aint it ?"

" You 're right," I replied, when I had recovered from the last run sufficiently to speak. " I couldn't have gone any farther at that pace."

" Wall, I 'd about gi'n out myself ; but it 's a heap better 'n 'twas back thar at Columby, 'nd we 're 'n a heap better condition ter whoop 'em up fer ther Johnnies, 'f they trouble us. Say, comrade," speaking to one of the party we had just overtaken, " what was that firin' fer, a while ago ?"

" Skirmish, I reckon. Rebs is thick all around us, and they 're thick on the other side of the Pike."

" Did yer have a hand in ther skirmish ?"

" No, ' twas way ahead o' us."

" Where are we ?"

" Don' know ! Some on em says we ain't far from

[231]

Spring Hill ; though what they knows about it, I 'm blamed 'f I know ! Some on 'em says, too, that ther rebs are camped ahead 'f us on ther other side 'f ther Pike 'nd that we 'll see their fires pretty quick !"

"Shouldn't be s'prised 'f we did !" responded Nick. "'Nd 'f we don't see more 'n fires we 'll be lucky ! It 's goin' ter be a close rub ! Mighty close ! That 's what 's ther matter !"

Here we halted, and it was with difficulty I could resist the impulse to unroll my blanket and lie down to sleep. As it was I sat down, stretched my weary limbs and dozed until shaken into wakefulness by Nick, who informed me word had been passed along the line that, when started again, we must move together quickly and noiselessly. Every man was to be alert and ready for an attack at any moment.

There had been some speculation as to our whereabouts and what our chances were of getting by the enemy without being seen and reaching Franklin in safety. Whatever the differences may have been as to minor details, all were agreed on one point, and that was, we were about half way between Columbia and Franklin, and if our presence and strength were discovered by the enemy we would be " gobbled." With this comforting assurance we resume our march.

Ears are strained to catch the slightest sound of the enemy. Eyes ache as we attempt, in vain, to pierce the pitchy darkness which shuts us in. Hardly a word is spoken. Matches are not lighted by smokers. Each man feels that upon him rests the responsibility for the · safety of every other man.

We had not been on the road more than half an hour when it seemed to me I heard a sound behind us as if we were being pursued. Once I stopped an instant and listened, but heard nothing.

"What is it, Dan?" asked Nick, noting the pause.

"Thought I heard the rebs after us, double quick."

"'T wouldn't be no great s'prise 'f we did have a little scrimmage 'fore we git out er this. Rebs is all around us, 'nd—" hesitatingly—"there they are, sure 's you 're born."

"Where?" I asked, quickly, expecting to hear a volley of musketry before a reply could be made.

"Jest over the hill yonder. See that light loomin' up thar, ter the left?"

I looked and plainly saw the hill outlined against the red glow beyond.

"No doubt er them bein' rebs," said Nick; "'nd I reckon they 're not more 'n half a mile away."

"Good thing for us they haven't tried to control the road."

"Reckon they don't b'lieve there 's any need er lookin' arter ther road. Ther rebs 's tired 's we be, 'nd they 're not goin' ter bother their heads 'bout a few stragglers; 'nd that 's all there is of us, 'nd they know it. Hark! What was that? Halt!"

Nick turned quickly, bringing his gun to a ready. There was no mistake this time. We not only heard the tramp of feet; we also heard the rattle and click of accouterments.

"Halt, thar, I say!" repeated Nick, in a louder tone, as the party showed no disposition to stop. "'F yer don't stand whar yer be, we 'll blow yer ter pieces. Who be yer?"

"Stragglers from th' Sixteenth and Twelfth Kentucky, from Columbia."

"Come on, then. Dogged 'f yer ain't hed ter leg it. Seen any 'f ther rebs?"

"Only a few pieces of artillery that passed a couple of miles back."

" Which way 'd they go ?"

" Crossed the road and moved off to the left."

" Didn't see nobody else, no pickets, nor nothin' ?"

" No."

" That 's all right then, they won't bother us."

The newcomers proved to be three men from the Sixteenth Kentucky and four men from the Twelfth Kentucky, the latter belonging to Company C. They had all been left behind in the hurry of departure, but no one questioned them particularly, as a few moments later we came in full view of the camp fires of large bodies of troops.

It was suggested that Schofield was in bivouac there, but there was no one who cared to investigate. The camp was almost parallel with the turnpike for a long distance, and we hurried by like phantoms.

Once we saw a body of horsemen passing between us and the light, but they were going in an opposite direction and quickly disappeared from view. Before losing sight of the bivouac of our foes, we dimly saw between it and us a force of some sort. Nearer to the road, we pass a few of our men silently standing beside a barricade of rails, evidently watching for some movement in opposition to our own.

The darkness deepens and again becomes blackness ; only the red gleams from a few of the distant fires break it here and there in swaying rifts. Not a word is spoken, while we are passing this point, though many an anxious eye is turned in the direction of the rebel camp.

All doubts as to whether we would get beyond reach of the enemy without being discovered were settled a few moments later by sharp firing in our rear. We were soon overtaken by the party we had seen standing at the barricade of rails. From this squad we learn that they had been fired upon by the enemy's skirmish line.

" They 'll chase us up, see 'f they don't," said Nick, upon learning the fire had been returned.

" So long as they don't know how many there are of us, we are just as good as a whole division would be," said I.

" Yer right, Dan ; and it will make ther Johnnies er little careful, arter we once get a crack at 'em. 'F we only had er few big guns, 'twould be all ther better."

A few minutes later and another volley was heard from the same direction.

"They won't get an answer this time ; ther coon ain't thar," said Nick.

" No, but as you said, just now, they'll follow us up."

Weary and worn we pressed onward, now with sway-ing step and half closed eyes, now breaking into a double quick, now slowing down to a rapid walk, every step bringing us nearer to Franklin, every man carrying his gun ready for instant action. A short interval passed, and then, within easy range, from our left came a light volley of musketry, which did us no harm.

Halting for a moment, we vigorously returned the fire and then resumed our march. It soon became apparent, from the method of attack, that the enemy were not present in large numbers. Possibly it was only a skirmish line or, perhaps, a small body of cav-alry. Whatever it was, the force continued to harass us at intervals.

Just before the day dawned, we saw the glowing embers of a baggage-wagon that had been destroyed. We gave this spot a wide berth. A little later and our eyes penetrated farther into the darkness with which we had been surrounded. A faint glow appeared in the east. Daylight came. The darkness broke and dissolved. The mists rose from the earth like ragged curtains.

In the morning light I saw the anxious, careworn faces of the men around me—soldiers bound together by the feeling of sympathy and comradeship, the natural accompaniment of a common danger and duty.

Close beside me was Nick—tall, awkward, gaunt, with a kindly, honest face and big gray eyes, which I found were curiously turned toward me.

As the sun rose we reached the friendly shelter of woods. Here we hurried along at a rapid pace. Our safety now depended on our speed. Tired, hungry and exhausted as we were, there was no time for halting, and, if there had been, breakfast was impossible, for there was nothing to eat.

Fifteen or twenty miles are nothing for strong, well-fed soldiers, breaking camp in the freshness of the early morning, but we were in no condition for it. We had not slept for two nights, and our haversacks were empty.

Many a time I was tempted to drop out of line and rest. What odds if I were taken prisoner and carried to Andersonville? I might as well die there as anywhere.

Hour after hour slipped away. Mile after mile we covered in this toilsome march, stimulated only to still greater effort by occasional shots from the enemy. At last the breastworks thrown up by Schofield's force on the crest of the hill between us and Franklin came into view.

A half-hour later we passed through the opening in the works at the turnpike, where we were welcomed as from the dead. The greeting was a cordial one, but it was interrupted by Nick, who quietly said :

" Dan, thar 's our cook in the rear 'f that old cotton-gin yonder. Come, my boy, 'nd we 'll feed."

A glance to the right refreshed my eyes with the sight of blazing wood and steaming kettles. Thither we went and, through Nick's cleverness, succeeded in obtaining a bit of bacon, a pot of hot, black coffee and sugar with which to sweeten it. It was a feast for a hungry man ; such a meal as I had not enjoyed in a long time, and it was quickly devoured.

While eating, I asked the cook if he had seen any of the Twelfth Kentucky, and was informed that a lot of our men had passed only a short time before and that they were now asleep in a little hollow only a few steps away in the rear and on the right of the road.

After I had finished eating, I left Nick at the fire and started in search of the boys, finding them where the cook had directed me. Captain Hartees was there and, only a few feet away, Fred, Jake and Taylor, all with their accouterments on, sleeping just as they had thrown themselves, on reaching the spot where they lay. I was soon beside them and, without my blanket under my head for a pillow, speedily became oblivious to all surroundings.

CHAPTER XXIII.

Franklin, Tennessee, the county seat of Williamson, is on the south bank of the Little Harpeth. This stream winds nearly around the town, holding it as it were in the lap of a crescent.

Within the arms of this crescent, that is, across from one point to the other, is a ridge, known as Carter's Hill, the crest of which commands a fine view of the surrounding country. From this ridge, toward the north, the ground gradually slopes to the river bank, where the town is located. Franklin, therefore, is bounded by the river on the north, east and west and by the ridge on the south.

To the south of this ridge is also a gradual slope which for little less than a mile on the right and directly in front was clear of timber. This elevated ground was occupied by our troops and, as I stood by the cook's fire and drank my coffee, a few hours before, I saw that the line selected for defense, and along which our men were rapidly throwing up earth works, was a curve extending from river to river.

The center of this intrenchment, part of which de-. scribed an angle, was at the Columbia Turnpike, where a space, the whole width of the road, was left open, and through which the artillery and baggage wagons had passed on their way to Nashville.

After sleeping two or three hours, I was suddenly awakened. Expecting to find that some of my comrades had disturbed me, I raised my head ; but a glance satisfied me they were still sleeping, and there was no one else near. Closing my eyes, I again tried to sleep, but the subtle influence had fled, and, in spite of my tired, worn-out condition, would not return. At last I arose, buckled on my accouterments and, with rifle in hand, walked toward the works.

Here I found most of our forces in position and awaiting the appearance of the enemy. On the left of the road I noticed a part of our brigade. A little way in the rear were parked the ammunition wagons. Crossing the road, a short distance away, a retrenchment commanded the opening in the works and its approach. A few rods south of the cotton gin, a battery of six field pieces had been stationed. West of this, and on the other side of the Pike, were Opdycke's men in reserve.

Just outside the works, beyond the angle, a detail of men were hurriedly constructing a thorny abatis of osage orange. East of this, Henderson's men held the line to the Lewisburg Pike ; then Casement's Second Brigade to the river.

Passing through the opening, I stood for a few moments gazing at the landscape before me. The afternoon was surpassingly lovely, and an Indian-summer haze, which pervaded the warm atmosphere, had settled on the distant hills. Nature was peacefully sinking into her winter sleep, undisturbed by any noise save the caw of a crow which lazily winged its way toward the leafless trees on the other side of the river.

"Caw ! Caw ! Caw !"

Like a hungry ghoul, impatient for a feast of human flesh, this "thing of evil" turned suddenly and sailed

in a circle above us. There was something almost
prophetic in the action. Death was at hand. In less
than an hour, perhaps, the air would be thick with
hissing bullets and the earth in front of me made red
with blood.

"Caw! Caw! Caw!"

Pitiless and mocking came the hoarse response to my
thought. Was it a warning? The query thrilled me, and
I saw others shiver as we watched this uneasy spirit
winging higher and still higher. Was it possible that
from his dizzy height he saw the moment of battle
drawing near?

"Caw! Caw! Caw!" came the answer.

"What a place for a stand!" thought I. "If Hood
will only dare attack us here!"

In front of me was an unobstructed slope of open
fields, skirted at the base by a belt of woods. Beyond,
and nestling among the hills, a few farm houses were
to be seen.

Less than half a mile in front of our center and
stretching across the Turnpike were stationed two
brigades of Wagner's Division.

Why they were there I could not understand, but
supposed it must be for some good purpose. I noticed
every one in that line was alert and evidently scanning
the woods at the foot of the slope.

In the intrenchments, too, men were anxiously watching. Now that their work was nearly finished, they
gathered in groups to discuss the probability of an attack. The solitary worker, with pick or shovel here
and there, stopped occasionally between the motions of
his occupation and viewed the scene.

"Will Hood attack us here or will he march around
us and once more get in our rear?" was the question of
the moment.

We had not long to wait for an answer to this query, for, presently, a skirmish line, emerging from the woods, gave signal that the enemy were approaching.

An awful stillness fell upon the scene ; a quiet I had experienced, and which every one who has been in battle knows better than can be described. The pulse-beat of the line quickened. Men dropped pick and spade and grasped their rifles. Gunners stood by their guns, silently awaiting the solid ranks which everybody knew were but a little distance behind the skirmishers. I scanned the faces of the veterans near me, and saw pictured there confidence and determination to settle their account with Hood.

Suddenly, from a dozen throats, there arose the cry : " There they come !"

Almost at the same instant, from out of the woods near the river, on our left, and stretching to a considerable distance beyond the Columbia Turnpike, I saw the dark gray lines and glittering bayonets of the Confederate army. In heavily massed column they advanced, as gayly, it seemed to me, as if they were entering a parade-ground instead of a battle-field. Marching toward us for a short distance, they wheeled into line, halted, and were at once ready for the order, " Forward !"

Two detachments of artillery thundered out of the woods, galloped forward, unlimbered, and established themselves in positions, covering different roads. There was no counter-marching, no shifting of pieces. The formation was made with accuracy and dispatch.

Leaving my post of observation in front, I turned, went inside the works and joined a group from my brigade, who were also watching the scene.

When the enemy began to move they manifested even more deliberation than at first ; the lines, which appeared to be six or seven regiments deep, in the center, assumed better shape and advanced with a precision and military bearing seldom seen on a holiday parade. It was one of the most impressive sights I ever witnessed and occasioned much favorable comment from the veterans near me.

Later, as the enemy increased their speed to a double-quick, one of the group in front of me said :

"That's what I call a handsome line of battle."

"You 're right, it is !" said another. "And they mean business, too !"

"The best thing Wagner can do," said a third, "is to git out er that place, and do it quick, too ! He 'd better git in here out er the way."

"He 's no good where he is," rejoined the first speaker, "and we can't use a piece of artillery or fire a musket while they stand between us and the enemy."

"There 's a terrible mistake somewhere !" added still another speaker.

It was true, we could not fire without injury to our men. It was also true and painfully apparent that some one had seriously blundered in placing that line. Yet there it stood, two brigades of dazed, undisciplined men, opposed to nearly forty thousand of the flower of the Confederate Army.

When the enemy approached within a short distance, these bridgades opened a rattling fire ; but the enemy, without pause or, so far as we could see, the loss of a man, hurried on, firing as they came, their line extending half a mile beyond either flank of the panic-stricken. brigades, who now broke and fled—a confused, disorganized crowd, flying in terror and streaming directly up the Turnpike, toward our center, as fast as their legs could carry them.

"There 's a foot-race for yer !" exclaimed the familiar

voice of Jake Bence. "But it's just what we might expect. Somehow we never get half a chance at the Johnnies, but somebody up and spoils it all. What business 'd that line out there, any way? The idea! Hanging on till the last minute, 'nd what right had they to fire, any how? Our line's got to break now to let 'em in. The rebs are close onto 'em, 'nd if they don't look out they'll all come in together. There's rebs enough to eat us, if they ever get a chance. Come, Dan, we'd better go and wake up the boys."

Together we hurried to our company in the rear of the cotton-gin, roused man after man and set these to work waking others. I ran to Captain Hartees, who was lying with his head resting on his overcoat, and attempted to shake him into wakefulness. He did not respond.

"Captain!" I shouted. "Wake up! The rebs are coming!"

By this time the noise of artillery and musketry on our left gave evidence that the battle had commenced; and, as I stooped and again took the sleeping officer by the shoulder, I could hear the loud, ringing yells of the enemy added to the roar of the oncoming storm.

"Captain!" I cried again. "Captain! Wake up! The rebs are here! The've attacked us—are coming close to the works! Come, come, get up, or it will be too late!" Saying which, I took hold of the shoulders of the sleeper and raised him almost to his feet before he awoke.

When the captain finally became conscious that he was wanted the fleetest runners of the retreating brigades had reached the ditch in front of the works, jumped into it, and were coming up on the other side and through our lines, which had opened to receive them.

From one end of our line of defense to the other, excepting that portion covering the turnpike, a flame of fire flashed a moment, fitfully, and the white smoke of the burned powder hung like a curtain for an instant between us and the enemy, only to drift away and reveal the long lines of graycoats rapidly advancing and pouring into our ranks a fire no less rapid. In front I saw a wide area, literally crammed with Confederates ; their lines, being thicker at this point than at any other, were mixed with our own men, all running together.

The enemy fully appreciated the situation, knew they were completely covered by our men, and that so long as this condition of things continued, we could not fire. They also understood that our line would open to let in this hapless crowd, and that that break in our center would be their opportunity.

Toward this point they were running, careless, confident, their muskets at a charge, and their faces beaming with satisfaction, as if they were anticipating a grand rout to come and were even then enjoying it. Nearer and nearer, like a drove of brown sheep, crowding by and trying to run over each other, in their eagerness to be first through our center, they jump into the ditch with our men, and with them enter our lines.

In their rear, a perfect sea of heads and glistening steel, is moving forward with the same desperate eagerness, forcing those who are in front continually forward, whether they will or not.

The charge of the enemy was so impetuous, and the bewilderment of the men, who should have held this important point, so great, that our line, like a huge gate opening inward, yielded. The enemy saw it, and with a deafening yell, rushed for the gap, which immediately becomes wider as the One hundredth and a part of the One hundred and Fourth Ohio left their post of duty and ran.

Panic stricken, men and officers fled in dismay; the wildest confusion prevailed. Every one seemed bent on getting to the rear at the earliest moment. It looked as if no human power could check this disastrous stampede. A moment longer and our whole line, already in great peril, would have been hopelessly broken and Hood victorious; but just as the color-bearer of the One hundredth Ohio came running by us, Captain Hartees snatched the flag and, waving it aloft an instant, shouted in a tone heard above the tumult:

"Break for the works!"

With a loud cheer company after company of the Twelfth Kentucky follow the man whose bravery had stimulated them so many times in emergencies. Colonel White, with voice and gesture, urged on the Sixteenth Kentucky and the Eighth Tennessee, and rallied the flying Ohio regiments. All together we struggle for the abandoned positions, while Wagner's men, with the One Hundred and Seventy-fifth Ohio and Opdyke's Brigade, filled with the enthusiasm of their leader, also hurry to our support.

I had never before, in conflict, been so close to the enemy; never before had been able to look in men's faces and note their expression. The countenances of these men were not unpleasant to look upon. There was nothing to excite fear—nothing brutal—about them; rather an expression of indifference, as I look back at them now, like men who might, perhaps, have been dispossessed of their sensibilities, and were merely executing an order, without the faintest thought or care of consequences. There were many gray, weather-beaten faces, telling tales of hardship, of privation and of suffering.

As the main body of the two lines met, I heard, from the opposite side :

"We 've got 'em on the run, boys. The works are ours ! Hold all you get !"

In response came the cheering voice of Hartees :

"Forward, men ! Drive 'em back ! Clean 'em out !"

I saw Jake, at this instant, jump quickly forward, knock down a Confederate color-bearer, wrench away the flag he carried, throw it on the ground, trample it under foot and leave it there.

Immediately a desperate hand-to-hand fight, with bayonets and clubbed muskets, ensued, and the standards of both armies waved within the line of works.

I found myself defending blows that a burly fellow was aiming at my head. The features of his dust-blackened and heated face were quivering with ferocious joy. His sharp white teeth were laid bare in a wolfish grin, and I saw blazing, in his small gray eyes, a determination to kill me or any one else who opposed him.

He had clubbed his gun and was striking at me with all the strength he could command. My rifle was loaded, but so rapidly did this man handle his weapon that I could do nothing but ward off his blows.

Once, twice, thrice he brought down the butt of his musket, aiming to strike my head ; but each time I successfully fenced it off. Again and again, faster and faster, he followed blow on blow. I seemed to have been left alone to take care of this man. My comrades were by my side; so near that I could feel the movements of their bodies against my own, yet each man was defending, with his life, the ground he stood upon, as I was. Each was held equally close to his perilous duty by the dogged determination of his antagonist. I could help no one, others could not help me.

The man confronting me was larger and stronger than I, and I felt that I could not stand before him very long. My defense weakened rapidly, but there set in now a backward movement of the enemy—the line in front of me becoming, if possible, more dense than ever. As his comrades crowded against my antagonist he wavered, failed to recover from the last blow quick enough to deliver another. My rifle was at his breast in an instant. I fired. A flash, a burning flame; then, with a look of disappoitment on his face, intensified as he clutched his rifle with firmer grip, he fell at my feet.

At this moment I discovered beside me Nick Searle, who, with others of the Sixteenth Kentucky, in their eagerness to meet the enemy, had separated from their comrades in that first rush for the works and were now fighting with us, side by side.

Nick was striving desperately to free his gun from the control of an assailant who had locked bayonets with him.

They were well matched in strength, Nick having advantage only by being the more active and fresher of the two. There could be no doubt as to the result of this individual encounter, I thought, glancing for an instant at the combatants.

But another of the enemy jumped to the relief of his comrade and, with the butt of his musket raised in the air, was about to decide the content against my friend.

Quickly thrusting forward my rifle, I warded off the blow which descended with crushing force on the arm of Nick's foe, causing him to lose hold of his musket and leaving Nick free to act in his own defense.

There was no method of action in that encounter; all we thought of or cared for or strove to accomplish, was to check, if possible, the progress of the enemy. Men discharged their muskets in the faces of other men; they ran each other through the body with bayonets; they clubbed their guns and brought them down upon the head of the enemy who stood nearest. Others used the butts of their guns, as one might use a battering-ram, and struck their opponents in the face.

Rifle struck rifle, bayonet locked with bayonet, and men panted as they wildly struggled with each other for possession of this central point in the line of our defense. Back, step by step, the enemy are forced into the ditch. They fought like madmen to hold all they had gained; but, in spite of their undaunted courage, the gap through which they had expected to pass "on the run" closed and was now well defended.

Among the many prisoners taken and hurried to the rear, I saw the Confederate general, Gordon, in charge of Captain Hartees.

It was while leading his division in this charge that the Confederate general, Cleburn was shot, not more than thirty paces in front of us. The horse from which he fell advanced to the top of our works, where he was shot and dropped with his feet hanging over the headlogs.

Our line was once more unbroken, and we were

thinking that the worst was over, when the cry was sounded:

"There they come again!"

Another line of battle, stronger than the first, had advanced at a double quick, under cover of the smoke, and were now upon us.

On they come, shoulder touching shoulder, loading and firing as they advanced. But their assault was met with the firmness of a rock, and the living wave was dashed back. Bruised, torn and bleeding, they staggered and fell in heaps under our fire, which was now crossed at a left oblique by the fire from a part of our brigade, on the other side of the Pike.

The discharge of small arms was so incessant that dense masses of smoke settled upon us, partly obscuring the field, and veiled the movements of the assaulting lines, excepting when the sulphurous vapor was lifted into rifts. Then we saw battle-flags waving, lines charging and men reeling and falling to earth. Great swaths of human beings fell, as grass falls before a scythe; but the horrible gaps closed again, and tramping, slipping, stumbling over the fallen bodies of their dead and wounded comrades, with the powder flame from our guns almost burning their faces, they pressed toward the death which they knew awaited them.

Again and again the assault was made, with similar results; and the piles of dead and wounded attested the heroic determination of the enemy to carry our works at any cost.

One Confederate color-bearer reached the crest of our works with his flag, stood with it above his head an instant; then, burying its pointed staff deep in the 'oose earth, and amid a storm of bullets, leaving his colors flying in our faces, he jumped back among his comrades, laughing and unharmed.

Hardly had he disappeared when, with a prolonged yell, the enemy attacked us with such fury that it seemed as if not only Hood's but Lee's army, also, was behind those gallant fellows, forcing them on. But they need no spur. Their standard was planted upon our works and beckoned to them. Volley upon volley we direct at the staff of this banner, but it continued to wave, defiantly, mockingly.

Captain Hartees forces his way toward this point, shouting at the same time:

"Cut down that flag! Down with it!"

"Cut it down! Cut it down!" echoed a score of voices.

A heavy fire was centered upon it, tearing the banner into shreds. The staff splintered, bit by bit. Oh, so slowly! It bent, it broke, and the emblem of treason at last dropped to the earth.

Faster the rear ranks loaded, faster the front ranks fired, until at times our whole front was one continuous line of blazing musketry. The enemy in our immediate front could endure it no longer, and during a brief lull cry out:

"For God's sake, stop firing! Let us come in! We surrender!"

"Stay where you are!" thunders back a voice. "Lie down! Keep out of the way!"

We could not let them in. Other lines were still advancing upon us, and we had no time to spare in taking prisoners. Worst of all, our ammunition was giving out.

Captain Hartees discovered this fact and ordered me

to carry the information to General Reilly, and tell him we must have more ammunition, and at once.

I left my place in line, went to the rear, found the general, and delivered the message.

"Tell him," said our brigade commander, "he shall have it, and all he wants at once," upon which he turned and rode away.

It appeared to me as I stood alone for a moment, trying to take in the scene, that the bullets were flying thicker there, than at the front. Shot and shell were whistling through the air from all directions ; while along the whole line of our defense, enveloped in thick smoke, which was dispersed above in a thin canopy of bluish vapor, I heard the hoarse shout of contending armies, and the angry report of musketry as it flashed and tore along from right and left to center and back again, lighting up the smoke clouds as the lightning's flash illumines the dark cloud on a summer's night.

Wounded men everywhere ; some, leaning on their guns for support, were limping away ; some, crawling to a place of safety ; others, too weak to move further, were dying where loss of blood had compelled them to stop.

A wounded, riderless horse, frantic with pain, and wild with the furious tumult, bounded over the field, seeking to fly from the peril which surrounded us.

I wonder now that I ever had the courage to return to my post ; but the idea that my life was in danger never occurred to me. The scene I witnessed from the rear impressed me, but it inspired no feeling of fear ; I had delivered my message, and satisfied myself that things were yet well with us, and returned to my duty.

My nerves were strung to the highest tension, and I was conscious that my excitement was intense, but the controlling influence, that which moved me quickly forward, was the fear that some of my comrades should miss me, and not understand why I had left them.

Once more in line, I glanced backward toward the ammunition-wagons, and there saw a man take a box of ammunition on his shoulder and start toward us on the run. He had covered nearly half the distance when he fell, pierced with the enemy's bullets. Another man picked up the box, but carried it only a few yards when he, too, fell. At that moment some one from brigade headquarters, who had seen the second man fall, ran to the box, now wet with blood, picked it up and brought it in.

In a moment the cover was off and the contents of the box were distributed. Just then came another lull in the firing when the enemy, who had given up the fight, and had since been lying close under the hedge and in the ditch, jumped up, shouting :

" Let us come in now ! We surrender !"

" Come in ! Come in !" we shouted, without waiting for orders.

Instantly our works were swarming with the enemy, who threw down both colors, arms and ammunition, and hurried to the rear.

Two or three of our boys picked up a few of these battle flags, of which there was a large number, when a shout from some one stopped them.

" Leave these flags for the sutlers !" said the voice. " Look out for the flags in front !"

Only a brief pause in the roar of battle, just long enough to pass around the ammunition we had received and get our prisoners out of the way, when again "the rebel yell," from another of the successive lines of assailants, gave warning of a renewal of the contest.

Like men who were breasting a storm of hail, pulling their hats down over their eyes and inclining their heads forward to meet the leaden rain, they rush toward the red tongues of death that, simultaneously with the order, "Fire!" leaped forth to scorch and wither dozens and scores and hundreds.

I wonder how men dare rush in the face of death so calmly, so deliberately.

I fixed my eyes on a tall, sinewy fellow, with brown beard, a slouched hat, with the rim turned down and a ragged suit of brown and gray. His hands held his rifle firmly as he ran over the dead and wounded bodies of those who have gone before him. He looked not to see where he stepped; now upon the chest of some wounded comrade; now upon the neck or in the face of some one nearly dead, who writhed in agony at the fresh torture inflicted.

On, on he came. Bullets flew faster and yet faster around him; his companions fell on either side of him; he heeded them not. He stumbled at last, gathered himself, ran a few paces, stumbled again, staggered, dropped his gun and fell. Those behind were now running over his body as he ran over others but an instant before.

Meanwhile, the sun had set. It was becoming dark, but I could yet see across the Turnpike, where the battle was raging still no less fiercely than with us. There, also, the enemy are trying to storm the works.

But our line stood firm as the cliffs of the sea. An officer, leading the charge, rode to the ditch, leaped it and mounted the works, where the horse fell, riddled with bullets, and the rider tumbled headlong to the earth.

A howl of rage rose from the infuriated host which now sprang forward for revenge. The entire line was stimulated to desperation. Nearer and nearer they come. Another battle flag rose above the works within a feet few feet of me. The experience with that other flag was enough for one day, and I resolved that this banner should not wave over us if I could help it.

Impulsively I dropped my rifle, jumped toward the flag, seized it by the staff with both hands and exerted all my energy to wrench it from the hands of the man who carried it. A desperate struggle for the possession of the flag ensued. First victory seemed to be on one side, then on the other. But neither would yield.

Backward and forward, now brought nearly to my knees, now in danger of being thrown to the earth by the almost superhuman strength of my antagonist, we struggled for a moment on the works, the flag, just above our heads, swaying in all directions with the movements of our bodies, the thick smoke of the atmosphere around us, almost suffocating in its density, vibrating with the sounds of exploding rifles, clashing bayonets and the whistle and zip of swiftly flying bullets.

Suddenly I felt a burning sensation, as if a red hot iron had been laid on my head, and my eyes were quickly blinded with hot blood running over my face. Conscious that whatever I did must be done quickly, I summoned all the power that in me lay for a final

"I SEIZED THE FLAG WITH BOTH HANDS."—*See Page* 254.

effort. The staff yielded, and, amid wild shouts of triumph, though from which side I could not tell, I fall backward. Some one caught me as I fell, and hurried me to the rear.

I grew dizzy. My strength was fast leaving me, and it was with difficulty I kept my feet as we ran. The noise of battle increased. There was a roaring sound in my ears; a sharp, stinging pain in my right arm; a bursting sensation; then—blankness.

CHAPTER XXIV.

It was night when I returned to consciousness, and I found myself in bed, gazing at a small circle of light on the ceiling overhead. Directly beneath was a heavily-shaded lamp, which cast a luminous disk upon a table. Other parts of the room were in somber gloom.

In a low chair near the table, partly in light and partly in shadow, sat a woman reading. I could not see the woman's face nor tell if she was black or white.

An air of wholesome comfort and peace and quiet pervaded the place, and I wondered where it was; why I was lying in bed with my head so tightly bandaged; why my arms and limbs were so numb and void of feeling.

For some time my brain refused to act and I lay dazed, bewildered, utterly unable to recall the past. By degrees, however, it slowly came to me, and the picture of a powder-blackened face and a man carrying a bullet-rent battle flag presented itself. Then the conflict in which I was wounded flashed before me.

But this house. Why was I here? This was not a hospital. It must be far removed from the results of yesterday's battle; for, so far as I could see, there were no other wounded men near me.

[256]

I tried in various ways to account for my surroundings, but reached no satisfactory conclusion. Then my mind reverted to the battle; whether or not we were victorious; if I succeeded in taking that flag. I had hold of the staff and there was a confused recollection that I did not let go of it. Then came that terrible, burning pain in my head.

"Ah, if that had not come so soon, had only kept away a moment longer, the flag would have been mine, and I should have remembered all about it. Perhaps this woman can tell me something about it."

I tried to attract her attention and failed. She did not hear me; at least she did not move. My voice was weak and strange. I hardly recognized it. But I tried again; this time with what I considered a greater effort.

"Who got the flag?" I asked.

Still no response.

My voice was thick and hoarse, but she surely must have heard me. Why don't the woman answer me?

I lay and looked and waited and wondered what it all meant; where Fred was, and if it was he who helped me to the rear when I was wounded.

Now I think of it, I don't remember seeing him during the fight; but neither do I remember seeing any one else, except Bence and Hartees and Nick too, after the fight commenced. I wonder if they got out of the battle all right. Fred was with me when Hartees shouted for us to follow him, and we both started for the works together.

Hartees what became of him? He was a brave man, none braver; always at the front; never shirking. He and I were the only two in the regiment who were not Kentuckians. Where did he come from? Nobody ever seemed to know. Of course I had seen him at the Waytown Arms 'on the night we received the news that Fort Sumter had been fired upon, but he was a stranger, even there, as will be remembered.

Musing thus, I wearily watched the leaves of the book as the reader turned them one by one. I wished she would stop reading and look at me that I might attract her attention. But I was in darkness, and even if I should beckon she could not see me. While trying to arrange some plan by which I might call her, I fell asleep.

When I again awoke the sun was shining into the room, through partially closed shutters, and I saw a young woman sitting by an open window looking at me.

The face of this woman was familiar to me. I had seen it before. It is wonderfully like Mary's face. But how can that be possible. How came she here? Pshaw! I must be dreaming. And yet, I ought to know that face.

Resolved to prove at once if it were she, or at least attract attention before she turned her eyes from me, I said :

"Mary !"

"What !" rising suddenly. "Do you really know me, Dan ?"

"Yes, Mary, why shouldn't I know you ?"

"Thank God!" she fervently exclaimed, tears streaming down her face as she came rapidly to my bedside, bent over and kissed me.

Surely this is no dream, thought I, closing my eyes, and yet I cannot understand the reality of my situation. Yesterday in battle, in middle Tennessee; to-day at home in Northern Kentucky.

Distance is not so easily overcome as that, and if it were, how was it managed that I had been so speedily taken care of while others, in a worse condition, are left to suffer on that terrible battlefield?

I hardly dare speak lest the spell should break and I find, after all, it was only a dream. What if it should be so? I shuddered at the thought and opened my eyes A look from Mary inspired me with the confidence to speak.

"Mary," said I, hesitatingly, "Mary, tell me, is this a dream?"

"Oh, Dan, it is all real; but you must not dare talk. You are so weak. Let me—"

Here she turned to leave the room.

"Mary!" I cried, with all the strength at my command, determined not to let her pass out of sight; "Mary, don't leave me! Don't!"

"I won't, Dan, I won't. But your mother—"

Just then the door opened softly, and my mother entered the room. I looked into the dear, tired face, whose lips were quivering with suppressed emotion as she came toward me, and whatever else I tried to say, my voice failed to utter but the one word:

"Mother!"

"My dear child," she said, kneeling by my bed and putting her face lovingly against mine, "God is indeed good to give me back my boy. He will let you live now and get strong again."

"Yes, mother, I shall soon be well."

"It will take time, my son. But you are at home now, and in good hands. Please God, we will bring you out of this all right. But you will have to be perfectly quiet for some time yet. A dangerous operation has been performed on your head. The result, so far,

is successful. But the least excitement may undo all
that the doctors have done. So you will be patient,
my boy, and wait until you are stronger, before we can
talk to you or you can ask questions. Don't think of
the past. Sleep. Rest. Watch me or Mary, and
remember mother is with you."

"I'll try and obey orders," I answered, trying to
smile.

"That's right, my son. You shall know all we can
tell you in good time. Mary or I will be with you
night and day. You shall not want for anything, so
don't worry. The doctors will be here to-night. Until
then you must not talk any more. Let me fix your
pillow a little. There! You feel easier now, don't
you?"

"Yes, mother."

"Sleep now, if you can. The more you sleep the
faster you will gain strength."

With this comforting thought my mother kissed me
and quietly left the room. I watched her until the
door closed, assured myself that Mary was still with
me, then shut my eyes and slept.

When I awoke the doctors—three of them—were
present. They felt my pulse, ascertained the tempera-
ture of my body, examined the bandages on my head,
asked me if I knew where I was, what regiment I
belonged to, and a number of questions which, at the
time, seemed quite silly to me. They were all answered
promptly, however, and without confusion.

"Most encouraging," said a gray-haired doctor, one of
the trio, when the other two had finished with their
catechising. "Young man," he said, addressing me,
"you may thank God that you have remarkable recu-
perative powers."

During the conference which followed there was some talk of leaving opiates for me to take, but the gray-haired doctor objected, saying :

"The young man needs neither opiates nor tonics. We have only to look after these bandages, and with careful nursing"—here he glanced at Mary—"nature will do the rest."

After giving full instructions regarding my diet and forbidding me to talk, the doctors departed.

A week of studied silence followed ; days of sleeping and waiting and watching. In this time I rapidly gained in strength. The sensation of numbness in both lower limbs was gradually leaving them. My left hand and arm I could move a little, but not enough so that I could feed myself. My right side, however, seemed to have no sense of feeling whatever.

The doctors came every evening, noted the progress I had made and offered me words of encouragement. At last they informed us that I was strong enough to be talked to or that some one might read to me ; but only for a little while at a time ; not more than half an hour each day.

This was glorious liberty, and my first investment of it was with my mother. The next morning, after breakfast, she seated herself near the bed and said :

"Well, my son, now that we can talk to you, I suppose you want to know all about yourself and how you happen to be here !"

"Yes, mother !"

She began :

"Shortly after the Battle of Franklin I received a letter from Fred, at Nashville. He told me you had been wounded and needed more care than you could possibly get from army surgeons and nurses. The next morning, after receiving that letter, I was on my way to Nashville, where I found you in a temporary hospital. You were unconscious and, the doctor told me, had been so since the battle. Your condition, he said, was produced by two pieces of the fractured skull pressing upon the brain. The remedy was an extremely difficult operation which he intended to perform when you were strong enough. The shock your nervous system had received was great, and it would yet be weeks before he could think of doing anything more for you. Your arm was healing."

"My arm, mother?"

"Yes, my dear boy. The bone of your right arm was so shattered that amputation above the elbow was necessary."

"I didn't know that," I said. This accounted for the numbness in my right side. I had no arm and could not feel. "Well," I said, trying to look cheerful, "my left arm remains and my lower limbs," moving them. "Yes, they are yet sound."

"Better still, my son, the operation of ten days ago was successful, and your senses have been restored. As soon as the doctor at Nashville thought I could safely do so I had you brought home, where you have been ever since. Shortly after reaching home a fever set in and we almost despaired of your life; but careful nursing brought you safely through."

"You and Mary nursed me through it all?"

"Yes, my boy. Either she or I have been with you night and day."

"You are both very tired."

"We were both very anxious until after the operation ten days ago. Since then the improvement in your condition has been so marked that we have rested much, to say nothing of the mental relief we have enjoyed. But I must finish my story."

"What about the doctors here, mother? Who were they?"

"Several doctors were consulted as to performing the operation necessary to relieve that pressure on your brain, and, as no one here dared undertake it, a specialist—the old gentleman—was sent for from Cincinnati. He came, examined your head and appointed a day when he would perform the operation. He said the result all depended on the curative resources of nature. He could only give you the benefit of his art. Nature must provide for the rest."

"Did he say anything about the wounds?"

"There were two separate wounds, he said, at right angles with each other, and one very much deeper than the other. They were in a healthy condition, however, and that was in your favor. That was all he would say, except that it was a remarkable case. On the appointed day the doctors came, the specialist bringing two friends with him from Cincinnati. The operation was performed, and Doctor Cutler, who lives in town, said the old gentleman exhibited wonderful skill. I was not allowed in the room. They thought it better not. After the operation you went to sleep, and slept soundly for the rest of that day and night. The next morning you saw Mary sitting by the window, and spoke to her."

"Who was it seated at the table, reading, the night before?" I asked.

"It was I. Did Mary tell you some one was there?"

"No, mother. I saw you and tried to call you, but failed. I watched you turn the leaves of that book for a long time; wondered where I was and tried to make it all out, but finally went to sleep."

"The doctor thought you might wake up in the night, and he was right. But he warned us not to talk to you; that it would be better for you to sleep. I did not hear you, however. There, I must not talk any more. Mary will tell you all about the battle to-morrow. You have heard enough for to-day."

On the following morning, after disposing of the scanty allowance—one poached egg, two small slices of buttered toast and a glass of warm milk, which constituted my breakfast—I asked Mary to tell me all about the battle.

"Do you feel better this morning?" she asked.

"Much better," I replied. "Mary, yesterday morning mother told me that you and she have nursed me ever since I was brought home."

"It is true," replied Mary. "But I was glad to do it. Don't say anything about it. The danger is now passed, thank God, and you will soon be up and about."

"You have been very good to me and I must at least say I am grateful for what you have done," I persisted.

"Then have the goodness not to refer to it again, please. Is there not something I can do for you!"

"Yes; tell me about the battle, please, and how it went. I am anxious to know."

"You must let me tell you in my own way, then, as things occur to me. I can only tell you what Fred has told me and what I have read in the daily papers."

"Fred got out of it all right, then?" I asked.

"Yes, but you must not anticipate nor interrupt nor question me. Remember, sir," and her face assumed an expression of droll importance, "I am to do all the talking."

"All right, Mary, I will remember."

"In the first place, then, Hood was defeated, losing something over six thousand men. Schofield lost two thousand men. One thousand of these belonged to Wagner's two brigades, who were in front of your works before the battle commenced. The fight was about over by seven o'clock.; though there were occasional volleys from the enemy until ten o'clock. After that time, there being no further demonstration, Schofield sent out a skirmish line, and not finding the enemy, they returned, when our whole force quietly left the works and marched to Nashville. The flag you risked your life for—"

"Well?" I asked quickly, my pulses throbbing with excitement.

"Is in this drawer."

"What?" I exclaimed, as the thought of this trophy being so near, thrilled me.. "Then I did capture it after all?"

"Yes, but calm yourself, Dan. Be perfectly calm or I shall stop talking. It will not do to excite yourself. I ought not to have spoken of this."

"Show it to me Mary. Show it to me. See, I am calm."

With a look of distrust, Mary opened a drawer in the table standing near the head of my bed, took out and unfolded a tattered, blood-stained, cross-barred flag, the general appearance of which had been burned so vividly into my memory.

Hold it up, Mary. Hold it up! Let me look at it once more."

"Oh, Dan, how could you?" she said, holding the flag up as high as she could reach. "How could you dare so much for only a flag?"

"Only a flag, Mary; only a flag. Ah, if you had seen the hosts of brave men following that flag, through smoke and blood, to the jaws of death. If you had thrilled with the cheers of encouragement from comrades who were watching you; if you could know—"

"Hush, sir! Hush! Remember your promise; you are not to talk. It won't do any good. I have tried, but cannot understand it, and I don't believe any woman or even a man who has not been in battle can understand anything of the inspiration in a flag, that leads men to death. It was a daring thing to do. They say you jumped onto the works wrenched the flag from the hands of its bearer and that too after you had been wounded. It was a brave act, and as you were between two fires, it is a miracle you were not killed. After you had possession of the flag you fell backward. A man by the name of Searle caught you—"

"What, Nick?" I asked.

"Yes, I think that is his name."

"Where is he now?"

"Remember your promise, and please not interrupt. Let me finish the story in my own way. I mean to be arbitrary in this matter."

"I will be silent," I passively responded. "Go on!"

"Well, then, you were led to the rear as rapidly as possible, dragging the captured banner after you. Before reaching a place of safety your arm was shattered by a bullet; then you dropped the flag. At the same time you received another wound in your head and dropped as if dead. Searle dragged you to the ambulances, where you were examined by the doctor, who found you were living and, after dressing your wounds temporarily, sent you to Nashville. Fred and others saw you when you captured the flag and have many times told the story. Searle, on his return to the front, picked up the flag, tore it from the staff and put it in his pocket. He came to see you when the war closed."

"What!" I exclaimed in astonishment at this new revelation. "The war—the war—closed, did you say?"

"Yes, Dan. Lee surrendered on the 9th of April."

"And I—?"

"Have been battling for life and reason for nearly six months. It is now the 20th of May."

CHAPTER XXV.

"How is my boy to-day?" said mother, on entering my room one morning, a few days after the events narrated in the last chapter.

"Better, thank you," I replied. "I slept well last night, and am now equal to a good breakfast, and feel as if I might be up and dressed by and by."

Mother smiled good-naturedly, and said:

"There's nothing to be gained by hurrying. Better wait a few days longer. Mary is preparing breakfast, and, while you are waiting, I have a little story to tell which, I am sure, will surprise you, and I know will do you no harm."

"What is it, mother?" I asked, wondering how it was possible to bring forward anything more surprising than had been revealed to me during the days just passed.

"Well, I will tell you. About four weeks since I received from a lawyer in Memphis, Tennessee, a letter, which had been forwarded to me from Waytown. The letter was addressed to your father, and stated that father's brother—"

I did not know father had a brother?" I interrupted.

"He did, though. But he rarely ever mentioned him. His name was Daniel Nichols. He was a rich planter, owned a large number of slaves, and was so thoroughly aristocratic in his notions that father would have nothing to do with him."

"More 's the pity," I remarked. "His brother might have been a great help when father was sick and in trouble."

"Yes, he might, and no doubt would, if he had known. But your father was as proud, though not as successful, as his brother, and would not have asked for help to keep us out of the poor-house."

"But the lawyer's letter. What about it?" I asked, a little impatiently.

"I was about to tell you. It was a notice, in effect, that Daniel Nichols had died and that his property, by reason of the death of his son, had been willed to your father, and that the lawyers awaited further instructions and would be pleased to attend to all matters of transfer, record, *et cetera*."

"What is the property, mother?"

"A schedule of it accompanied the letter, and it amounts to almost one hundred and fifty thousand dollars."

"What?" I gasped. "One hundred and— Oh, pshaw! It cannot be. It is only a mistake. One hundred and fifty thous— Are you sure this is true?"

"Quite true, Daniel, and no mistake."

"And I am—mother, am I dreaming? Say that again, please," said I, reaching out and taking her hand in my own.

"It is all true, Daniel. Your uncle died and left all his property—that is, all the war had left him—to your father. As your father is dead the property passes, by terms of the will, to you. It is valued at a hundred and fifty thousand dollars in round numbers, and consists of a bank account of some fifty thousand, United States bonds, singularly enough, to the extent of fifty thousand more, and the balance represents the assessed valuation of the plantation, all of which have been duly transferred to you, his nephew and only living blood relation."

"And it is then really a fact that I am a—"

"A rich man, in your own right, Daniel."

I lay back upon my pillow, closed my eyes and tried to take in the situation. My father's brother! An uncle of whom I had never heard, in western Tennessee! Strangely enough, at that moment I heard a familiar tune being whistled by a passing boy on the street, and there came to my mind the old chant of Black Lige,

"Nebber min' de wedder so de win' don' blow."

Quickly following the resurrection of this old tune, there passed in mental review the stalwart form of the captain's cook, and his effort, the first time we met, to have me recognize him as the son of his old master. Lige was from Tennessee, they said. Yes, it must be so. No doubt I resembled that cousin, and Lige was moved to recognition by it. I wondered if I should ever see Lige again. If I should happen down there and welcome him back to the old plantation, where, no doubt, he was born and had passed all his young life— Mary's appearance at this instant put an end to my dreaming, and I asked if Mary knew of my good fortune.

"Yes, Daniel, Mary knows the whole story."

"It 's about my uncle in Tennessee," I replied in answer to a questioning look from Mary's eyes.

"I am glad for you," she said, simply, "but now we have something of vastly more importance to consider. Here are dainties fit for a king, and you have only to eat sir and be well."

What an appetizing breakfast that was, with Mary and mother to supply the needs of my missing hand; and what a delightful experience to watch these dear ones as they lovingly vied with each other in their efforts to please me.

After the meal was finished and mother had taken away the tray, Mary said:

"I wonder if you are now in a condition to bear another surprise?"

"What, another? Will wonders never cease?"

"I hope, Dan, we may never again have anything happen to us less pleasing than that which I am about to tell you of. But, perhaps, after all, I had better wait a day or two longer. You ought not to have too much to carry in your mind just yet."

"There you go, teasing again. You know I am strong enough now to bear almost anything. Besides, I have already been so thoroughly surprised at everything that has transpired that I do not see how it can be possible to startle me further; particularly if what you tell me is pleasing."

"Oh, it is decidedly pleasant, or you may be sure I would not tell you," Mary replied. "Perhaps, after all, I may as well tell you."

"Do, I implore you," said I, coaxingly.

Mary looked at me quietly for an instant and then said:

"Do you happen to have the least bit of curiosity to know whatever became of your captain?"

"Do I want to know where Captain Hartees is? Most emphatically, yes!"

"Ah, yes, Hartees! Yes, that's the name. I could not recall it."

"But what about him? Do you know where he is?"

"I can make a shrewd guess," as the Yankees say.

"Come, Mary, tell me what you have to tell, and don't tease me any longer? Was he wounded at Franklin?"

"No, he was not wounded!" she replied, smiling at my impatience.

"I'm glad of that," I said, taking hold of her hand and looking into her love-lit eyes.

"Well, we had a letter direct from Waytown one day last week, and—"

"Tell me about that some other time, Mary; but, just now, tell me where Captain Hartees is—or I'll cut you off without a shilling!"

"You are getting positively dangerous, and if you don't look out you shall have no dinner!"

"All right, Mary, have your own way; take your own time; I'm sure to know it later."

"You surely won't if you persist in interrupting me! This letter was dated at Waytown and was signed by John Hartees."

"Well, well, that is, indeed, a surprise. What is he doing there, pray?"

"That you will learn later, if you please."

"I should like to see him."

"It will be your own fault if you do not, as soon as you are able to travel!"

" How so ?"

" Because he has settled there. He has married Edith Miller, whom I suppose you have heard of."

" Married Edith Miller ?"

" Yes, sir ; and, what is more, he is very anxious to have you and your mother, when you recover, come back to Waytown and live there."

" We never could do that, Mary, and see our old home occupied by strangers."

" But couldn't you buy it back ?"

" Yes ; but mother would feel—"

" Well, it does not happen to be necessary. You interrupt me so that I don't make any progress at all."

" I promise I will not speak again," said I.

' " Listen, then. This letter was filled with kindest wishes for your speedy restoration to health, and expressed the hope that you would soon be able to come back to your old home and live near your friends. With this letter came a deed of transfer from Edith, turning over to your mother all the property which, by fore-closure, passed from the hands of your father into the possession of Edith's father. What do you think of that, sir ?" Mary concluded, with a smile.

" I do not know what to think of it, my dear, except that God has been very good to us and that we have very much to be thankful for."

*　　*　　*　　*　　*　　*　　*

Careful nursing hastened my recovery, and in six months from the date of the surgical operation which restored me to consciousness I stood with Mary at the altar, from which we went forth into the world as hus-band and wife.

In good time Mary and I and mother returned to

Waytown, where a series of pleasant surprises awaited us. As the train rolled into the station I caught sight of Captain Hartees with his wife Edith. Near by I also saw Dick Wentworth, the old station agent, and Billy Green. There, too, were big Joe Bentley and little Tommy Atkins, with a host of other old-time, familiar faces.

I also noticed that the station itself was decorated with bunting and flags.

As we stepped from the cars to the platform a salute was being fired in a neighboring field, and we were at once surrounded by loving friends, who gave us a royal welcome home.

What it all meant, what mother or Mary or I had done to entitle us to such a reception, or why the air was at this moment vibrating with patriotic music from the village band, I confess was beyond me to explain.

Carriages awaited us, in which, preceded by the band and followed by a crowd of villagers, we rode to the Waytown Arms, also gayly decked with flags and bunting.

At the tavern door we were received by the select men of the town, by whom we were conducted to the parlors, where a public reception was held. Here, every one seemed anxious to take me by the hand and offer me a word of congratulation—though it appeared, considering the fact that I had been only a humble private in the army, and was now only a citizen returning to the home of his boyhood, that my friends were making a greater demonstration over the event than my record or position would seem to warrant.

Mary, mother and I stood in one corner of the big double parlors, with Captain Hartees, his wife, the selectmen close by, and the villagers with extended hands and words of welcome passing before us.

At last the handshaking was finished, and the people—all who could be accommodated in the parlors —stood waiting, expectantly, as if there was something yet to be accomplished or said of which they desired to be listeners and observers.

To me it was an instant of awkward pause, for I could not anticipate what was coming ; but it was only for an instant, when Bert Smith, chairman of the selectmen, armed with an official-looking document, stepped in front of, and, in his most impressive manner, said :

" My brother, no doubt you have been surprised at the reception which has greeted your arrival home, and, perhaps, you have wondered not a little what it was all about. I do not know that I can offer a better explanation than to say that Waytown is happy this day to do honor to one of its heroes. At a meeting held in Town Hall, some months since, celebrating the close of war and the return of our brave sons, many of them scarred and maimed from Southern battle-fields, our beloved citizen, Captain Hartees, had something to offer in eulogy of what Waytown had done during the war, and there described the bravery exhibited at the Battle of Franklin by the son whom it is our delight to honor to-day. Words of mine cannot fitly describe the period of anxious waiting for the weekly reports that came to us during the weary months of your unconsciousness, nor can I express the joy we felt on learning the result of the surgical skill which restored your reason. We rejoiced that the lost was found, that the dead had been made alive again, and it now becomes my pleasure to hand you a medal of honor, presented by an act of Congress for gallantry and personal valor to Daniel Nichols, private Company D, Twelfth Kentucky Volunteers, at the Battle of Franklin, Tennessee, November 30, 1864. Wear it, as you alone can wear it, ever remembering, my brother, that while the United States may reward with medals the devotion and bravery of its loyal sons, Waytown will cherish in its heart of hearts a love for its heroes which can never grow dim and can never pass away."

As I took the medal in my hand, cheer upon cheer went up from the assembled villagers, and I, with a heart too full for utterance, could only feebly express in words the gratitude I felt for the honors bestowed upon me.

A banquet, such as the Waytown Arms had never before found occasion to spread was then served, and thus closed the experiences of an eventful day.

Years afterward, I attended a reunion of the Twelfth Kentucky at Louisville, and there met my cousin Fred, Nick Searle and Jake Bence. Black Lige also put in an appearance and was immediately taken charge of by Captain Hartees who succeeded in persuading his faithful servant of the past to return with him to Waytown.

Many and cordial were the greetings exchanged at that reunion ; and when, at its close, the comrades separated to go their different ways, as if in answer to the question I asked myself, "how many of us shall ever meet again," Black Lige sang softly,

" Nebber min' de wedder so de win' don' blow,
Don' yer bodder 'bout yer trouble till it comes."

THE END.

www.ingramcontent.com/pod-product-compliance
Lightning Source LLC
Chambersburg PA
CBHW021050030726
47496CB00006B/1767